My Friend My Lover My Stalker

Devonnia Levous

Black Print Publishing
289 Livingston St
Brooklyn, NY 11217

ISBN 09722771-9-6

ACKNOWLEDGEMENTS

Yes! Finally! It took a while, but after distractions, interruptions and procrastination, I've accomplished the goal to write a book. My first. There are so many people I'd like to thank for their support, prodding, and encouragement.

First and foremost I'd like to thank and dedicate this book to my mother, Delores. Without you there would be no me.

To the rest of my family; my sister, brother-in-law, niece, nephews, granddaughters, grandson, my sons, Kevin, Quentin, Marcus, and all other family members: thank you, I love you all.

To Mr. Chocolate Cookies, Vincent Tyler, thanks for your friendship and support. Keep on entertaining us with your tanta- lizing works.

To Michael Baisden, thanks for your inspiration, help, and all those wonderful seminars. Continued success to you.

To Ken O'Connor and Joella Johnson, thanks for your input and encouragement, for insisting that I finish the book. Now you can find out how it ends. Sorry I left you hanging.

To my friends and family at the 'Tower'. I miss you all: Frank Rios, Ken O'Connor, Tony Weathersby, John Bednarz, Lydell Wynne, Neil Williams, and all the other friends I made there over the years.

To my friends at UPS: Frank Rios, Keith Pittman, and everyone at the Madison Counter: Kim, Gwen, Shenell, Burt, Tina, Kyle, Eli, Chandra, Bennie, Tangila, Frank.

To my girl, Christina Barnes-Williams, you are without a doubt one of the classiest women I know. Thanks for your friendship and inspiration.

To all those who helped make the first printing a success: DeLisa, Quentin, Irma, Edward, Melvin, thanks for spreading the word and thanks to everyone who purchased copies.

A very special thanks to Carl Weber and Black Print Publishing.

ONE

MY FRIEND

"Hello Jeremy."

"Hey Tara! It's good to hear from you. What's up?"

"Jeremy, I need you."

"Is that right?"

"Yeah, that's right. I need the services of the great Jeremy Brennan, Attorney at Law."

"Tara, you must be in some deep doo-doo, but if you can afford me, then I'm all yours. Now please tell me what a lady as classy and sophisticated as yourself could possibly need with a criminal attorney."

"I'm at 17th and State and I'm being held for questioning about a disappearance and possible murder."

"Murder! Okay Tara, who'd you kill this time?" he asked.

"Look Jeremy, cut the comedy, ok? I'm being held for questioning in the disappearance and possible murder of Stan, even though they don't have a body."

"Damn, baby! Look, I'm on my way. Just sit tight. Are you alright?"

"Yeah, I'm fine."

"Okay, I'm on my way," Jeremy said excitedly.

"Thank you Jeremy. And by the way, Johnnie C. was my first choice but unfortunately he's not available; so if I can afford him I certainly have no problem affording you, Mr. Hotshot," I laughed while hanging up the phone.

Now I felt as if I could breathe and was relieved to know that Jeremy was on his way. Not only was he one of the most sought after, competent criminal attorneys in the

Midwest, who could very easily hold his own against the legendary Johnnie C., but he was also one of my dearest friends whom I'd known since we were 13 years old growing up in the Henry Horner Projects.

Who could have ever imagined the roads our lives would take over the past twenty years, with Jeremy becoming one hell of a criminal attorney after being one hell of a criminal for so many years. Back then he was by far one of the smoothest, slickest boosters on the Westside of Chicago. There was nothing he couldn't or wouldn't steal. His game was so tight he had people placing orders with him. Everybody liked, respected, and some people even feared him, because along with being extremely attractive, he was also one of the toughest, get all up in your face, ass-kickingest brothers in the projects. There were some people who questioned Jeremy's sexuality behind his back, but no one—and I do mean no one—dared say anything to his face about what his preferences might be. Besides, everyone was just too damn happy with the deals he would give them on his merchandise to even care. But fortunately for Jeremy, a stint in the penitentiary was all that was needed for him to give up his life of crime and do something productive with himself. I suspect it was in the penitentiary where Jeremy did come to terms with his sexuality. I'm just happy that he's now in a loving and happy relationship with an intelligent, sexy linebacker of an NFL team. (But I'm not telling who it is.)

As for me, I followed my passion of becoming a writer, and now I'm a well-known, very highly paid suspense novelist with four books to my credit. And I'm sitting in jail, accused of having something to do with the disappearance and possible murder of a man who was once my friend, my lover and who then, unfortunately, became my stalker.

"Damn! I wish Jeremy would hurry up and get here. I would like to take a long, hot bubble bath and have a cold glass of Chablis," I mumbled.

"Excuse me, Ms. St. Pierre."

"Yes, officer?"

"I just wanted to know if I could get you some coffee or anything," said the officer who was standing in front of my cell. "My wife and I are big fans of yours and I just hate seeing you in this situation."

"Thank you officer, but I'm fine. My lawyer should be here shortly."

"Alright, but if you need anything in the meantime, just give me a call. I'm officer Johnson, and I'll be sitting right down the hall."

"Thank you, officer Johnson, for being so kind and courteous."

Now please don't get me wrong, I don't mean to sound cold and callous because a man I once loved and cared so much about is missing and presumed to be dead, and my focus is on a bath and a drink; but considering the fact that Stan and I have known each other since he was 10 and I was 12, he knew better than anyone that I am not a person to be messed with. Obviously he thought good sex could make me overlook the fact that what was once a great relationship had turned into something cruel and evil. No, we were not having sex when we were 10 and 12. That happened much later.

As I sat back and waited for Jeremy to arrive, I remembered when I'd first met Stan. It was at the wedding. He was 10 and his father was marrying my Aunt June.

Mr. Bishop had been raising Stan alone ever since he was 5 and his mother just upped and walked out on them. Now he was marrying my aunt, whom I had always been very close to. I felt honored to be their flower girl and was ecstatic to know that they had been able to get an apartment on the 12th floor of the same building in which I lived with my mother and sister, Denise. That was back in the day when the projects were a fun place in which to live; with two parent families, clean breezeways, hallways and working elevators that didn't smell eternally of piss. The playgrounds were actually places where a child could play and have fun. There was never a shortage of kids to play with. I remember how we would stay in the playground playing Red Light, Green Light, Simon Says, or just jumping rope until the porch lights came on. Every kid knew that once those lights came on, you'd better have your butt on the elevator heading home or else you'd be one sorry ass. But we didn't mind, because once we'd gone home, had dinner and taken our baths, our parents would let us sit out on the breezeways where we could watch the older guys playing basketball, signifying, or doing what I loved seeing them do most; acting like doo-woppers and throwing down on hits by the Platters, Temptations, Smokey, or other soul groups. Man! Did we have some talented brothers in that building. But I won't even bother going into where most of them are today. (I guess I have a lot of nerve, sitting here in a jail cell.) But anyway.

Since Aunt June had moved into my building, I would hang out at her apartment and that was how Stan and I became friends. Stan was quiet and kind of shy, which is why Aunt June and Uncle B. (which is what I called him) encouraged him to hang out with me. They knew I was very outgoing, talkative, and was well liked. Not only that, but even though I was a skinny kid, I never backed down from a confrontation and could throw down with the best of 'em, so they didn't have to worry about anyone picking on Stan.

Once you got to know Stan and he let his guard down and stopped being shy and quiet, the kid was a blast to be around. He had a great sense of humor, was very creative, and had a hell of an imagination. Now mind you, this was before Playstation, Sega and cable tv; so you had to be creative and imaginative in order to keep yourself entertained. Stan was a master at coming up with some great games to play. I remember once when he, my sister Denise, who was 14 at the time (this was one of the rare occasions when she hung out with us, as she had discovered boys and getting high by this time), and I were at my house. My mother was at work. Ever since my father had been killed in a car crash two years earlier, my mother worked tirelessly, so she was rarely at home. Anyway, we were bored and had nothing to do so Stan came up with a game called Penny Pool. Two people would sit at opposite ends of the table and one player would spot his penny. The other player would have to line up his penny and flick it across the table, trying to knock the first player's penny off the table. I guess it was the poor man's version of Air Hockey. Stan also liked taking things apart: clocks, toasters, radios. Anything he could get his hands on. But fortunately for him, when he put them back together, they worked better than before. So before long, he just grew on me and we became inseparable and the best of friends. I was as protective of him as if he were my little brother. There's one incident in particular which stands out in my mind. It happened about seven months after I'd first met the little knucklehead.

TWO

"Hey Tara, ain't that your little cousin Stan sitting over there crying?" asked my girl Deanne as we were coming off of the elevator.

"Yeah, that's him," I said as I hurried over to where he was sitting. "Stan, what's wrong?"

"Melody took the dollar my Daddy gave me," he sniffled.

"Where that heifer at?" I yelled.

"She ran down Lake St. after the ice cream truck," he said.

I looked down Lake St. and sure enough, there that wench was, standing at the truck getting her an ice cream cone. I immediately took off and ran up six flights of stairs to my apartment where I grabbed a jar with a lid. I ran back downstairs and went to a side of the building where there always seemed to be an overabundance of ants. I hurriedly scooped about 20 or 30 ants into the jar and put the lid on it. "Come on!" I said to Stan, who along with Deanne was looking at me is if I'd lost my mind. By this time Melody was coming down the street, happily eating her ill-gotten ice cream cone.

"Hey Melody," I smiled as I walked up to her, holding the jar behind my back and unscrewing the lid. "Where'd you get the ice cream?"

"Off the truck," she said, rolling her eyes.

"I can't believe you'd get a plain ole vanilla cone. Here, let me spice it up for you," I said as I dumped the ants all over her ice cream. She screamed and tried to drop it but I grabbed her hand and made her hold onto it. "Now eat it, you simple bitch!" I yelled while glaring at her.

"Nooo, please. I'm sorry," she cried.

"Eat it!" I said, smashing it into her face.

By this time she was gagging and throwing up, so I casually turned around and started walking back to the building with Stan and Deanne following me, cracking up laughing. Needless to say, Miss Melody never messed with Stan again.

"Come on," I said when we got back to the building. "Let's go up to my apartment and play."

* * *

"Ugh, what's that smell?" Stan said as I opened the door.

"That's weed!" Deanne yelled.

"What tha!..." I shouted as I walked into the house. Apparently, somewhere between the time that I'd come upstairs to get the jar and now, my trifling sister Denise had come home. She was sitting in the living room with three guys, two of whom I knew, and they weren't shit. The other guy I'd never seen before, but even in my rage I did notice how cute he was. Denise was sitting in the chair smoking a joint and one of the guys, named JT, was standing behind her chair with his hands on the two things that seemed to mean the world to Denise; her breasts.

"Why the hell are y'all in here disrespecting my mother's house like this?" I yelled.

"Look, little girl," Denise said as she jumped up, "don't come in here with this bullshit."

I just stood there looking at her crazy ass, because we both knew that even though she was older and bigger than me, I would still have no problem mopping the floor with her ass. But since I'd already had one altercation that day, I figured I'd met my quota.

"Your damn friends better be gone when I get back," I said to her. "Come on Stan, let's go up to your house," I said as I stalked out the door with Stan and Deanne right behind me.

"Are you gonna tell your mom or Momma June when we get upstairs?" Stan asked.

"No. I'm not." As much as I hated Denise for what she was doing, I didn't believe in tricking on her or anyone else for that matter. I felt as if I was capable of dealing with any problems I had without bringing Momma into it. When we got upstairs, a different smell greeted us as we entered Stan's house. This one was of fried chicken, greens, and yams. Aunt June was an excellent cook and she always cooked enough for me and Denise since our mother was always working and didn't have time to cook.

"Hey Auntie June," I said as I gave her a big hug. "Where's Uncle B.?"

"Oh, he's downstairs fixing Ms. Austin's fan. He'll be up in a little while."

I'm certain Stan got his talent for fixing things from Uncle B., because that man could fix anything; electrical work, plumbing, carpentry, he could do it all. I'm sure if you looked in the dictionary under "Handy-Man" you'd see a picture of Uncle B. Yeah, Uncle B. was a Godsend in the neighborhood and that's how he made a living. But for all his talents and skills, wouldn't you know it, he couldn't get a real J-O-B with benefits so that he could support his family in a manner that any self-respecting man would want to. But Uncle B. never blamed or complained. He just did what he had to do, held his head up, and never let the unfairness of society get to him. Or so it appeared.

"Boy! Don't you go in that refrigerator without washing your hands," Aunt June said as she smacked Stan with the dish towel. "That Kool-Aid ain't goin' nowhere. You kids go wash your hands now so y'all can eat."

Needless to say, Deanne was the first one in the bathroom and the first one to the table. Unlike my mother who didn't cook because she was always working,

Deanne's mother sat on her fat ass at home every day and rarely cooked. *How she manages to stay so big is beyond me,* I thought as I went to the cabinet to get the dishes and help set the table. As I got the dishes down, I briefly thanked God for Aunt June and Uncle B. Ever since my father's death, my mother's long hours away from home, and my dear sister's jump onto the fast road to nowhere, I felt blessed to have family that I could turn to for support, love, and a good, home cooked meal. I never let my mom or anyone know just how much I hurt inside over the loss of what was once a very stable home life with two loving parents.

"Hey, how's my favorite people?" Uncle B. bellowed as he walked into the house.

Uncle B. was a slight man who stood "5'6" and weighed about 140 lbs., but boy was he loud and boisterous.

"Hey Uncle B.," I said as I ran over to give him a hug.

"Hi Daddy," Stan said, gulping down a glass of Kool-Aid.

"Hello Mr. Bishop," Deanne softly said. Deanne had developed a teen-aged crush on Uncle B. and it was very obvious.

"Damn! Something sho' smells good, and somebody sho' looks good," he said as he set down his tool box and went over to hug and kiss Aunt June.

"Man, watch your mouth," she said as she smiled at him. They were always hugging and kissing, acting like a couple of love struck teenagers.

"And how is the finest woman in the building doing?" he asked while trying to cop a feel on Aunt June's ample behind.

"What do you mean 'the building'? I'm the finest woman on the Westside of Chicago," she said as she put her hands on her hips. By this time we kids were cracking up. Aunt June, who indeed was a very pretty woman, stood

"5'3", weighed 150 lbs., and had a figure like a black Betty-Boop. Men were always hitting on her, but it seemed she only had eyes for Uncle B. (I said 'it seemed'.)

"Now go wash up so we can eat," she said while pushing Uncle B. toward the bathroom. "These kids are hungry."

After Uncle B. had washed up, we all sat down, said grace, and for the next twenty minutes the only thing that could be heard was smacking lips, teeth being sucked, and fingers being licked.

"Girl, that was delicious!" Uncle B. said as he pushed his chair back and belched. "Aunt Bee from Mayberry ain't got nothing on my baby. Do she, kids?"

"No sir," Deanne said while carrying her plate to the sink and trying to switch what little butt she had. "Mrs. Bishop, do you mind if I take my Momma a plate?" she asked. "She probably didn't get a chance to cook today."

"No baby, I don't mind. Go ahead and fix her a plate," Aunt June said as she cut her eye over at Uncle B.

"I'll wash the dishes, Aunt June," I said as Stan began clearing the table.

"Okay baby, but when you're done, you go on home. Tomorrow's a school day," Aunt June said as her and Uncle B. headed for the living room. I noticed how at the mention of washing dishes, Deanne seemed to speed it up with fixing her mother's plate—a BIG plate—of food. The girl was not a fan of housework.

"Goodnight everyone," she said while hurrying out the door.

"That girl know she looks out for her mother," Uncle B. said.

"Yeah, if only her mother would look out for her kids instead of giving her money to some man. Maybe then she would have some money to buy food and get up off her ass and cook sometimes," Aunt June whispered to Uncle B. Well, at least she thought she was whispering, but I have a keen sense of hearing. And besides, it was common knowledge that Deanne's mother had questionable morals and she changed men more often than she probably changed her underwear. And not surprisingly, they only managed to come around at check time.

"I hope Mr. Bell comes to school tomorrow. I don't like our substitute teacher," Stan said as he played with the suds from the dishwater. Mr. Bell was Stan's 6th grade teacher and he'd been my 6th and 7th grade teacher. He was the best thing to ever happen to me as far as my schooling went. Mr. Bell always encouraged his students to excel and believe in themselves and their abilities. He also didn't take any shit off his students. This was at a time when a teacher was no different than a parent. You got out of line, you got your ass whipped. I smiled as I remembered how many Fridays I went to school wearing two pairs of pants to absorb the pain from the blows of his thick ruler. Mr. Bell, like so many parents, couldn't just whip you at the time when you messed up. Noooo, he would keep a list of who had messed up, what they'd done wrong, and how many licks they were scheduled to receive, and on Fridays at exactly 2:00, he would line us up, tell us how many licks we were getting and then proceed to mete out his brand of justice.

Now I know what you're thinking: Why not just pretend to be sick and stay home on Friday if you'd had the misfortune of making Mr. Bell's hit list, right? Uh, uh, that was not happening, because unless there'd been a death in your family—YOUR OWN—you had better be in school on Friday or you would really find out the meaning of corporal punishment.

It was because of Mr. Bell's mixture of love, encouragement and discipline, that many of his students had a love for learning and realized that knowledge truly was power. A large percentage of his students went on to become very successful. It was Mr. Bell who first noticed I had a talent for writing when he gave the class a creative writing project and I wrote a play. He was so impressed that he allowed the class to perform my play for a school assembly. I loved every minute of it. First, I held auditions for the parts and I felt really honored that so many of my classmates approached me about being in the play, which was titled "Pollution – What's Your Solution?" Yes, I was a child with a social conscience. I even wrote a song about pollution. The play was a success, and since then I've been hooked on writing. "Pollution" was the only play I ever wrote, but after that I started writing short stories. It was truly a blessing that the school board allowed Mr. Bell to work with the same group of students for two years in a row. At first I was sad when I went on to the 8th grade because I wanted to have Mr. Bell as my teacher for the rest of my school years, but eventually I grew to like the idea of being in the 8th grade and now I was eagerly looking forward to graduating and going to Lane Tech High School.

"Stan, I hope you appreciate having Mr. Bell for a teacher," I said as I finished washing the dishes.

"Yeah, I appreciate having him for a teacher, but my butt don't appreciate having him for a teacher," he said as he rubbed his backside and laughed.

"Yeah, I heard that! Now that's one thing I don't miss about the man," I laughed.

"Aunt June, I'm finished with the dishes, so I'm gonna head home now. Momma should be home by now," I said as I walked into the living room.

"Okay baby. Fix some food to take home to your Momma and Denise and give my big sister a hug for me."

"Okay," I said as I got a plate out of the cabinet and filled it with food. "Stan, stop by and get me in the morning," I said to him as I went to give Aunt June and Uncle B. a goodnight hug. "I'll see y'all tomorrow."

I was really happy to see that Aunt June and Uncle B. had each other and that they always seemed to be so happy. Sometimes I would get sad and lonely when I remembered all the fun times I'd had with my father. But now he was dead, my mother was rarely home, and my sister seemed to be losing her mind.

THREE

"Stan, go run your bath water."

"Okay, Momma June," Stan said as he headed for the bathroom. He didn't know why every night she would tell him to take a bath. He thought by now she should know how much he enjoyed bathing. Stan couldn't figure out why so many other little boys hated taking them. He loved being clean, and bath time for him was a time when he would just lay back, relax and let his mind wander. Stan guessed the reason he enjoyed baths so much was because his real mother hardly ever gave him any. Hell, she hardly ever did anything for him except to yell at him or hit him for anything he did or did not do. He was only five when she left, but he could still clearly remember the mean things she would do to him. Like the time he spilled Kool-Aid and she grabbed him, dragged him over to the open window, put his head on the window sill, and threatened to slam the window down on his head. Stan's father was hardly ever at home and Stan assumed it was because his father was afraid of her too. Instead of being there to protect Stan from her, he just left him there to suffer her abuse. But Stan didn't feel any hatred toward him, because after she left, he was always there for Stan and he started being both a father and a mother. He made sure Stan ate well, taught him how to keep his body clean, and hardly ever yelled at or hit him. He also started taking him along when he had a job to do for someone, where Stan would intently watch everything he did. But even though his mother treated him like shit when she was there, he still loved her and always wondered where she was and if she ever thought about him.

As Stan got into the tub, he remembered when his father started dating Momma June. He was eight years old and one day his father came home with this really pretty lady whose name he said was June. She seemed nice and his dad would sometimes take him places with them so that he could get to know her better. Stan did like her, but whenever she was at their house he would get real quiet or go in his room. He didn't want her to get mad at him about something and start yelling at or hitting him like his mother did, so he figured if he was quiet she wouldn't notice him.

His father seemed really happy and after about five months, he asked her to move in with them. They had been going together for about a year when Stan noticed that they had started arguing about his father not being able to find a stable job, even though he was always doing work for people in the neighborhood. Stan guessed Momma June didn't think he was making enough money. Stan would get scared whenever Momma June got mad at his father. He worried she might get mad and start yelling at him too. He was also afraid that like his mother, she too would leave them. But even though they argued, they would always kiss and make up and be happy again.

His father eventually got a job at the A&P grocery store so they had more money and his father and Momma June didn't argue anymore. Then one day his father asked Momma June to marry him, and she said yes. She had already applied for an apartment in the projects and it came through about a month after they'd gotten married. They had been married about three months when Stan's father got laid off from the A&P, and then they started arguing again. They never let anyone else see them arguing. Everyone thought they were two happy lovebirds. Stan wanted to talk to Tara about their arguing, but he knew she had her own problems dealing with the loss of her father. So he just kept it to himself and hoped that his father would find another job soon.

Since the walls in the projects were so thin, it was easy to hear someone talking in another room in the house, especially from the bathroom. Stan could hear his father and Momma June in the living room talking.

"So did you get Ms. Austin's fan working?" Momma June asked.

"Yeah, I fixed it, but she said she couldn't pay me until next Friday when she gets her check," Stan heard his father say.

"Goddammit, Henry! When are you gonna stop being so nice to these damn people? Hell, we got bills to pay, too!" Momma June exploded. "The way you go around giving all these women credit, I'm beginning to wonder if you ain't fixing more than their appliances."

"Look June, I don't know what you're trying to say, but I know I don't like it. Hell, you act as if I'm not trying to do anything to make some money, when you know damn well I'm out here every day busting my ass. I give these people time to pay me because I know they out here struggling trying to make ends meet!" he yelled.

"Struggling! Hell, I was struggling when I was single. I didn't get married to continue struggling. I watch my sister, Geneva, struggling trying to take care of two kids since her husband was killed. At least when James was alive he made sure his family was taken care of. That's all I want."

"Well June, I thought you married me because you loved me. I thought you married me for better or for worse. I didn't know you just wanted someone to take care of you and who you could compare to your brother-in-law."

"I'm not trying to compare you to anyone. And I don't need anyone to take care of me, because I was doing it before I met you and I can continue to do it. As a matter of fact," she said, "I got a job interview scheduled for Monday."

"Look June, I'm sick of this conversation. You do whatever makes you happy, okay? I'm going down to Bob's for a drink."

"Yeah, whatever. Just don't show your ass back up here drunk."

By that time Stan's bath water had gotten cold so he decided to get out. As he was coming out of the bathroom, he heard his father leaving the house. Momma June was still sitting on the couch with tears in her eyes. Stan just went in his room and closed the door, worried that he was about to lose another mother.

FOUR

"Momma, I'm home," I said as I walked into the house.

"Hey baby," my mother said as she came out of her bedroom. "What you got there?"

"Aunt June sent you some food," I said, sitting the plate on the stove. "Her and Uncle B. said hi. How was your day at work?"

"Girl! There are people walking the streets these days who should seriously consider turning themselves in to the nearest mental institution," my mother said as she shook her head and laughed.

"I guess you had some crazy clients come into the Social Security Office today."

"Clients! Hell, I'm talking about those crazy women I work with. They sit around all day discussing their personal business, acting as if they're fifteen years old. And then they have the nerve to talk about anybody who's got enough self-respect not to put their own business out in the streets. I just hope you and Denise have enough sense not to go around acting like you were raised with no morals. And speaking of Denise, what's wrong with her? Why is she in bed so early talking about she got a headache?"

"I don't know Momma. She seemed fine when I saw her earlier. Maybe she got a headache from all of the air freshener she sprayed in here."

"I don't know why that girl always sprays so much of that stuff," Momma said.

I can't believe my mother is this naïve, I thought as I got up to give her a hug. "Well Momma, I'm gonna take my bath and get ready for bed," I said as I headed for my room.

When I walked into the bedroom, Denise was laying across her bed with the pillow over her head.

"Hey Denise, what's up," I yelled.

"You think that shit's funny," she said, glaring at me.

"Denise, ain't nothing funny about a fourteen-year-old girl whose goal is to smoke as much weed and screw as many no good niggers as she can. You wouldn't be doing this shit if daddy were still alive."

"But he ain't alive now, is he? And even if he were he wouldn't give a damn anyway. You're the only one he cared anything about. His precious little baby."

"Oh please, Denise. Take my name off the invitation list," I shot at her.

"What damn invitation list?" she shot back at me.

"The list of people you're inviting to your pity party, 'cause I don't even wanna hear it. You know good and well Daddy treated us both the same. But you're just looking for any excuse to justify the fact that you're starting to act like some of the slutty ass girls in this building who aren't nothing but doorknobs—everybody gets a turn! And look at them, they're either pregnant or they already have kids. And some of them aren't even eighteen yet."

"Tara, you need to freeze on that bullshit. You walk around acting like you so much better than everybody else, writing your silly little stories and shit, like you white or some-thing. You need to wake up. You live on the Westside of Chicago, in the projects. You black and po' like everybody else in here."

"Where I live don't have nothing to do with who I am," I calmly said. "I have goals and dreams and I'm gonna do some-thing with my life. I believe in aiming high. But you, your motto seems to be 'aim low and avoid disappointments'. And I don't aspire to be a pot smoking ho like you."

"Who the hell you calling a ho?" she screamed as she jumped off the bed, reached underneath it and grabbed the box in which I kept my stories. "Let's see what your smart ass got to say when I start ripping these dumb ass stories up!"

Just then Momma stormed into the room. "What the hell is going on in here?"

"Momma," I said while glaring at Denise, "you know I love you and I would never want to see you sad or hurt, but if your daughter doesn't take her hands off my belongings she's gonna leave this house wearing a toe tag and I'm gonna leave here wearing metal bracelets."

And with that I calmly turned around and walked out of the bedroom into the bathroom, with both Momma and Denise looking at me as if I'd lost my mind. But since Momma knew me better than anyone, she knew I always had a flair for the dramatic and would say things just to make my point. I just hoped I hadn't gone too far this time.

Oh well, I'll just have to apologize to her and Denise when I finish my bath, I thought as I started running the water. No matter what, I still loved my sister and I knew she was hurting just as I was over our loss. I'd said some pretty mean things to her—true, but mean nonetheless. As I waited for the tub to fill, I stood in front of the mirror scowling and making faces, trying to look tough. It was amazing how much you could frighten and intimidate someone simply by giving a piercing stare or a nasty scowl; which is why I would periodically practice making mean faces. Heck, it had just worked with Denise, because she looked scared to death when I stared her down. "Oh well, a girl's got to do what a girl's got to do," I said as I sank into the tub.

After twenty minutes of soaking, I decided to get out as I wanted to apologize to Momma and Denise before they went to sleep. I also wanted to work on the story I was currently writing, which was about a girl who woke up one morning to find that her parents had been replaced by purple, three-eyed aliens who walked on their hands and spoke in riddles. (Sometimes my imagination took a sharp detour.)

As soon as I finished up in the bathroom, I went into Momma's room. "Momma, I'm sorry for getting you upset and for talking to Denise like I did," I said as I sat on the side of her bed.

"You should be ashamed of yourself for carrying on like that. I can't believe you would have the nerve to threaten to kill your own sister when you know your Momma is just too tired to be stepping over dead bodies or cleaning up spilled blood. But I accept your apology. Now get out of my room so I can watch a little TV before I go to sleep."

"Momma, you so crazy," I said as I gave her a hug and kiss. I walked into our bedroom smiling, but the smile imme-diately left my face when I saw Denise was still sitting on her bed, huffing and puffing with her face all screwed up. I could have sworn there was steam coming out of her ears. *Oh boy, this is not going to be easy,* I thought as I stood facing her. "Denise, I want to apologize for the mean things I said to you. I shouldn't have went off on you like that."

"Yeah, whatever," she said while giving me a look that could kill. Maybe she had been practicing faces also.

"Well, I'm gonna go in the living room and do some writing," I said as I got my box from underneath the bed and headed out of the room.

"Bitch," I heard her mumble.

"Heifer," I mumbled back at her.

FIVE

"Deanne, would you hurry up? We're not gonna be late for school waiting around for you," I yelled as me and Stan sat in Deanne's living room waiting for her.

"I'm trying to find some decent socks," she yelled back.

Finally after about five minutes she came out of her bedroom, which she shared with her 16-year-old sister and her 7- year-old brother.

"Aren't Beverly and Jason going to school?" Stan asked as we were leaving the house.

"Naw, Jason talking about he tired, and Beverly says school is too boring. Hell, if Momma let them stay home, I might as well stay home too," Deanne pouted.

"Deanne, are you stupid or just dumb?" I asked her. "Being a drop-out and an underachiever should not be a goal. Dag, I swear you'd think hanging out with me by now some of my good qualities would have rubbed off on you. Not that I have any bad qualities," I laughed.

"Do you consider them chicken legs of yours to be a good quality?" she shot at me.

"Oh, so now you want to play the dozens, huh?"

"Hey Tara, look! Ain't that the dude who was at your house yesterday with JT and Lil Man?" Stan said.

"Yeah, that's him," I said as I watched him heading in our direction.

"Man, look at those cold threads dude got on," Stan ex-claimed. "His people must have money."

"Yeah, and he's fine too," Deanne said.

By this time he had walked up to us and he stood directly in front of me. "Hey shorty, what's up?" he said.

"First off, my name is not shorty, and second, you're blocking my path," I said as I stared directly into his eyes. And they were very lovely eyes, which were attached to a very lovely face, but the expression on my face was the opposite of the thoughts that were going through my head.

"Well, I guess I should get out of your path," he said as he stepped aside and held out his hand. "My name's Jeremy."

"Hello, Jeremy. Goodbye, Jeremy," I said as I started walking away.

"Hey, wait a minute shorty. What's with all the attitude?" he asked as he grabbed my arm.

"Maybe smoking so much weed has eaten away your brain cells," I said, snatching my arm away, "but as I recall, yesterday you had the nerve to be sitting in my mother's house getting high. That's what's with all this attitude. And like I said before, my name ain't shorty."

"Well, maybe if you told me your name, shorty, then I would stop calling you shorty," he said as he smiled at me.

"Her name's Tara," Deanne piped in with her big mouth.

"Look Tara," he said, "I wasn't disrespecting your mom's house, because I don't smoke that shit. Maybe you're the one with damaged brain cells because as I recall it was your sister who was smoking weed. I was just there with my cousin JT, who wanted to introduce me to some of his friends since I'm gonna be living with him and my Aunt. But I'm sorry if you thought we were disrespecting your house," he said as he started walking beside me toward school.

"Jeremy, those are some sharp clothes you got on," Stan said as he and Deanne fell into step behind us. "You got a job or something?"

"It's probably the 'or something'," I said, looking at Jeremy.

"So what's that supposed to mean?" he asked.

"Well, let's see," I said, "JT is your cousin, you're now living with and hanging out with him, he wears expensive clothes, you wear expensive clothes, he sells drugs; okay, you do the math."

"Well little miss mathematician, I don't use drugs and I don't sell drugs. I'm a businessman and a hustler."

"Yeah, right, a 13-year-old businessman," I said. "And just what is your business?"

"I'll put it like this," he said. "If someone sees something in a store and they can't afford the store's inflated prices, then I just get it for them at a discount price."

"So in other words, you're a common thief," I said.

"No, I'm a businessman."

"Hey, I saw this sharp warm-up suit at Fields," Deanne said. "You think you can get it for me?"

I just looked back and rolled my eyes at her.

"So will you be going to our school?" Stan asked.

"Naw man, I'm already in high school."

"What school do you go to?" Deanne asked.

"Lane Tech," Jeremy said as he winked at me.

"Get out of here! That's the same school Tara's going to in September," Stan said.

"Is that right," Jeremy said, smiling.

By this time we were at the entrance to the school. "If you go to Lane, why aren't you there now?" I asked.

"Hey, school is cool, but I'd rather be down on the corner shooting a little pool," he said, laughing. "Naw, on the real though, I have to go pick up the rest of my clothes from home, so I'm not going to school today."

"Well I hope you're a better 'businessman' than you are a poet," I said as we headed inside the school.

"I'll check y'all later," Jeremy said, heading down the street.

"Yeah, I hope that's much later," I responded.

SIX

The next two months seemed to fly by as I prepared for my 13th birthday, which was on June 20th. I was also busy writing my speech for the 8th grade graduation as I had been chosen Valedictorian.

Looking back now, it seems as if so many chaotic events took place during those two months. Since I'd been so caught up in my own life, I hadn't had much time to spend at Stan's house. My Aunt June had gotten the job as a receptionist for a law firm downtown, which meant she didn't get much chance to cook anymore. But I wasn't sweating it because both her and Momma made sure I paid attention when they cooked, so I was looking forward to trying out my culinary skills and cooking for them for a change. Momma said the food I cooked tasted good and since Stan was now spending more time at my house, I assumed it was because he was looking forward to my cooking also. Boy was I wrong, as I found out one evening when I happened to stop by his house.

Even though it had only been a little over a month since I'd last seen Uncle B., I was shocked at the change in him. As I walked up to give him a hug, the smell of alcohol was so over- whelming I almost gagged. And his appearance! Man, he looked as if he hadn't shaven or bathed in a long time. I looked over at Stan and could tell that he was embarrassed, so I held my breath and went ahead and gave Uncle B. a hug.

"Where's Aunt June?" I asked as the phone rang.

"I don't know. She should have been here two hours ago," Uncle B. said as he answered the phone. "Hello....hello," he said as he apparently received no reply. "Look goddammit, don't call here if you ain't gonna say shit!"

he yelled into the phone before slamming it down. "She think I don't know what the hell is going on," he mumbled as he headed for the door. "Stan, I'll be back in a couple of hours."

"Okay Daddy," Stan said with a sad look on his face.

As soon as Uncle B. was out of the house I walked over to Stan. "Stan, what in the world is going on around here?"

"*Your aunt* is ruining our family, that's what!"

"Okay Stan, let's try this again. What's going on? You're talking crazy, Uncle B. is looking crazy, and it's almost 8:30 and my aunt hasn't made it home from work yet."

"Look Tara, I've never told you this, but *your aunt* was riding my dad's ass even before they got married about him not having a steady job and making enough money, and you know my dad is always hustling trying to make some money," Stan said with tears in his eyes.

"Yeah, you're right about that. Your dad is always fixing things for people, but what do you mean about my aunt riding him? Every time I see them they're always kissing and acting all lovey-dovey."

"They never let anyone see them arguing. Most of the time they are cool with each other, but then *your aunt* just snaps on him about him not having enough money."

"Okay, Stan! Just hold up one minute because you're beginning to piss me off. My aunt has always been 'Momma June' to you, but now all of a sudden she's *'your aunt'*. What's up with that?"

"Well I'm sorry," Stan said, "but she makes me sick the way she treats my dad now. Ever since she started working she acts like she so much better than Daddy. Always yelling at him and calling him stupid and ripple-head. And you know what else?"

"What?" I asked.

"She got a boyfriend!"

"Stop lying, Stan," I said angrily.

"I'm not lying. Didn't you see what happened when Daddy answered the phone? And don't even bother saying it was probably a wrong number, 'cause it happens a lot, especially whenever *your aunt,* excuse me, I mean Momma June, is late getting home."

"Well Stan, that doesn't mean she has a boyfriend."

"Okay, remember last week when I went to visit my grand- mother?"

"Yeah, and?"

"Well, when I was coming home I was walking down Washington St., and I saw this really nice car. I think it was a Lincoln. It was parked and I could see the couple all hugged up and kissing. At first I didn't pay them any attention 'cause I was checking out the car, but as I got closer I saw who it was. It was Momma June."

"Who was the man?" I asked, incredulously.

"I don't know. I've never seen him before, but he was a really big, black dude. I hope he's not a pimp," Stan said with a smirk on his face.

"Look Stan, don't get your little ass whipped," I said, pointing my finger in his face. "Did they see you?"

"Naw, they were too busy playing tongue hockey. I'm telling you Tara, Momma June has changed. All she care about is getting her hair and nails done and buying new clothes."

"Stan, I've known my Aunt almost thirteen years now and she's always been the nicest, most loving person you could ever meet. So I'm not even hearing this smack you're telling me, okay?"

"You believe what you want, but I'm telling you, she's changed." Just then the door opened and Aunt June walked in.

"Girl, what in the world are you doing up here? It's almost 9:00," Aunt June said as she kicked off her shoes.

"We were just talking and I lost track of time," I said as I stared at her. It seemed as if she had changed. While her appearance was immaculate, she seemed to be short-tempered and impatient. *Maybe,* I thought, *she's just tired and I'm just imagining things and letting what Stan said get to me.*

"You look really nice, Aunt June. How was your day at work?" I asked. "Are you working overtime now?"

"Tara, my day was just fine, but why are you asking me all these questions? Am I on trial or something?" she said, hands on hips.

I noticed Stan looking at me with an 'I told you so' look on his face. "I'm sorry, Aunt June. I was just trying to be polite," I said as I headed for the door.

"Yeah, well I didn't mean to be short with you. I'm just worn out from today," she said as she turned to Stan.

I wonder what's got her worn out, I thought, closing the door.

"Stan, shouldn't you be getting ready for bed?"

"I just wanted to wait up for my Daddy."

"Boy, ain't no telling when that man might drag his ass in here drunk and talking crazy. Go on to bed," she said, not bothering to tell Stan to take a bath first—like she usually did.

Man, I thought as I walked downstairs to my apartment, *Aunt June has changed.* I couldn't wait to get home so I could talk to Momma about what was going on; but that was one conversation that never took place. Little did I know that the drama taking place at Stan's home was nothing compared to what was going on in my home at that moment.

As I neared my apartment I could hear Momma yelling, so I rushed in to see what was going on. Momma was pacing back and forth looking mad enough to kill. Denise was sitting on the couch crying. "Momma, I'm sorry. I didn't mean for it to happen," she cried.

"What the hell you mean, you didn't mean for it to happen? Don't you know if you lay down, open your legs and let some nasty ass boy do his business in you, then you stand a good chance of getting pregnant? What part of that have you been unclear about?" Momma yelled.

Oh shit! I thought as I stood there with my mouth wide open. *Denise is pregnant!*

Now, no one could ever accuse my sister of being the brightest bulb in the pack and she proved it when she added insult to injury by looking up at Momma and saying. "Well, at least now I can get a welfare check and stop having to ask you for money."

When she said that, my jaw literally hit the floor and so did Momma's. But unfortunately for Denise it didn't take long for Momma to recover, because as soon as she did she grabbed Denise by her collar with one hand and with the other one she reached back and slapped the girl so hard I'm sure our ancestors must have felt it. In order to keep Momma from killing the girl, I ran over and grabbed her. "Momma, please don't hit her again, you're gonna hurt her!" I cried.

"Take your hands off me," Momma said, glaring at me. And I did exactly that, with a quickness. I was too pretty to have a hand print forever embedded on my face.

"Her ass need to be hurt. And she will be, because if you think having a baby and taking care of one is easy, then you're about to find out different," Momma said, storming into her room.

I just stood there looking at my sister as she lay on the couch crying rivers of tears.

"Denise, why don't you go lay down in the bed and I'll bring you some aspirin and a cold towel. Momma will be okay, she just needs some time to accept this," I said as I rubbed Denise's back. *Hell,* I thought, *why should she accept this? I know I don't think I can accept the fact that there will be a crying, smelly baby here in an apartment that's already too small and cluttered for the three of us. I'm certainly not looking forward to this, but I guess I don't have a choice in the matter. Oh well,* I thought as I sat down, *I'm sure things can't get any crazier. I just hope I don't wake up next week to find out a mistake had been made and I won't be graduating. Now that would be some serious craziness.* Little did I know that the summer of '79 would get crazier.

SEVEN

"Hey Tara, wait up," I heard as I walked to the bus stop.

"Jeremy, what's up?" I said as he ran up to me.

"So how was your first day as a freshman?" he asked.

"It was okay, I guess. High school is a lot different from grammar school."

"You'll be alright. Just keep your eyes open and your guard up and don't fall in with the wrong crowd," he said as the bus pulled up.

"I'm already in with the wrong crowd," I laughed, pointing at him.

"That's real funny, shorty," he said, punching me in the arm.

"Aren't you getting on?" I asked, stepping up on the bus.

"Naw, I got some business to take care of."

"Well, be careful while you're taking care of your business," I said as the doors closed. I couldn't believe how close me and Jeremy had grown over the past couple of months. Even though I was totally against what he was doing to make money, he was still a good person and he was so much fun to be around. As I sat back and prepared for the long ride home, which included one bus and two trains, I thought about the events that had taken place over the summer.

First, there was no mistake. I did graduate—at the top of my class—and I was the Valedictorian. My speech was very stirring and emotional and it dealt with the issues of being a young person growing up in the inner city; of taking responsibility for our lives and making wise choices;

of not letting the circumstances of where we live dictate who we are or who we become, or stop us from dreaming, having goals, and making every effort to excel while keeping God first and foremost in our lives, and always loving and respecting our parents and families. When I'd finished, there wasn't a dry eye in the auditorium. As I looked around, I was happy to see the people I loved and cared most about were there.

Momma looked so proud and elegant in her white designer suit, which she'd saved up for. Mr. Bell, my favorite teacher, was there beaming and looking as happy as if he were watching his own children graduating. I'm sure Daddy was up in heaven smoking a cigar with his chest poked out saying, "That's my baby girl!"

Jeremy somehow managed to get a ticket and he was sitting next to Denise. I could see so many emotions crossing my sister's face and I knew she was hurting. Ever since the night she'd told Momma about her pregnancy, things hadn't been the same between them and the tension at home was so thick you could cut it with a knife. There were times when I felt guilty being so happy and knowing my sister was so miserable, but seeing her here trying to be happy for me made me want to cry.

I'll never forget the smile on her face when I was handed my diploma. That was the first time I'd seen her smile in about a week. Every time I think of her I remember that smile because it was also the last time I would see her smile for a long time. When my sister walked out of that auditorium, she kept right on walking. The next time I heard from her was a month after my graduation when she phoned one day while Momma was at work, to let me know that she was alright. So I just said a lot of prayers for her and her baby and ask God to watch over them and bring them home. I also asked him to forgive me for the negative thoughts I had about them.

Stan was also there, along with Aunt June and Uncle B., who was sober, clean, and huggable. They looked like a family again and appeared to be happy. They were laughing and joking with each other and it seemed as if they had worked things out and were enjoying each other's company. I was hoping that everything was now fine between them. For about two months everything was, but then one day about ten days before school resumed, all hell broke loose.

As I got off the bus to transfer to the Red Line Train, I thought about that day and how I saw a side of my aunt that would change my opinion of her. I had turned 13 (and it was a memorable 13th birthday—memorable in a negative way because my sister was not there, and in a positive way because Momma gave me a bank book with my very own savings account in which she'd deposited $1,000.) I had also been able to get a summer job at the park and Stan was going there for summer camp. Well anyway, one day Stan got sick and they'd tried to contact Aunt June at work but she wasn't there. By this time Uncle B. had cleaned himself up and found a job as a security guard, but they weren't able to reach him either. So I volunteered to take Stan home and watch him until we could contact Aunt June or Uncle B. When we walked into the house, at first everything was quiet, but then all of a sudden we hear these noises coming from the bedroom. It sounded like someone was hurt, in agony. (Heck, I was 13. I didn't know ecstasy could sometimes sound like agony). Stan and I thought maybe Aunt June was in there sick or something so we went running into the room. There on the bed was my aunt, though I couldn't see her face. I assumed it was her, because all I could see was this humongous ass going up and down on top of a man who was not Uncle B. Hell, not only was he not Uncle B., he was a white man. The first thing that ran through my mind after the shock of seeing my aunt's big naked ass, was how in the world did a white man get this far in the building, and how he must have really wanted a piece of Aunt June to even risk coming in here.

They were so involved in what they were doing that at first they had no idea we were standing there. But then Aunt June looked around and when she saw us she instantly jumped up. Since I'd never seen a man's genitals before, I couldn't help but take a peek. I wanted to see what had Aunt June making all those silly noises. What I saw did not impress me at all; a skinny pale thing that looked like it was sneezing. (Okay, I had no idea what semen was or what it looked like. I guess Momma was way overdue for having that little talk with me.) I just hoped black men's things didn't look like that, because if they did then I knew I'd never get a chance to make disgusting noises.

By this time the white guy had jumped up also and just as Aunt June was about to say something, we heard the front door slam shut.

"Uh-huh, goddammit! I knew somethin' was going on here!"

Oh shit! I thought as I looked around to see Uncle B. standing there shaking with rage.

"You no good, lousy, stankin' ass bitch!" he spat.

Pencil dick had somehow managed to get his pants on by now and was babbling. "Mister, I'm sorry. She didn't tell me she was married. I'm sorry, man. Please don't hurt me!"

"Motherfucker! I'm go' toss your ugly white ass out this 12th floor window!" Uncle B. screamed as he moved toward the guy. As soon as Uncle B. moved, the man lunged, grabbed his jacket and pulled out a gun.

"Look, I don't want to hurt anyone. I just want to get the hell out of here," he said as he backed up in the direction of the door. As soon as he got to the door, he yanked it open and was out of the house and probably out of the building in the blink of an eye. While all of this had been going on, I'd been so stunned that I had almost forgotten about Stan. I turned to look at him and my heart literally broke into a thousand pieces. He was just standing there, not moving, not blinking, just staring directly at Aunt June, who by now had had the decency to put on a robe, with tears streaming down his face.

"Why June? Why are you doing this to me?" Uncle B. asked as he started to cry. "I thought you loved me. I thought we were working our problems out. I stopped drinking, I got a job. Everything I do, I do for you. So why?" he sobbed. "Why are you in our bed screwing a goddamn white man? Ain't they done took enough from us?"

"Look Henry," she said as she glared at him (can you believe she was actually acting as if she was the one who had been wronged?), I do love you, but I'm tired of your drinking and only working every now and then. I'm sick of living in these damn projects. You ain't taking care of me, I'm taking care of myself!"

"June, all I want is for us to be happy," Uncle B. said as he hung his head.

"Well Henry, it's too late for that because all I want is out. Out of this house, out of this building, out of this marriage!"

"So what are you saying, June? You want me to leave?"

"No Henry, I don't want you to leave. I'm leaving!" And with that she walked in the bathroom and slammed the door. At that moment, so many different emotions were going through my body that I thought I would explode. I wanted to cry, I wanted to scream, I wanted to grab Stan, who was still silently crying, and just hug him and make the hurt go away. I wanted to comfort Uncle B., who looked as if his whole world had come crashing down, but most of all I wanted to kick down that bathroom door and slowly and methodically drown my aunt in the toilet; a place where at the moment I felt she needed to be. Aunt or no aunt, I felt at that moment as if she was the equivalent of shit. What had happened to the aunt I loved and respected? *How could she be so cold and heartless?* I thought as I stood there like a deer caught in the glare of headlights.

"Tara, take Stan down to your place," Uncle B. said as he stood staring at the bathroom door. "I'll come get him later." As I took Stan by the hand and led him out of the house, I wished that Uncle B. would stop staring at that damn bathroom door and hug Stan or say something, anything, to him. But he didn't, so I just walked out with Stan beside me.

* * *

As I got off the Red Line Train at State St. and went upstairs to catch the Green Line Train, I recalled the events that happened next, which would forever seal my friendship with Jeremy.

Once we'd gotten to my house, I took Stan to my room and told him to lay down while I got some tissue and a towel to clean his face. It seemed as if lately I'd been doing a lot of tear wiping. "Stan," I said as I sat on the bed, "I thought you said the man you saw my Aunt with was black."

"He was," Stan said.

"Then who was that she was with upstairs?"

"I don't know, and I don't care!"

"I can't believe this," I said as I looked at Stan.

"Look Tara, I don't want to talk about what we just saw and heard, now or ever." he said, rolling over.

"Stan, I just need to talk about it," I said. But he only laid there facing the wall, refusing to say anything else, so I got up and went into the living room. I was glad Momma wasn't home yet; although I wanted to talk to someone, I didn't think I could bring myself to tell Momma about her only sister. I sat on the couch for about a half hour reliving everything that had just happened until finally I could take it no longer. I went back into the bedroom to try to talk to Stan again, but he was sound asleep. I decided to go up to Deanne's house. I knew I couldn't tell her everything that had happened, but I needed to talk to someone. When I got to Deanne's, she wasn't home so I stood on the porch staring off into space.

"Tara, are you okay?"

Dag, I thought as I looked up and saw Jeremy heading toward me. The last thing I needed was to hear him trying to be funny and cracking on me. "Yeah, I'm alright."

"No you're not," he said. "I've been in my doorway watching you standing here for the past five minutes, staring off into space."

I'd forgotten that he lived on the same floor as Deanne. "I'm okay," I said, trying to mask my feelings. But as I looked into Jeremy's face I saw nothing but concern written there.

"Okay," he said. "Look, I was about to fix one of my delicious Dagwood sandwiches. Would you like one?"

At that moment it dawned on me that I hadn't eaten all day, and since I really wasn't ready to go back home yet, I said okay.

"Why don't you go in the living room and watch TV while I fix our sandwiches?" he said. "Besides, I can't have you seeing the special ingredients I use on my sandwiches; then I'd have to kill you." I looked at him and laughed. Boy, did that feel good.

We sat on the couch side by side eating our sandwiches, drinking apple juice and watching television. Jeremy wasn't kidding when he said his sandwiches were delicious. Dagwood would have been impressed. As I sat there smacking my lips, I wanted so bad to take the sandwich apart piece by piece to see what he'd put on it to make it taste so good. But I could see him cutting his eye at me, smiling, as if he could read my mind. So I managed to resist the temptation and sat there enjoying it, wondering how I was gonna go back to those sorry bologna and cheese sandwiches I'd been making, after eating one of these. Once we'd finished eating, Jeremy cleaned up and sat back down on the couch facing me. "Tara," he said, "did you know my father's white?"

"Get out of here!" I exclaimed.

"What, you thought I got this light from taking bleach baths?" he smiled.

"Well you know, we do come in all different shades and that doesn't mean we necessarily have to have a parent who's white."

"Yeah, my father's white. He owns his own consulting firm and he and my mother have a home in Highland Park. But you know what? Even though my parents have been married fifteen years, his family still won't accept the fact that he married a black woman. Hell, I got cousins I've never met and grandparents who won't even acknowledge me."

"I'm sorry, Jeremy," I said sadly.

"Hey, it's alright. It's their loss, not mine."

"Jeremy, I can't understand why it is you come from a family with money and a home and you're out here being a businessman."

"Naw Tara, you can call it what it is. I'm a shoplifter. A thief. It has nothing to do with my people having money. When I first started shoplifting I just wanted to get my father's attention and piss him off because I blamed him for his parents not wanting to have anything to do with me. But after awhile, I did it because it was fun and I liked the thrill and challenge of being able to go in a store and walk out with anything I wanted without having to pay for it. Since I wasn't really doing it for the money, I would sell the stuff I'd stolen dirt cheap. Hell, some of my parents' high-class friends were customers of mine. They'd shit if they knew that."

"So what happened? Why are you here living with your Aunt?" I asked.

"Well, I'd been ditching school and my parents were hearing rumors that I was shoplifting. One day my mother found two Rolex watches in my room. She wanted to kick my ass, but my dad was like, 'Ruthie, we will not hit our child. We have to talk to him and find out why he's rebelling and acting out in this fashion.' Then he says to me, 'Jeremy, your mother and I will not tolerate this atrocious behavior. We are going to have to ground you, young man'," Jeremy said, laughing as he imitated his father.

"Dag, your dad talks like that?" I laughed.

"I told you he's white."

"If my father found out I'd been stealing and ditching school, he would have beat me like a runaway slave," I said. "But Jeremy, I still don't understand why being grounded would make you want to leave home and come live in the pj's."

"Actually, it was my dad's idea. He said I was ungrateful and didn't appreciate how good I had it, so he wanted me to come live here so that I could see what it's like for people who have to struggle to make ends meet. Maybe then I would get my act together and appreciate what I had."

"Oh, I understand," I said. But really I didn't. Jeremy's explanation just didn't make sense to me. *Maybe white folks react to things differently than we do,* I thought to myself. It would be a year later when I would find out the real reason Jeremy's father sent him to live elsewhere.

"Aren't you afraid of getting arrested?" I asked him.

"Girl, I am too smooth to get caught. And besides, if I do, Pops will take care of it."

As we sat there watching television, I thought about how I was beginning to like Jeremy. Although I didn't know much about boys, Jeremy seemed different. He was sensitive and con- cerned and I was touched that he would open up to me about his family. I felt so comfortable with him that before I knew it, I started telling him about what had happened at Stan's house. The more I talked the more I cried, but Jeremy never made fun about my crying like a little baby. He just wrapped his arms around me and let me talk and cry until I was done.

"I'm sorry," I said. "I got tears and snot all over your shirt."

"That's alright. It'll wash out. Well, I know the tears will, but that's some pretty thick snot you left on my shoulder. So, do you feel better now?"

"Yeah, I do. I feel a lot better now."

"Good. Then you'll be getting my bill for one meal and one counseling session," he said while smiling.

"Well, I can pay you now if you have change for a dollar."

"That's real funny, shorty," he said, thunking me upside my head.

"Well, I'd better go home now and find out what's going on with Stan," I said, standing up.

"Okay," he said, "I'll catch you later."

"Thanks Jeremy."

* * *

When I walked in the house, Momma was on the phone and I could tell she was upset. I guess she'd found out about what had happened. I waved to her and went to my room to see how Stan was doing, but he was gone. At first I wasn't paying much attention to Momma's conversation until I heard her say Aunt June's name.

"June," she said, "how could you dog out a good man like Henry? You know that man loves you and would do anything for you! And what about Stan? Hasn't that child been through enough? Now he got to deal with seeing your whorish ass in bed with some white man, and now you're talking about leaving him and Henry. What the hell is the matter with you. Do you think some white man's gonna let you come live with him! What do you mean he's not the man you're gonna live with? And who in the hell is Robert?"

I didn't hear Momma say anything for a few minutes. I guess Aunt June was trying to explain things to her, and I sure wanted to know who Robert was and who the white man was.

"I don't believe this shit!" I heard Momma explode. "You mean to tell me you're gonna leave your husband for some nigger named Robert just because he's cute and drives a Lincoln? If you're leaving Henry for this Robert dude, then who the hell was that white man my daughter and Stan saw you fucking? You know what, June, I don't even wanna know who he was. All I got to say to you is that you a low-life bitch and the next time I see you, both of us will be going to the hospital. You, to have your ass sewn up, and me to have my foot surgically removed from your ass, because I intend to kick your ass until I get tired! You have no right messing over a good man like Henry and allowing Tara and Stan to catch your trifling ass in bed screwing some asshole."

I heard Momma slam the phone down. *Man,* I thought, *Aunt June is leaving Uncle B. for that man Stan saw her in the car with, but she was just in bed with another man. I sure hope 'Robert with the Lincoln' know's what kind of woman he's hooking up with.* Just then Momma walked in my room.

"Baby, are you alright? I'm sorry you had to see that and to hear me lose my temper just now."

"Yeah Momma I'm alright. But where's Stan?"

"Henry came to get him. That's when he told me about this mess. He took Stan to his grandmother's to stay for a couple of days while he gets things straightened out."

"Momma, I don't understand why this is happening," I said as for the second time that day I started to cry.

"I know baby, I know," Momma said as she held me on her lap and for the second time that day I also told her everything that had happened.

* * *

As I got off the train and walked to my building, I reflected on how that day I'd learned a lot, but the one lesson I would always remember was how much it helped to talk about, and if necessary cry about, things which were troubling and too much to deal with on your own. I felt so much better after pouring my heart out to Jeremy and Momma. I knew I would never hold in anything I felt I needed to get off my chest. I just hoped that one day Stan would realize the importance of talking to someone he could trust instead of holding in his anger and letting it eat away at him. As I got on the elevator and rode up to my house, I wondered if other 13 year old kids had as much drama in their lives as I seemed to be having in mine.

* * *

The next two years were pretty much uneventful, with me settling into my high school classes. Denise eventually started getting her life together even though she still refused to come home. I rarely heard from Stan, who was still staying with his grandmother. On the occasions when I would run into Uncle B., I'd ask about him and when he might be coming back home. Uncle B. would just shrug his shoulders. As for Uncle B., he would manage to clean himself up for a little while, but then he would sink back down into his hopeless world of alcoholism. My friendship with Jeremy continued to grow and we became the best of friends.

EIGHT

"Michelle, would you care to tell me what happened?" Principal Greer asked as we sat in her office.

"Nothing," Michelle said as she stared at the floor. "I slipped in the bathroom, fell and hit my face on the sink."

"Michelle, do I look stupid? Your face is swollen, you have a black eye and a bloody nose. All of those injuries could not have occurred simply from you falling."

As I sat there staring straight ahead, I thought to myself that Michelle was telling the truth, sort of. She did hit her face on the sink, but I was the one responsible for hitting her face on the sink. But if she chose not to tell, I certainly wasn't going to volunteer the information.

"Tara St. Pierre, you're sitting here looking all innocent, but I'm certain you had something to do with this. Mr. Jackson saw the two of you arguing yesterday; but since Michelle claims she fell, I can't do anything but to let it go," Principal Greer said as she looked directly at me. "If it weren't for the fact that you've been a model student for the two years you've been here at Lane Tech, I would make it a point to pursue this further. If I ever find out you had something to do with this, I won't hesitate to take whatever action deemed necessary, even if it means expelling you from this school. I'm sure your mother would very much like for you to finish your two remaining years here."

"Yes ma'am, she would. And so would I," I said while trying to look as sincere as possible.

"You two young ladies are dismissed," she said as I stood up, grabbed my books and headed off to my honors English class. As I walked down the hall to class, my thoughts went back to the previous day in gym class, Michelle and some of her friends were talking about the upcoming Junior Prom and who in our Sophomore class had been invited.

"I don't care how many guys ask me, I'm turning all of 'em down if Jeremy asks me to go," Rachel said.

"Girl, you know he ain't gonna ask your ass. Tara's his woman. That's who he's gonna take," I heard Jean say. I tried hard to ignore them because I knew they were just talking shit trying to piss me off. But then Michelle decided to take it one step further.

"Y'all know damn well Tara ain't his girlfriend. She's just his front. Hell, we've all but thrown pussy Jeremy's way and he acts like he's allergic to it. But I guess fags are allergic to pussy," she laughed. "Shit, Tara's probably a dyke, 'cause you sho' don't see her with any guys." As they started laughing, I got up and walked out of the gym while trying to ignore their silly asses. As I walked out, I knew the first chance I got I was gonna fuck Michelle up. And whadda you know? I got that chance. I was in the washroom when I heard Michelle come in talking to Jean. "Girl, come on in here and wait for me while I smoke this joint," she said. "Ain't but one person in here. Come on." Unfortunately for her, she didn't know who that one person was.

"Naw girl, I got to go talk to my counselor," Jean said.

I decided to stay in the stall for a minute to let her smoke some of her joint. That way, I could totally mess up her high. I didn't want to wait too long and have someone come in, so after about a minute or two I came out of the stall. I didn't waste any time talking to her. I just walked up to her and immediately started punching her in the face. She tried to run but I grabbed her by her hair, and that's when I smashed her face into the sink. As she fell to the floor crying, I bent down and picked up her joint. "Here," I said, "don't forget your joint." I patted her on the head and strolled out of the washroom.

* * *

As I headed home after school, I decided it was time I con- fronted Jeremy about what Michelle and her friends were saying about him. Not only were those idiots saying Jeremy was gay, but I had been hearing whispered rumors about his sexuality from others. I had always assumed the guys were talking shit because they were jealous that Jeremy was handsome and dressed better than they did. As for the girls, I figured they were pissed because he wouldn't date any of them. But as I thought about it, I'd only known him to have one girlfriend and that was a very short relationship. When I'd asked him why they'd split up he said she was always asking him for money. I figured that maybe he wasn't interested in dating just yet. I know I certainly had no interest in having a boyfriend at that time.

I remembered an incident that had happened a couple of months earlier. Philip had bought a watch from Jeremy and brought it back saying it didn't work. Jeremy probably would have gladly given him back his money. But Philip had had the watch for about three months and it was all scratched up, so Jeremy refused to give him a refund. Philip started cussing and getting all up in Jeremy's face, calling him soft and a punk. Jeremy just stood staring at him; but then Philip said to Jeremy, "Maybe if I let you suck my dick then you'll be happy to give me back my money and yours too!" Before I knew it, Jeremy had grabbed him by the throat with one hand and lifted him off the ground. He kept applying more pressure until Philip's eyes started to bulge. When Jeremy saw he was near unconsciousness, he let him go. While Philip lay on the ground gasping for air, Jeremy stood over him patiently waiting for him to regain his composure. As soon as he did, Jeremy started unmercifully kicking his ass until his cousin JT ran up and stopped him.

Just thinking about that incident convinced me that I needed to talk to Jeremy about these rumors.

When I got to the building, I went straight to Jeremy's apartment. Since he had fewer classes than I did, I knew he would probably be at home.

"Hey girl, what's up?" Jeremy said as he opened the door. He obviously had been working out since he was wearing a pair of biker shorts with a towel draped around his neck. His body was glistening with sweat and he was drinking a bottle of Gatorade. *Hell, naw!* I thought as I looked at him. *This boy cannot be gay. Not with a body like that.*

"Jeremy, I need to talk to you," I said, walking in and taking a seat.

"Okay, what's up?"

"Well, I haven't had anything to eat all day. You think you could rustle me up a sandwich?"

"That's what you wanted to talk to me about?" he asked, snapping me with the towel.

"Uh uh, but you know I never pass up an opportunity for one of your mahvelous sandwiches, dahling."

"Well since you put it like that, then I guess that's one Jeremy Special coming up."

"Okay, so what's up?" he asked when I'd finished eating. "You look like you got some heavy shit on your mind. I hope nothing's happened to Denise or Stan."

"No. I talked to Denise a couple of weeks ago and she's doing fine. It's been about three months since I've spoken to Stan, but he says he's doing good."

"Well I'm glad to hear that. So what's got you so uptight?"

"I got into a fight today with Michelle. Well, actually it wasn't really a fight. It was more like a serious Muhammad Ali style ass-kicking.

"Good! That slut is always up in somebody's business," he said, giving me five. "So what did she do to unleash the fury of Ms. Tara?"

"Her and her girls were calling you a fag the other day. That's not the first time I've heard this shit about you being gay. So I'm asking you straight up: Jeremy, are you gay?"

"So what, you got something against gay people?" he asked while looking me straight in the eye.

"Hell naw, that doesn't bother me. What would bother me would be knowing that you didn't trust me enough to tell me," I said with my hands on my hips.

"Okay, Tara," Jeremy said as he sat down next to me. "You're my friend, so I know I can trust you. Remember when I told you my parents got upset when I was caught with two Rolex's in my room?"

"Yeah, and?"

"Well, what I didn't tell you was that the Rolex's happened to be on the arms of two 'friends' of mine. When my mom walked in the room, that's all they were wearing and the three of us were in a compromising position."

"Get the hell out of here, Jeremy!" I shouted. "You mean to tell me you had two boyfriends and you were only 12 or 13?"

"They weren't my boyfriends. We were just experimenting."

"Sooo, who were they? Were they black or white?" I asked, excitedly.

"Damn Tara, slow down! Jonathan was 15, white, and he lived across the street from me. Robert was 16, black, and he lived next door."

"Well, how did you all become involved?" I anxiously asked.

"They were sort of like my mentors. They're the ones who schooled me on the shoplifting game."

"Obviously they were your mentors in more ways than one," I laughed. "But how did you go from shoplifting together to freaking together?"

"I never knew they were gay. One day we were at my house wrestling and rough-housing around when Jonathan said it was hot in my room, so he strips down to his briefs. So Robert says he wants to get comfortable too, but he's not wearing any underwear. Jonathan says 'so what' and dared him to take off his clothes—so Robert did. I was sitting there checking them out. I didn't think he would do it, but he did. He had such a firm, hard, muscular body and I found myself getting aroused. By the time they'd started wrestling again, I was so turned on that I took off my clothes and joined in the fun. Next thing I know, Jonathan's blowing me while Robert's behind me rubbing his body up against mine. I was so into what was happening that I didn't hear the door open."

"Oh shit!" I said. "Your moms walked in!"

"Yep, she sure did."

"So what happened?"

As soon as she was able to breathe again, she started cussing and calling us every nasty name she could think of. Then she turned around and headed for her room. Hell, I thought she was going for her gun. So I threw on my clothes—by this time Jonathan and Robert were already dressed—and we got the hell out of there. I waited until about 7:00 that night and called home to find out what was going on. My dad answered the phone and told me he loved me but that I was not welcome in his home ever again. So I called my Aunt, and here I am."

"Damn Jeremy, that's some deep shit!"

"Yeah, tell me about it."

"Jeremy, can I ask you something?"

"Yeah, what?"

"Don't that shit hurt?"

"Don't what hurt?" he asked.

"Well to put it nicely, having anal sex?" I asked.

"I wouldn't know if it hurts or not," he responded. "I haven't indulged in that—yet. All I know is that I was turned on being with another guy. And even though I've tried being with girls, they just don't excite me like guys do. Besides, if so many people—both men and women—are having anal sex, it couldn't be all that painful. But if you should ever let a man knock on your back door, then you let me know how it felt and if it was painful," he laughed.

"Now that's some shit that will never happen. Heck, I haven't met anyone I like well enough to let knock on my front door."

"Maybe that's because you're a dyke," he said, wagging his tongue at me.

"No way! I like beef, not fish. I just haven't found a guy I like well enough to give the panties up to," I said, throwing a pillow at him.

"So now that you know my 'dirty little secret', does that mean you're not going to my Junior Prom with me?"

"Get real," I said. "As long as you promise not to wear a dress and pumps, then I'm there." Jeremy and I had made a pact that we would be each other's date at our Junior Proms, but now that he had admitted to being gay, I couldn't help but wonder who he planned on taking to his Senior Prom. But that would forever remain a mystery. Not only would he not be attending his Senior Prom, but our date for his Junior Prom would not be happening either, as it would only be a matter of time before Jeremy's shoplifting would catch up with him and land him in the penitentiary.

"Jeremy, you and JT seem pretty close," I said. "It doesn't bother him that you're gay?"

"Believe it or not...."

But before Jeremy could finish—as if on cue—JT came running into the house.

"Damn, man, the cops at Deanne's house!" JT exclaimed.

As the three of us went outside to see what was going on, we saw the police coming out of Deanne's house carrying a bag with a large quantity of marijuana, cocaine, and two guns inside. A female officer came out leading Deanne, who had her head down and her hands cuffed behind her. I stood there looking at her, shaking my head. I know I should have felt sorry for her, but I didn't. I couldn't understand how she could be so stupid as to let JT use her like he did.

For the past two years, ever since our 8th grade graduation, Deanne had been working for JT, selling drugs. She thought she was a high-roller; walking around wearing expensive clothes, flexing and letting everybody know her business. JT would stash the drugs and guns at her house while her mom pretended she didn't know what was going on. Not only did she know, but she encouraged it. And now look at her; standing over there ranting and raving about how she don't know how that shit got in her house. But she was just worried because not only was her 'goose that laid the golden egg' gone, but the housing authority was gonna terminate her lease for having drugs and guns in her apartment. *Oh well,* I thought, *they brought it on themselves.*

"Shit!" JT mumbled as the police got on the elevator with Deanne, "I'm gonna miss that damn girl. She was the best worker I had and she never fucked with the stash."

"Jeremy, I'll check you later," I said as I headed for the elevator, rolling my eyes at JT. Normally, I would take the stairs, but for some reason I decided to take the elevator. As soon as the doors opened, I regretted my choice.

"Tara! Girl, how you doing? Come here and give me a hug. How come you don't come see your Uncle B. anymore?"

"Uncle B., it's good to see you (boy was that a lie). I've been busy with school and all," I said while trying to keep as much distance between us as was possible in that small-ass elevator. "How is Stan doing?"

"He's just fine," Uncle B. said. "He's down in Louisiana with my sister, you know."

"Yeah, I know," I said as the doors opened on my floor. "Well, I gotta go. I'll see you later Uncle B.," I said as I hurried off the elevator. *Damn! How could a man let himself sink that low over a woman?* I thought as I walked to my apartment. Uncle B. looked like hell and smelled worse. He only cared about two things; getting drunk, and then getting drunker. And that's what he'd devoted all of his time to doing since the day my Aunt left him. He had no interest in his appearance, his apartment—which was in worse condition than he was—or in his son. What started out as Stan staying with his grandmother for a couple of days, turned into him living with her for over a year, until her death. Then Stan went to stay with his Aunt in Louisiana. During the time Stan stayed with his grand- mother, he never came back to the building to visit either his father or me. I tried visiting him on a few occasions, but he always seemed so distant and withdrawn that eventually I stopped visiting him. "Man, I miss him," I said aloud as I opened the door, rushing inside to catch the phone before it stopped ringing.

"Hello?"

"Tara, what's up, sis?"

"Denise!" I shouted. "How you doing girl?"

"Girl, I'm blessed. The Lord is good," she said.

"Amen to that," I said as I prepared myself for one of her religious tangents. Not that I was knocking her—for she did have a lot to be thankful for—but like a lot of people who suddenly discover religion, the girl had a tendency to sometimes go overboard. But I was just glad to hear her voice as it had been about six months since the last time we'd spoken, when she'd called to say how much living in Montana at the Youth Transitional House had changed her life. It allowed her to find God and be at peace with herself. After running away from home, she'd had a miscarriage and lost her baby. She then hooked up with a 30-year-old man who turned her out and had her prostituting herself. When Momma found out where she was staying and what she was doing, she would either call the police or go by the house herself, but Denise always managed to stay a step ahead of her. Sometimes she would phone home and tell Momma to leave her alone. As much as Momma wanted to believe that the guy was holding Denise against her will and forcing her to prostitute herself, she had to finally accept the fact that Denise was as much responsible for what she was doing as her boyfriend was. So Momma, knowing that you can't help a person who doesn't want to be helped, put it in God's hands. Finally, Denise was arrested and sent to the Audy Home for Juveniles for three months, during which time Momma went to court and made her a ward of the state so that she could qualify for placement in the Transitional House in Montana. Since being there, Denise had totally turned her life around. She'd been taking GED classes, was an "A" student, worked part-time in a clothing store, did volunteer work at the local hospital, and as I said before, she'd found God. So, no, I didn't mind listening to her preach—not one bit.

We talked for about an hour and I filled her in on what was happening in the 'hood. I told her about Deanne being arrested and my running into Uncle B. on the elevator. I did not, however, share with her what Jeremy had revealed to me. That would have certainly got her to quoting scriptures. So I kept that juicy tidbit to myself.

"So, how's Aunt June doing?" Denise asked.

"Oh, she's doing good," I lied.

"Well I'm happy to hear that. So, baby sis, I've got to go," she said. "Give my love to Momma and take care of yourself. I love you."

"I love you too, Denise," I said as I hung up. I definitely didn't want to get into a conversation about Aunt June. Even though two years had passed since she'd been caught ass up, she was still on my 'Tara's Most Hated List.' I couldn't help but smile as I wondered if she was happy now. She'd said she was leaving Uncle B. for a man who would give her the things Uncle B. couldn't. And 'Robert with the Lincoln' was doing just that. Uncle B. couldn't give her a house in the suburbs, but Robert did. Uncle B. couldn't give her lots of money, clothes and a nice car, but Robert did. Uncle B. wouldn't beat her up on a daily basis, but Robert did. (I don't think she quite bargained for that one!) It seems as if Aunt June's full-time job was at the law firm, and her part-time job was going home and being abused by Robert. How do I know this, you ask? Well, even though Momma wanted to beat the crap out of Aunt June, that was still her baby sister; so whenever Aunt June would call—which wasn't often since Robert monitored her calls—she would tell Momma what was going on. Since she wasn't really able to go into detail over the phone, she would write Momma letters about twice a month and give her the details of her sick relationship. Momma didn't know I'd found where she kept the letters, but being a black Nancy Drew, I was able to find them. Once, when they were talking on the phone—I guess the warden wasn't home—I picked up the extension in my room (quite by accident, wink-wink) and heard Momma asking her why she didn't just leave.

"And do what?" Aunt June asked. "Move back to the projects? Hell, I got a nice car, a beautiful home and money in my pockets."

"Yeah," Momma said, "ain't nothing in life free, and you're paying dearly for your material luxuries."

"I'll be alright. Robert just needs time to adjust and realize he's got a good woman," Aunt June said.

Hello! I thought, almost dropping the phone. *Aunt June must be on drugs or something. This is the same 'good woman' who left her husband for a man because he was cute and drove a nice car. This after being caught in bed with another man!*

That's when I (carefully) hung up the phone. Whatever illness Aunt June was suffering from, I didn't want to take a chance on it being transmitted through the phone lines. I certainly didn't want to become that stupid over a man.

NINE

"Tara! Tara!" Momma shouted as she rushed in the house.

"Momma! What's wrong?" I asked as I jumped up. Momma plopped down in a chair, breathing hard and out of breath. She obviously had run up six flights of stairs, so I knew whatever had her all charged up had to be pretty serious.

"Here....read this," she gasped while handing me a letter. The letter was from an attorney and it basically stated that after five years, the CTA had finally reached a settlement in the wrongful death of my father who had been killed in a head-on collision with a CTA bus which had been driven by a drunken employee.

"Momma," I said as I continued to read, "this says the settlement is for the amount of thr... thr... thr..."

"THREE HUNDRED THOUSAND DOLLARS!!" Momma shouted as she jumped up. I stood there speechless for about a minute while I read and re-read the letter. Then we hugged each other and started dancing through the house singing, "Oh yes, we're moving on up, to the East Side, to that deluxe apartment in the sky...." We danced, hugged, sang and cried until we were exhausted. "Baby," Momma said, "now I know you're as happy as I am, but we gotta be careful and not let anyone know about this money. You know how triflin' niggas around here are."

"Yeah Momma, I know what you mean. But don't worry, I'm not saying a thing to anyone."

"Good. Now look, I have to go to the attorney's office on Friday to handle the paperwork, then we're going house shopping," Momma said, beaming from ear to ear.

"Alrighty now. And let's not forget about a nice ride for your baby girl." I sat in the chair, pretending it was a car and getting my lean on.

* * *

And wouldn't you know it, no matter how much you try to keep something on the down low, somehow a triflin' ass nigga always manages to find out. That triflin' ass nigga turned out to be Jerome—a part-time drug dealer, full-time drug user. How he managed to find out about the money is a mystery to me. Maybe he was standing outside with his ear pasted to our paper-thin ass door. But nevertheless, somehow he knew and he planned on taking advantage of the situation. On Friday as my mother was returning home from the lawyer's office, Jerome made his move.

* * *

"Man, I wonder what's going on now." Jeremy said as we walked through the playground and saw a police car and an ambulance pulled up near the building entrance. We could see the paramedics coming off the elevator with someone on a stretcher. "Momma?" I shouted as I took off running toward the stretcher. I couldn't see my mother's face but I recognized her shoes. As I pushed and shoved people out of my way, an officer grabbed me. "Hold on, young lady," he said. "That's my mother!" I yelled at him.

"Tara?" Momma said as she struggled to look around, sounding disoriented. It was hard for her to see as blood was streaming down her face from a gash in her head.

"Will you be riding to the hospital with her?" the paramedic asked as they loaded the stretcher into the ambulance. "You damn right!" I answered.

While we rode to the hospital and the paramedic worked to stop the bleeding, I wondered what had happened to Momma and prayed that she would be alright. The thought that this may have had anything to do with the money never crossed my mind.

When we arrived at Cook County Hospital, I sat in the waiting room while they took Momma in to examine her and give her stitches. After about forty minutes, Jeremy and JT came into the waiting room.

"Tara! Is everything okay? How's your mom? What happened?" Jeremy excitedly asked.

"They're giving her stitches now, but I still don't know what happened. The police are going to talk to her as soon as the doctor is finished."

Five minutes later the doctor walked in and informed us that he was done but that they would be keeping Momma overnight for observation. He told me that I could go in and see her now. When I entered the room the police were there questioning Momma.

"Well," Momma said, "I had just come from downtown and I had some things on my mind so I wasn't paying attention to what was going on around me like I normally do. I was getting on the elevator when all of a sudden someone pushed me from behind and slammed me into the elevator wall. Then he grabbed me by my hair and spun me around."

"Did you recognize him?" one of the officers asked.

"No. He had on one of those caps that cover your face with the eyes cut out, so I couldn't see his face."

"Okay, what happened then?"

"He grabbed me by the throat and said 'give it up bitch!' I asked him what the hell was he talking about and he said he wanted the money. So I reached in my pocket and gave him about $20.00. So he slaps me and says 'you know what money I'm talking about.'"

That's when it dawned on me that somehow he knew about the settlement money.

"I told him that I would give him the money," Momma continued. "So I handed him my purse with one hand, and with the other one I reached into my pocket and grabbed my straight razor. As the elevator door opened and he was about to run off, I slashed him across the face. That's when he turned around and hit me in the head."

"What did he hit you with?" Officer Perez asked.

"I'm not sure. I didn't see it, but I know it was small, heavy, and it hurt like hell. After he hit me he took off running."

"Alright, Ms. St. Pierre. We'll let you get some rest now and head back over to the building to see if we can find out who did this."

"Well he shouldn't be hard to find. He'll be the one walk-ing around with a sliced cheek," Momma said.

As the officers left the room, I went over and hugged Momma. "Momma," I cried, holding her tightly, "I'm sorry I wasn't there with you."

"Aw, that's alright, baby. I'm fine. But Tara, please tell me you didn't tell anyone about the money."

"No Momma, I swear to you, I didn't tell anyone. Not even Jeremy."

"Well I don't know how that slime bucket found out, but somehow he did."

"Do you think maybe he just chose you at random?"

"Naw baby, he knew about the money and his stupid ass actually thought I'd be walking around with $300,000 in my purse. Now my favorite Gucci purse is gone."

"What did you have in the purse, Momma?"

"My lipstick, a comb, a book and some candy. I had my I.D. and the papers from the attorney along with the check stub in the inside pocket of my jacket."

"Good thinking Momma," I said as I hugged her again.

"Well baby, it's about to get dark. I want you to go on home now. You're not afraid to go home, are you?"

"Of course not, Momma. I'll be alright. You just get some rest."

"Why don't you take a cab home, Tara."

"Momma, now you know no cab's gonna go to the projects. Besides, Jeremy and JT are in the waiting room, so I'll be fine."

"Alright then," Momma said as she kissed me on the fore- head. "I'll see you tomorrow then."

As I left Momma's room, my mind was racing as I thought of the things I was gonna do to the punk who had attacked my mother. I was determined to find out who it was and mete out a little project justice before turning him over to the police.

"Tara!" Jeremy shouted when he saw me. "Is your mom alright?"

"Yeah, she's fine. She'll be home tomorrow."

"Did she say what happened?" JT asked.

"Yeah," I said as I proceeded to tell them what she'd told the police. I didn't, however, tell them the reason why she'd been targeted.

"Don't worry, Tara. We'll find that motherfucker!" Jeremy angrily said.

"Oh without a doubt," I said as we walked to the bus stop.

TEN

Six weeks had passed since my mother's assault and the consensus around the building was that Jerome had done it since he'd been seen with a deep slash on his cheek. But he was keeping a low profile since that day. Being a patient person, I knew he'd turn up sooner or later. In the mean- time, we'd found our dream home and would be moving soon to a gorgeous split-level, four bedroom home in Schaumburg. I was extremely excited and was looking forward to moving, even though I was gonna miss going to Lane Tech. But I was sure the schools in Schaumburg were just as good, if not better. I'd also decided to major in Journalism when I got to college, so I knew I had to really apply myself for the remainder of my high school years. Not that I was worried about anything, because brains was definitely one of my best assets. I knew I would also miss Jeremy. We had grown so close. But I was certain I would be able to talk him into coming out to spend a weekend sometime. That way he could get out of this environment and maybe think about giving up his little business, which I must say was very profitable.

I wondered if there were a lot of fine boys in Schaumburg. It seemed that lately since my body had started developing, I'd become more interested in boys. Momma said it was just a hormonal thing and she had *that talk* with me again. I assured her that even though boys were on my mind, sex wasn't. Well, that wasn't exactly true. I had been thinking about sex and wondering what it felt like, but I wasn't about to let some guy use me as his own personal cum dump; that's for sure. So for the time being, the only thing the guys would be getting from me would be the chance to admire, from afar, my cute little tight body, which I was very proud of. My breasts were perky and needed no assistance from a bra. My legs were long and shapely and looked as if I ran track. And my booty was oh so cutey! Not trying to sound conceited, but on a scale of 1 to 10, I was definitely a 9.9. Momma said I was pretty enough to be a model, but she's my mother, she's supposed to say things like that.

KNOCK, KNOCK, KNOCK, KNOCK!! Suddenly I was snapped out of my daydream by loud knocking on the front door and Jeremy calling out my name. "Tara! Tara! Open up!"

"Man, Jeremy! What's going on?" I asked as I yanked open the door.

"JT and Lil' Man caught Jerome. They have him in that vacant apartment on the 3rd floor. Come on!"

"Does JT have his piece on him?" I asked as I closed the door and we took off down the stairs.

"I got one. But Tara, that motherfucker ain't worth us killing him and going to jail."

"I know that," I said as I held out my hand. "I'm not gonna kill him, I'm just gonna scare the shit out of him. Trust me," I said as Jeremy handed me his piece. When we got to the apart-ment Jerome was sitting in a chair trembling and looking like a man who'd just had his last meal and was waiting to be strapped into the chair for execution. I slowly walked over to where he was seated, grabbed his face in my hand, and turned it so that I could get a good look at the scar.

"My mother does nice work," I said as I glared at him. "Did it hurt, Jerome?"

"Tara, I'm sorry. I didn't know what I was doing. I was high!"

"I didn't ask you all that shit! I said, did it hurt?"

"Yeah, it hurt!" he cried.

"Good! Then I'm gonna stay with the program and make sure what I do to you hurts just as bad," I said as I walked over to Jeremy. Jerome jumped up and tried to run but Lil' Man, who stood only 5'3" but was built like a bull and looked like one too, punched him in his bird-like chest and knocked him back down. "Watch this," I whispered to Jeremy as I turned around and walked back over to Jerome. I stood in front of him and reached around and grabbed the gun, which was in the small of my back.

"Hey, whadda ya know? It's fully loaded," I said as I snapped it open. "JT, do you think I should unload all six of these bullets in his punk ass?"

"Shit, why waste five bullets? One bullet straight to the head will do the job just as well."

"You're right," I said as I proceeded to remove five bullets, counting them as I took them out. "We'll just leave one in and find out if your guardian angels are watching over you today," I said, snapping the gun shut and spinning the chamber. By this time, Jerome was crying and pleading like a little baby.

"Man, shut yo' sissy ass up," Jeremy said. "Hell, Tara's mom wasn't crying like that when your rotten ass stuck her up and hit her in the head, now was she?"

"I said I was sorry, man. What more do you want from me?" Jerome blubbered.

"I want blood! Your blood all over this floor!" I said as I raised the gun. "So let's see how lucky you are," I said, aiming the gun at his knee and pulling the trigger. *Click.*

"Damn! You would have looked so nice missing a kneecap," I smiled at him. By this time a large stain had formed on the front of Jerome's pants and there was the unmistakable stench of urine in the air, mixed with the smell of fear.

"Damn Tara, go ahead and get this shit over with," JT said, "before this motherfucker shit on himself. Then I'm gonna shoot his ass for assaulting my nostrils."

"Yeah, you're right. I'm tired of looking at this piece of shit." I said as I aimed the gun at his head and again pulled the trigger. *Click.*

"Tara! Please don't kill me! I'm sorry! I don't care what you do to me, just please don't kill me!" Jerome cried.

"Okay, now here's what's gonna happen," I said, putting the barrel in his mouth, "I'm gonna pull this trigger again and either your brains are gonna be scattered all over this room, or this will be your lucky day and you'll be able to crawl outta here with a well kicked ass. *Click.*

"Okay, I guess you win. It looks like you'll be getting off easy. Well, not entirely easy, because we about to beat the ever loving shit out of you." Jeremy said as the four of us commenced to whupping his ass, beating, punching and kicking the shit out of him for the next ten minutes. When we were done, JT told him he could go, but all Jerome would do was to crawl over to a corner of the room, curl up in a fetal position and continue to whimper like a scared puppy.

"Oh well, he'll be okay—one day," I said as we left our little torture chamber.

"Damn, Tara!" Lil Man said when we got outside. "You one crazy bitch! Now what if that gun had gone off? All of our asses would be looking at life in prison."

"I might be crazy, but I ain't stupid," I said as I opened the gun to reveal that it was empty. "The hand is quicker than the eye. I took out all of the bullets," I laughed as I gave the gun back to Jeremy.

* * *

During the next two weeks as we packed and prepared for our move to Schaumburg, no one saw or heard from Jerome. Rumor had it that he'd checked into a drug rehab center on the southside, so I guess he had us to thank for motivating him to get himself clean. Maybe we'd receive a community service award.

ELEVEN

It had been one month since we moved into our new home and I was loving it. My new school was pretty cool. I just needed time to adjust to being around so many boring white kids, though some of them were pretty fly. There was an opening for a writer with the school newspaper so I applied and was accepted. Now I could give a little flavor to the paper and spice it up with my commentaries on issues in the school and the community. Momma agreed to let Jeremy come spend the upcoming weekend. Since I'd told her he was gay, she wasn't tripping about us getting into any 'trouble.'

I'd been worried about Momma lately, though. For the past two weeks she'd complained about being tired and she didn't look well. Maybe she was just worn out from the move and all of the shopping we'd been doing. We'd know what was going on next week when she went to her doctor for a complete physical. I just hoped it was nothing serious.

I decided to call Jeremy to find out what time he planned on coming for the weekend. I wanted to break the news to him that he had to go to the mall with me on Saturday to help me pick out the dress I'd be wearing to his prom, which was in three weeks. As I waited for someone to answer the phone, I smiled, remembering that day when we'd given Jerome the ass kicking that his Momma should have given him a long time ago.

"Talk to me."

"Hey JT, what's up? This is Tara. Is Jeremy home?"

"Girl, Jeremy's in jail."

"What!" I exclaimed. "What happened?"

"Well, Monday him and one of his homeboys was down-town taking care of their business and there was a plainclothes cop watching them. He waited until they'd finished and were heading home then he called for backup and pulled them over. They had about $30,000 in merchandise in the car."

"Hold up JT," I yelled. "How come you didn't call me and let me know what happened?"

"I wanted to Tara, but I don't know your new number, and Jeremy wouldn't give it to me when I asked him for it. He said he didn't want you to know what had happened."

"So, is he gonna get out soon?"

" *He* thinks so. He thinks his asshole father is gonna get him out, but my ole girl said she talked to his folks and they basically said 'fuck him; it'll teach him a lesson.'"

"Now that's some cold shit!" I said angrily. "So what's gonna happen now?"

"Well, he's at 26th and California and he'll stay there until his court date, which is next month."

"Man, I can't believe this," I said. "JT, take down my number. Keep in touch and let me know what's going on."

"Okay Tara, I will. You be cool. Peace out."

"Damn! There's got to be something I can do to help Jeremy," I said out loud. I wished I could ask Momma to bond him out, but even though she liked Jeremy I knew she didn't approve of what he'd been doing. I wasn't sure what her reaction would be if I asked her for the money. Besides, I'd forgotten to ask JT if he even had a bond. Maybe Jeremy's folks would change their minds and get him out. If not, then I'd definitely have to tell Momma what happened when she asked why he didn't come out for the weekend.

As it turned out, Jeremy stayed in the county jail for five months, at which time he was sentenced to six years at the Menard Correctional Facility. During that time, we wrote each other constantly and talked on the phone occasionally. Once I turned 18, I tried to make it down there at least three times a year to visit him. At first he had a hard time accepting the fact that his parents weren't going to be there for him, but once he dealt with it he decided to move on and do whatever he could to make the best of his time. He took advantage of the classes that were offered and discovered he had a real passion for law. When he wrote and told me he planned on going to law school when he got out, I was proud of him even though, I must admit, I didn't think he was serious. Boy was I ever wrong! I'd also managed to reconnect with Stan briefly. We talked occasionally and he told me he was happy and planned on marrying his high school sweetheart. Although he said he was happy, he still refused to acknowledge what had happened between his father and my aunt. Whenever we talked, it seemed that no matter what the conversation was, he always managed to take it back to his girlfriend Gina and how much he loved and adored her. He some- times gave me the impression that he was more obsessed with her than in love with her. I wondered how she felt about him. But Stan was my friend and if he was happy, then I was happy for him. When he came to Chicago in the summer of 1987 to attend my mother's funeral, I couldn't believe how much he'd changed and how handsome he'd become.

* * *

It took years for me to deal with the anger I felt when my mother was diagnosed with colon cancer just when life was getting good for her. She spent years struggling to make ends meet and was finally able to relax a little, then the cancer ruined everything. She fought for four years until the pain and wasting away was more than she could bear and she finally gave in. I think she held on for so long because she was afraid for me and Denise and what would happen to us after she was gone. The doctor explained to us that sometimes when a person is near death they fear leaving their loved ones and so they hang on. At first when he told us to assure her that we would be alright and that it was okay for her to let go, I couldn't do it. I didn't want to tell my mother that it was okay for her to die. But when I was finally able to come to terms with the fact that she was in excruciating pain and there was nothing that could be done to save her, I was able to sit on her bed and cradle her in my arms as she had done me on countless occasions. I assured her that we would be fine and she should go ahead and receive her angel wings. Two days later, my mother quietly passed away in her sleep.

The following months left me with mixed emotions. I was hurting from my loss, but Momma's death brought our family closer again. Aunt June offered to come stay with us five months prior to Momma's passing. At first I was reluctant to have her around since I didn't know what kind of drama she might bring into our home, but Momma said it was alright. Aunt June had managed to get her life back on track, so I hesitantly agreed because I really did need help caring for Momma. The stress of taking care of her and going to DePaul University, where I was majoring in Journalism, was beginning to take its toll on me. I found out all the fears I had about Aunt June moving in with us were unwarranted as she had indeed managed to regain her senses and had left behind all the BS that had caused me to grow distant from her. Her number one concern now was her sister and she did everything possible to keep Momma happy and comfortable. She seemed to really take pleasure in keeping the house immaculate, even going so far as to clean my bedroom, which I had to explain to her was totally unnecessary. Aunt or no aunt, I didn't want anyone going through my personal things.

When Denise found out how sick Momma was, she imme- diately made plans to come home. She also brought a big surprise home with her; her *husband.* Even in her weakened state, Momma managed to snap on Denise for not letting us know about her marriage. I couldn't believe she didn't tell us she'd been married for three months. But her husband, Houston, took no time in getting Momma wrapped around his little finger—and me too, for that matter. Houston was a beautiful man; not just on the outside—because the man was definitely fine—but on the inside where it really counted. He doted on and catered to Momma as if she were his own mother. He was such a caring, considerate and loving man who stood 6'2", weighed about 240 lbs and had the most gorgeous hazel colored eyes I'd ever seen. His copper colored skin always seemed to glow. Maybe it was just his inner beauty shining through. He and Denise totally complemented one another and they seemed to be genuinely in love with each other.

I was so happy to see my sister again that some nights I would go to bed and cry a river of tears. I shed tears of happiness because I was glad to have my sister back in my life again and to see that she was so happy. I shed tears over the joy of having my favorite aunt out of an abusive relationship and back in my life. But most of all, I shed tears of sorrow knowing that it was my mother's rapidly declining health that had brought the family closer together again.

It was amazing how the four of us managed to live together under the same roof without any conflicts or problems. We all had a true love and respect for one another. Houston found a job as a Chemical Engineer and Denise went to school three days a week, studying to become a Registered Nurse so that she could be better equipped to help out with Momma. Aunt June was at home full-time to take care of Momma, and I continued my classes at DePaul.

As Momma got sicker, I started losing interest in my classes. After she passed, I lost all interest in school so I decided to take some time off after my second year to allow myself time to grieve. I knew I would go crazy with nothing to do, so I took a job as a columnist with a local magazine. The magazine was black owned and operated and catered to a broad spectrum of African-Americans; from baby-boomers, to generation X, to generation next. I totally enjoyed my job. My column focused on community news and events. Once a month I would spotlight one particular neighborhood or community and address the issues the residents had, be it good, bad, or funny. Everything from citizens' concerns about the police, to housing issues, to local talent. It was, to say the least, a very interesting job and my co-workers were great people to be around. But after about 2½ years, I found myself growing restless and wanted to do something else. That's when I decided to follow my passion and try my hand at writing a book, which surprisingly only took me seven months to write.

My first book, *Whispers of Silence* was about a 27-year-old woman who'd inherited a house, which was haunted. Every night at exactly 12:30 a.m. (it was obviously haunted by black ghosts on CP time, who couldn't make it on time for the 12:00 haunting), the walls would seem to come to life and she would hear whisperings coming from the walls. Needless to say, when she asked friends or family over to witness it, she was the only one able to hear it. Except for her 10-year-old niece. And so began her quest to find out what was happening in her home.

The success of the book was unexpected and overwhelming. Within four months of its release it had made the bestsellers list. I wished Momma and Daddy could have been around to see it. I knew they would have been so proud of me. I was sure they were up in heaven smiling down saying, "That's our baby girl!"

* * *

"Ms. St. Pierre. Ms. St. Pierre, excuse me," I heard someone saying. I looked up to see Officer Johnson standing in the doorway of the office where he'd allowed me to wait for Jeremy.

"I'm sorry Officer, I was daydreaming," I said as I stood up to straighten out my skirt.

"I'm sorry, Ms. St. Pierre. Your attorney, Mr. Brennan, called to say an emergency had come up but that he would be here as soon as possible."

"An emergency! Hell, this is an emergency," I said as I sat back down and took the Coke and sandwich Officer Johnson offered me.

"I have a portable television I can bring in here for you to watch if you'd like."

"Thank you, but I'm fine," I said as I began eating my sandwich and reliving the events which had led up to this 'emergency.'

TWELVE

MY LOVER

"So Tara, are you excited about your big date tonight with Stan?" Sherita asked.

"Not as excited as you seem to be about it," I responded. "Now would you please hurry up and get dressed so we can get out of here." Sherita and I had met at DePaul and we'd become close friends. We would try to make it to the health club at least three times a week for a strenuous workout. Since I had a date for tonight, I wanted my body to be toned and fit so I put in an extra half hour on the Stairmaster.

"So, did he tell you why his wife divorced him?" Sherita asked as we headed for her car.

"No, I haven't asked him yet, but as soon as I know I'll be sure to tell your nosy ass." Sherita was my girl, but damn was she nosy. And a 100% drama queen in all aspects of her life, especially when it came to men. Sometimes I think she purposely sought out men who weren't right for her just so she could have a little extra drama in her life. "Okay, enough about Stan," I said as she headed for my Gold Coast condo, "what's up with you and Bobby?"

"Girlfriend, check this out! You know I told you he can-celled our date for last Saturday because his wife insisted he take her out?"

"Yeah Sherita, that's usually what husbands do. They take their wives out," I responded.

"Uh-huh, whatever. Well anyway, I knew he would take her to the same restaurant he always takes her to. So guess who just happened to be there?"

"Girl, no you did not take your low down ass to that restaurant!"

"Oh yes I did, and Reggie was my date," she said with a smirk on her face. Reggie is my cousin on my father's side of the family. We'd had a chance to reconnect when he attended my mother's funeral and had managed to become pretty close since then, even though we were as different as night and day. In fact, he and Sherita were so much alike, they should have been related. Reggie was as much a drama king as Sherita was a drama queen. He wasn't happy unless he had some woman or women stressed out with all the drama and bullshit he would bring to a relationship.

"So what happened?" I asked. I knew if those two were together then there was definitely some crazy mess going down.

"Well, we sat where they wouldn't be able to see us. When Ms. Thang got up to go to the ladies' room, Reggie walks up to her and starts giving her some weak lines about how radiant she looks and how her dress compliments her lovely figure, and asked if she'd like to have dinner with him sometime. So, of course, she thanks him but tells him she's married. He tells her if her status should ever change to look him up, that he's a regular at that restaurant. Then he heads to the men's room. Okay, so I give her a few minutes, then I stroll into the ladies' room singing "If He's Your Boyfriend, He Wasn't Last Night". Well, we're standing at the sink and she notices the necklace I was wearing."

"That's a very beautiful and unique necklace you're wearing," she says.

"Why thank you," I smile at her, "my boyfriend gave it to me. Says he had it 'specially made just for me."

"That's strange," she says while staring at me.

"Sherita! Please don't tell me you were wearing that woman's necklace!" I said in shock.

"And you know this," Sherita's crazy ass said, laughing.

"How did you manage to get ahold of her necklace?" I asked, not really sure if I wanted to hear the answer.

"Well one day while me and Bobby were at their house getting our freak on and I'd laid some of this juicy kitt-katt on him, I was looking in her jewelry box, saw it, and tried it on. I told Bobby I liked it and wanted one. He said he'd had it 'specially made for his wife and she didn't even appreciate it enough to wear it. So he told me I could have it, that she wouldn't miss it. Can you believe that shit?"

"No, his trifling ass didn't! And your trifling ass took it!"

"Yes, his trifling ass did. And yes my trifling ass did too," she laughed.

"So, do you think she recognized it?"

"Hell yeah, she recognized it. I could see it all over her face."

"Did she say anything to you?"

"Uh-uh. She just stared then stormed out of the washroom. Reggie just happened to be leaving the men's room at the same time and he told her not to forget his offer. And do you know what she did?"

"I'm afraid to ask," I said while shaking my head.

"She gave Reggie her cell phone number. Can you believe that?"

"Sherita, one day somebody's gonna seriously hurt you and Reggie," I said as she pulled up in front of my building.

"Yeah whatever, Ms. Goody Two Shoes. I bet you haven't told Myles about your date tonight with Stan, have you?"

"Sweetheart, are you on drugs or something? I don't need Myles' permission to do anything. And besides, that man is history.

"All the more reason for you to give Stan some rhythm."

"Look Sherita, Stan and I are old friends just going out on a date to get reacquainted. There is no way I'm about to end one relationship and jump into another one. Hell, who has time for a relationship anyway."

"Shit, Tara, you don't seem to know what you're looking for in a relationship. Just look at your last three so-called serious flings. First there was Raheem, a pork-eating, loud-mouthed Muslim. Then there was Wendi, and I still don't know whatever possessed you to get involved with a woman," she laughed.

"I don't believe you," I said incredulously. "It was you and Reggie who took me to that club where I met Wendi."

"Shit! Nobody told your ass to go and fall in love with her."

"Yeah, you got a point there. I guess I got caught up."

"You got caught up, alright. You're still sweet on Miss Wendi," Sherita said as she blew me a kiss. "And now you're messing around with dough boy's tired ass. Girl, I can't believe someone as smart and fine as you keeps choosing the wrong lovers," she said with mock pity in her voice.

"I cannot believe I'm hearing this. Sherita, you refuse to date a man unless he's married, a thug, or has some kind of serious issues going on. And I'll have you know that I have had some good relationships."

"Name one, Tara."

"Okay, Davon. We had a strong, loving relationship," I reminded her.

"Yeah, right up until you really started to blow up and his fragile ego couldn't take it."

"Well that doesn't change the fact that he was a good man. He was honest, hard-working, a damn good lover, and he was crazy about me. He just couldn't handle the fact that my income made his look like lunch money. Now that's some stupid, macho shit," I said as I grabbed my gym bag off the back seat, getting out of the car.

"Call me tomorrow and give me the 411 on your date," Sherita yelled as I closed the door.

"That girl is a damn trip," I mumbled as I walked up to the door and was greeted by Ralph, the doorman.

"Good afternoon Ms. St. Pierre, did you enjoy your work-out?" he asked as he winked at me.

"Yes Ralph, I did. Thank you. How's your wife doing these days?" Ralph had to be all of 70 years old, but he was constantly flirting, and I was constantly reminding him of his wife. It seems since Viagra hit the market, there are more lecherous, horny old men on the loose.

"My wife's the same as always," he responded, "old and cranky."

"I can understand why," I said, entering the elevator. "Give her my regards."

As I entered my condo, which was on the 20th floor over-looking Lake Michigan with a magnificent view of the city, a peace and calm immediately overtook me. Entering my 'Palace,' as I referred to it, always managed to have a calming effect on me. I guess I had my interior decorator to thank for that, because he definitely hooked the place up. After letting Andre know what my favorite colors were and cutting pictures out of magazines of various furnishings that appealed to me, I gave him carte blanche and told him to spare no expense in making my condo feel like home. And that's exactly what Andre did. From the marble floors, chandeliers, various exquisite pieces of artwork which adorned the walls and easels, to the exotic plants and tropical fish which were in a wall-enclosed tank and the antique furnishings, my 'Palace' was certainly a place I was always happy to be. At first when Andre started talking about 'Feng Shui,' I had no idea what he was talking about. "Dahling, your home should be an expression of you," he said. "Each piece should reflect your essence and should be placed in just the right location."

"Okay," I said, not knowing what the heck he was talking about. But since he had come highly recommended and I'd seen some of his work, I knew I was in good hands. Now, as I walked in and dropped my gym bag while heading to the phone to check my messages, I was grateful for Feng Shui, Feng Way, and any other Fengs out there because this place was the shit!

As I checked my voicemail, I saw I had 7 messages. Four of them were business related. One was from Denise, calling to see if I was coming to Sunday dinner. I tried to make it home for Sunday dinners at least twice a month to visit with my family who still lived in Schaumburg. Aunt June was still there and currently dating a very nice, handsome 58-year-old doctor. Houston, with his fine self, was still working as a Chemical Engineer and treating Denise like a queen, especially since the addition to their family of the twins, Kyle and Kianna, who were now 2 years old. I loved my niece and nephew and enjoyed spoiling them rotten. They were wise beyond their years and always into something. They made me realize as much as I love kids, I was in no hurry to have any.

The next message was from Myles, calling to see if I'd 'come to my senses.' I thought I'd made it clear to him last Saturday at dinner that our relationship was going nowhere and he should move on. *I guess I'll have to spell it out for him, again,* I thought as I listened to my next message which was from Stan. It was kinda ironic that I had run into Stan Saturday at the same restaurant Myles and I were at. "Hello Ms. St. Pierre," Stan's message began, "I just want to say how much I'm looking forward to seeing you tonight. I'll pick you up at 7:00."

"Damn that man has a deep, sexy, melodic voice," I said aloud. "I can't believe he's back in Chicago." I smiled as I headed into my study to check my e-mail. The study contained numerous books by various authors whose works I loved, and although I didn't get much time to read, I still purchased books by my favorite authors to show my support. Eric J. Dickey, Shenesska Jackson, Michael Baisden, Omar Tyree, and, of course, the great Iyanla Vanzant, were some of my favorite authors. Sherita had given me a book last week of erotic poetry, written by a brother from the southside of Chicago named Vincent Tyler. While I'd never been much into poetry, I found myself intrigued by his writings and made a mental note to call him and tell him how much I enjoyed his book. Some of his writings were downright nasty and I found myself getting turned on reading them. "Maybe I'm in need of a Maintenance Man," I said, picking up the latest book I'd purchased. I'd had the pleasure of meeting the author, Michael Baisden, another brother from Chi-Town, when we were in New York at a writers' conference. "Now that's one crazy, off-the-hook man," I laughed as I remembered how much fun I'd had talking with him.

My lighted curio cabinet, which housed my four novels, was by far my pride and joy. Along with my books, it also held the various framed press clippings, book club reviews, awards and certificates I'd received from grammar school through college, in addition to the ones I'd received as an established writer. I always got a little misty eyed whenever I looked at my novels as they reminded me of all the love and hard work, not to mention the long hours, spent writing them. I thank God for blessing me with the gift for writing and I never take my success for granted. I make it a point to give back in various ways by hosting writers' seminars, being a guest speaker at various events for aspiring writers, or donating time or money. "Man, I'd better fix myself a snack," I said aloud as I listened to my stomach growl. "I've got five hours before Stan picks me up." As I turned to leave the den, I blew my books a kiss then headed for the bedroom to take off my sweats. One of the joys of living alone was being able to walk around butt naked if I chose to, and I chose to walk around naked most of the time. I totally enjoyed the freedom from clothes and being able to touch myself if I so felt like it, which I must admit was often. Guess that meant I needed to hurry up and get me some; I was starting to turn into a pervert. I tossed my sweats into the hamper and admired my figure in one of the various mirrors that adorned the walls of my bedroom. "Not too bad for a 33-year-old woman," I said, admiring my 5'8", 135 lb. frame. My breast were as firm as when I was 20. My stomach was flat, thanks to constant crunches. And my butt was tight and curvaceous. And thank the Lord, not an ounce of cellulite anywhere. "God is good!" I said, heading for the kitchen to fix myself a sandwich.

I decided to watch a movie to kill time before getting ready for my date. "Stan, back in Chicago and fine as wine, uh-uh-uh," I said as I thought back to the day when we'd run into one another at the restaurant.

"Myles, thanks for meeting me here," I said as we were finishing up our meal. I had managed to keep the conversation light and casual during dinner because I knew what I was about to say to him would not be pleasant.

"Tara, it's always a pleasure being with you. I missed you so much last week while you were in Washington. I thought about you every day," Myles said with a goofy look on his face.

"Yes, I guess you did miss me. I think it was the dozen roses you had delivered to my suite every day and the phone calls—three times a day—which gave it away," I sarcastically said.

"Tara," Myles said, taking my hand in his, "it's been awhile. Do you think we could get out of here and go to your place for a little intercourse?"

Okay, that's it, I thought to myself. As I sat there looking at that puppy dog expression on his face, I wondered what the hell it was I'd seen in Myles that made me date him the past 6 months. I must have either been extremely horny, or just vulnerable after my affair with Wendi. Myles was certainly not the type of man I generally date. Where I prefer tall athletic men, Myles was three inches shorter than I am and athleticism is not a word to be associated with him. A man doesn't necessarily have to have a six-pack to get my attention, but a keg—which is what Myles' stomach looks like—is certainly not an eye-catcher. I mean, if I can find time to work out to keep my stomach flat, how much trouble could it possibly be for anyone else to do it? Another thing Myles was lacking was a sense of humor. Witticisms seemed to go right over the man's head; not to mention he was corny as hell, which was obvious right now. Who the hell asks to have intercourse?

"So Tara, is that expression on your face to be taken as a yes? Will we be doing the horizontal boogie tonight?"

"Myles, sweetheart, it's fuck, okay? F-U-C-K. Do I want to fuck, screw, make love," I said, rolling my eyes at him. "And the answer is no."

"Okay Tara, I understand. You're tired from your trip."

"Myles, I am tired, but not from my trip. I'm tired of this relationship. You're a very interesting person, but we just aren't happening."

"Tara, I don't understand. What are you trying to tell me? What is it that you want? I try to give you everything. I'm willing to change to be the man you want. When you told me I wasn't funny and had no sense of humor, didn't I start reading joke books and going to comedy clubs? If saying intercourse bothers you, then I'll say 'fuck' from now on. Will fucking you make you happy? Will that make you happy, baby?"

"You know what'll make me happy?" I said exasperated.

"What?"

"If we could put your name between us," I answered, looking him directly in the eye.

"I don't understand," he responded. "What do you mean, 'put my name between us.?' "

"What I mean is I think it's time for us to put some miles between us—as in space. It's time we ended this relationship and moved on."

"Woman, you're tripping! I don't know what the hell's gotten into you, but call me when you've come to your senses. If it isn't too late by then," he said as he stood up, throwing his napkin on the table. "And since you've managed to spoil my dinner, you pay the bill," he said as he stormed out.

"Well, another one bites the dust," I said under my breath as I sat there sipping my strawberry iced tea. Now I know what you're thinking: If the man had so many flaws, why did I get involved with him in the first place?" I've asked myself the same question. But when I met Myles at a writers' conference in Rosemont, he seemed like a refreshing change of pace. I guess after having an affair with a woman, any man would have been a change of pace. Myles worked as an Events Coordinator for the Village of Rosemont and he was there making sure things went smoothly. It probably was his approach that appealed to me. No tired ass lines like "Is your husband married?" Just a straight- forward "Hi, I'm Myles Robertson and it would be my pleasure to have lunch with you sometime." And from there we managed to have an interesting and engaging conversation. When he asked if he could have my number, at first I was hesitant, but then I said 'what the hell' and gave it to him. Okay, I confess, the *real* reason I dated him for six months, even though he was short, out of shape and boring, was because the brother could work magic with his tongue. His penis, which I referred to as mini-me, left a lot to be desired, but he had no problem making me reach my 'cum quota'—which was a minimum 3 times—with his tongue. My motto has always been: "If I'm not cummin', then your ass will be going—out the door." Myles was, without a doubt, a brother with a Ph.D in Clitology, and his face and my clit were a perfect match. Hell, just thinking about it was getting me moist.

"Tara! I can't believe this. It is you!"

Damn! Now what? I thought, looking up. "Oh my God! Stan!" I couldn't believe it. Standing before me was my friend Stan Bishop, whom I had not seen in 12 years.

"Well, aren't you going to give me a hug?" he said as I sat there with my mouth hanging open.

"Yes! Yes! Yes!" I said as I jumped up, tightly hugging him. "Have a seat. I've just finished eating and I have a meeting to attend in an hour, but I certainly have time to talk with you. How long have you been in Chicago, and why haven't you looked me up?"

"I've been here about two months and I had every intention of looking you up. I just needed some time to get settled into my new house and take care of some business."

"So you've moved back to Chicago," I said excitedly. "That's great. Does your wife like it here? Where are you guys living?"

"Tara, my wife and I are divorced. It's been about 8 months now. She's living in Rockford with our daughter, Brie, who's now 7 years old. I purchased a home in Oak Park and I'm having some work done on it. That's why I hadn't had a chance to contact you yet. Gina had no right moving my daughter from Louisiana to here. That's why I decided to move back, to be close to my daughter," Stan said as a look of anger quickly crossed his face.

"It must've been a pretty messy divorce for her to do some- thing that extreme," I said sympathetically.

"Yeah, it was. Full of accusations, anger and bitterness. But things will be alright now. I can still be close to my daughter," he said. "But enough about me, congratulations on your success. I've been following your career and I am so proud of you," Stan said as he took my hands in his. "You are so beautiful."

"You're looking pretty hot yourself," I said to lighten up the moment a little. But that was no lie. Stan looked good, like he had just stepped off the cover of GQ Magazine.

* * *

And now here it was one week later and I was anticipating going out with him tonight. "We'll I'd better pick out something to wear," I said as I turned off the movie that I hadn't been watching in the first place.

* * *

"Hello! Hello! Stan, I know it's you," Gina angrily said. "I wish you would stop playing these childish ass games and just leave me alone!" As soon as she slammed the phone down, it rang again. "Look, dammit! I left Louisiana to get away from your crazy ass and I'm not gonna keep running. If I have to, I will go to the police and you'll never see Brie again."

"You can't get away from me, Gina. Don't you know that by now? I don't care where you go, I'll find you," Stan calmly said as he hung up the phone.

As he stood in his attic, he looked around at the room which he had turned into a shrine. Everywhere were photos of Tara, articles about Tara, and letters to Tara which had never been mailed. Stan had taken all the photos of Gina and cut her head off and replaced them with photos of Tara. He'd also taken one of his wedding pictures and had it blown up into a life sized cardboard cut-out and replaced Gina's head with an enlarged photo of Tara. As Stan stood staring at the cut-out with a glazed look on his face, he softly said, "Tara, I've always loved you. You're nothing like all the other women who've been in my life. I'll never let you out of my life again." As he turned to leave the attic, he blew a kiss to his shrine and walked downstairs to prepare for his date.

THIRTEEN

"Hello, Ms. St. Pierre, there's a gentleman down here, calls himself Stan Bishop, asking for you. I've never seen him before," Ralph's nosy ass said over the intercom.

"Thank you, Ralph. Tell him I'll be right down. No! As a matter of fact, send him up," I said. I'd always been very care-ful about who I let in my apartment, but Stan was a good friend. "What am I thinking about," I said aloud as I ran my fingers through my hair and waited for him to make it upstairs.

"Ohhhh, look at you," I said as I opened the door. "With your fine chocolate self."

"Tara, it's so good to see you again," Stan said as he grabbed me in a bear hug, lifting me off my feet and spinning me around.

"Okay, put me down. You're getting me dizzy."

"This is a beautiful place you got here," he said as he walked over to the 6ft. simulated waterfall that stood in the foyer.

"Well come on, let me give you the guided tour so you can check out the rest of the place before we leave. As I took him from room to room, he commented on and admired various items.

"That's a beautiful tapestry on that wall; and I could just sink into that bearskin rug by the fireplace and sleep like a baby."

"Well I hope you got some Pampers," I laughed, "because I don't want your big ass soiling my rug."

"Tara, you are such a fool," he said, softly pinching my nose. Stan seemed to really be taken with the study as he stood there looking around in awe at the numerous articles, pictures, and awards that were proudly displayed.

"You know, I have a lot of these articles about you and I have all of your books."

"Is that right, now? So I guess you're my number one fan, huh?"

"Yes, without a doubt I am your number one fan," he fondly said.

"Well alrighty then, I guess we'd better get out of here. My stomach is starting to sing songs," I said as we headed for the door. When we got downstairs, Ralph was standing in the lobby talking to the second shift doorman, Manny. Even though Ralph's shift had ended at 6:30, I'm sure he hung around just so he could see how long Stan was in my apartment.

"My, Ms. St. Pierre, you're looking very lovely this evening. Going out for a night on the town, huh?" nosy Ralph asked.

"Goodnight Ralph," I responded. "Say hello to your wife for me."

* * *

As we made the drive from my condo to the Green Dolphin on Ashland, we reminisced about our childhood (the good parts) and talked about our friends.

"So how is Jeremy doing?" Stan asked.

"Jeremy is great," I said. He's a hot shot attorney in L.A. now."

"Is that right? Now there's one brother who really turned his life around. Do you two still keep in touch?" Stan asked as he pulled into the parking lot.

"It's been about three years since we last saw each other, but we call one another when we can. We mainly keep in touch through e-mail; thank God for that invention. Jeremy's talking about coming back to Chicago to set up his practice here. Now wouldn't that be great, having my two good friends living back here," I said as we entered the restaurant and were seated.

"Yeah, that would be great," Stan said with what sounded like a hint of sarcasm. As we enjoyed our meal, I couldn't help but notice how much Stan had changed. Gone was the quiet, shy little boy. He had been replaced by an assertive, outgoing, charming and extremely handsome man whom I was finding myself becoming drawn to.

"So Tara," Stan said as if on cue, "who's the lucky man in your life?"

"Believe it or not, when we ran into each other last week at Spago's, I was there giving the guy I'd been dating his dismissal papers. Didn't you notice all the water around my table?" I laughed. "That was from the tears he shed upon hearing the devastating news."

"Now what on Earth did that brother do to cause you to un-mercifully kick him to the curb?"

"Well, I'll put it like this, you know how when you first light a candle and the fire is strong and it's burning brightly, but eventually the wick gets shorter and the fire dies down then goes out? Well, let's just say he was a small candle with a short wick."

"Tara, you are too crazy, you know that, woman?" Stan said as he smiled an absolutely radiant smile.

God, that man looks good, I thought to myself. *I guess now would be as good a time as any to ask him about his divorce.* "Stan, do you mind if I ask what happened between you and Gina? I know at one time you practically worshipped her."

"Tara, you can ask me anything," Stan said as he looked deeply into my eyes. "You're right, I did worship Gina. I loved that woman with every fiber of my soul and there was nothing I wouldn't do for her. But after I started my own construction company, she just seemed to change. She only seemed to care about shopping and hanging out with her friends. She never had time for me anymore. I just figured she was going through a phase or something. So I tried to talk to her about her behavior, but all she would say was that as long as she was a good mother and kept the house clean then that's all that should matter. I guess I didn't fit into her equation any longer, because by that time our sex life was pretty much nonexistent. But I still wanted to make our marriage work."

"So what happened?" I asked.

"I came home early one day and caught her in bed with one of my employees."

"Stan! No she didn't!" I said in shock. "What did you do?"

"My first impulse was to beat the shit out of both of them, but I managed to get ahold of myself and told her it was over; that she would be hearing from my lawyer. Of course I told Leroy to find himself another job and get the fuck out of my house, then I packed some clothes and went to a hotel. I stayed there until I was able to find an apartment. But the hardest part was explaining to my daughter that I wouldn't be living at home anymore."

"Why didn't you file for custody?"

"I seriously thought about it, but I know how close Brie is to her mother and I didn't want to hurt her. Besides, Gina never gave me any problems about seeing Brie. That is, not until she found out I was dating someone. Then she had the nerve to start trippin."

"Get out of here!" I exclaimed. "What'd she do?"

"Well, first she starts saying she didn't want her daughter around some strange woman, then when she saw I wasn't paying her any attention, then she really starts playing silly assed games. Sometimes when I'd go by to pick Brie up, she made sure Brie wasn't home; or she'd call and say she was bringing Brie by to spend time with me and never show up. So I threatened to take her to court and that's when she moved here."

"Now that's some deep shit, Stan. I'm sorry you had to go through that. But if you've moved back here, then what about your business back in Louisiana?"

"My cousin, William, is part owner, so he's running every- thing. We had been talking about expanding our business to another city, so I guess Chicago is as good as anywhere."

I wanted to ask Stan what made him think if Gina was trippin' in Louisiana that she wouldn't pull the same thing here, but I decided to let it rest for now.

"Well," Stan said after we'd finished our meal, "it's still early so what would you like to do now, lovely lady?"

"I'm enjoying sitting here talking with you and listening to the music. If you'd like to go dancing, we can do that."

"I'm enjoying sitting here talking with you, so let's just have a couple more drinks and continue our conversation."

"You know our old building has been torn down," I informed him.

"Yeah, I know. I drove past there the other day after I'd come from visiting my father at the nursing home."

"How is Uncle B. doing these days?" I asked.

"Not too good. He has cirrhosis and there's not much the doctors say can be done except to make him as comfortable as possible."

"That's too bad. I'm sorry to hear that. I'll go with you the next time you go to visit him," I said.

"I'm sure he would like that, though he probably won't remember you. Hey," Stan said, "why don't we go by my house for a while so you can see what I've done to the place."

"Okay," I said excitedly. "I can't wait to see the remodeling work you've done on it."

"Hey, you know me, always changing things, taking things apart and making them better and different," he said as we got into his car and headed for Oak Park.

* * *

"Here we are," he said as we pulled into the garage. As we left the garage, we walked into the laundry room and Stan stood watching me with an amused look on his face as I walked around, looking puzzled.

"Okay Stan, I give. Where the hell is the door and how do we get out of the laundry room?"

"You're standing right in front of the door," he said as he took a remote control out of his pocket and pressed a button. Sure enough, the wall that I had been standing in front of smoothly slid back to reveal a long, mirrored hallway.

"This is the master bedroom," Stan said as we walked down the hallway.

"What is the master bedroom?" I asked. "All I see is a mirrored wall."

"Now you see it, now you don't," he said as again he pressed the remote control and the wall slid back to reveal an enormous bedroom.

"I've heard of people wanting their homes to be different and unique, but this is crazy. Please don't tell me the bathroom is behind a sliding wall, because that could cause some serious problems for your guests."

"No, the bathroom is in plain sight," he said as we continued down the hall. Sure enough, there was the bathroom, with a real door.

"What a relief!" I said as we rounded a corner and went down three stairs to enter a huge, sparsely furnished sunken living room. To the left of the living room was, you guessed it, another hidden door, behind which was a short hallway that led to the kitchen and dining room.

"Well, that pretty much concludes the tour of the ground floor," Stan said as he led me back to the living room, "unless you'd like to see the upstairs. There are two guest bedrooms, a bath and a den."

"Maybe later," I said. "This house is making me dizzy."

"Then have a seat and make yourself comfortable. I'll get us something to drink. Oh yeah, I also have your favorite."

"And what would that be?" I curiously asked.

"Scrabble!" he said, walking over to the bookcase and picking up the game.

"I know you're not challenging me," I said, hands on hips.

"Oh yeah, that's a challenge. I just want you to know I'm no longer the little boy you used to beat up on when we played Scrabble as kids," he informed me.

"Well bring it on then," I said, rolling up my sleeves. "I take no prisoners."

We sat there playing Scrabble, drinking and talking, and before we knew it, it was 2:30 in the morning. "Aw man, I can't believe it's this late," I said as I looked at my watch.

"I can't believe you just kicked my butt three times," Stan said. "Girl, you know you still got it."

"And you know this, man," I laughed, imitating Chris Tucker. "Look Stan, I'm gonna call a cab and head home."

"No, Tara! Look, why don't you spend the night in one of the guestrooms? I have a 9:00 appointment in the morning downtown and I can drop you off then."

"You have an appointment on a Sunday morning?"

"Hey, you know how it goes; business never takes a day off. So what do you say?"

"Do I have to guess behind which wall are the stairs leading up to the guest rooms?" I asked with my arms folded across my chest.

"No beautiful, you don't. You'll also be pleased to know that those bedrooms have actual doors. And if it makes you more comfortable, I'll leave the doors leading upstairs and to the kitchen open, just in case you might want to come down for a drink or something," he said as he led me upstairs.

"Well, I probably would feel more comfortable with the doors open, but you don't have to worry about me coming down- stairs for anything. I sleep like a log. I can guarantee you as soon as my head hits the pillow, I will be out like a light."

"Well, goodnight," he said, gently kissing me on the forehead. "I'll see you in the morning."

"Goodnight," I said softly as I went in the room and gently closed the door—a real door. *Man, if I didn't know any better, I'd think Stan decorated this bedroom with me in mind,* I thought as I looked around. He'd decorated the room in all of my favorite colors and the artwork on the walls were by some of my favorite painters. Where most men would probably have chosen a floral patterned comforter (thinking all women like floral patterns), Stan had chosen a peach comforter with little cherubs adorning it. "I don't know how he knew I like cherubs, but I like this man's style," I said as I removed my clothes and hung them up in the closet. After quickly removing my makeup and washing my underwear, I promptly jumped in the bed.

* * *

"You are so beautiful, Tara," Stan said softly as he stood in the back of the closet caressing her clothes and watching Tara as she slept. He'd been standing in the same spot for over an hour, watching her and inhaling the scent from her clothes. When she rolled over and kicked the comforter off, exposing her naked- ness, Stan found himself getting aroused. As he stood there stroking himself and getting to the point where he was ready to explode, he decided it was time he got back downstairs. So he quietly closed the closet door, opened the hidden door in the back of the closet and went downstairs to his room.

* * *

"Hey sleepyhead, wake up. It's 7:30."

"What tha…." I said as I sat up in bed with a start. "Who the hell is in my house?" As I looked around disoriented, I remembered I wasn't at home but at Stan's. "Okay, Stan, I'll be down as soon as I shower and get dressed."

"Would you like some breakfast?" he asked through the door.

"Just some juice and a croissant."

"Okay, it'll be waiting for you when you come down."

As I got up and headed for the bathroom, I looked over at the closet door. "That's funny, I could have sworn I'd left that closet door open last night. I must be trippin."

* * *

"So, what's on your agenda for today?" Stan asked as we headed for my home.

"Well, I'm gonna do a little cleaning and laundry then work on a couple of chapters for my next book before heading out to Schaumburg for dinner at Momma's." It's funny, even though my mother had been gone for over ten years, I still referred to the house as hers. "You know what?" I said, turning to face Stan, "You should join me. I bet you hardly remember my sister Denise; but I know she would love to see you. She has a wonderful family. A really cool husband, and two gorgeous kids, and…. oh, oh," I said, trailing off.

"What's the matter?" he asked.

"I'm sorry Stan. I almost forgot about my Aunt June. She lives there, so she'll also be there."

"Tara," Stan said, pulling up to my building, "I hold no grudges against your aunt. As a matter of fact, I would love to see her. So if that offer still stands, then I would love to join you."

"Good! I'll tell you what, I plan on getting there around 3:00 and dinner is at 5:00, so why don't you come around 3:30 or 4:00?" I said, writing down the address. "I'm glad you've managed to forgive my Aunt," I said as I opened the car door.

"Time heals all wounds," he said as he smiled that heart- warming smile at me.

"Aunt June," Stan angrily said as he sped off, gripping the steering wheel so hard his knuckles turned red. "It's because of that bitch that my father is in the condition he's in today. But for Tara's sake, I'll be the charming, debonair gentleman when I see her rotten ass again."

FOURTEEN

"Whose is this, bitch? Huh, huh? Say my name!"

Damn! What is this dude's name? Sherita thought as she looked back at the super fine, chocolate man who'd been giving her endless hours of pleasure. "This is yo' pussy, daddy," she said as she bucked back to meet his thrusts. *I swear I'm gonna have to stop picking up complete strangers and bringing 'em home. This shit could get to be dangerous,* she thought as she felt him tense up and explode inside of her.

"Damn baby, that shit was the bomb," he said as he rolled off her, laying beside her, panting.

"The bathroom is through there," Sherita pointed. "You can shower first. I'll wait."

"Naw, baby, you can go first. I need a couple of minutes to lay here and catch my breath. You know you laid it on me," he said.

"Okay baby, *(damn, what is his name?),* I'll be back in a few."

"You know, I was thinking…" Sherita said as she emerged from the bathroom. "Hey daddy, where are you?" Sherita's *friend* was not in the bed, so she went into the kitchen thinking he might be there; but he wasn't. Sherita went back into the bedroom, and that's when she noticed his clothes were gone, along with her purse, which had been in the chair by the window. "That no good, low-down, dirty motherfucker!" she said as she walked over to the chair to pick up a sheet of paper which was where her purse had been.

It's bitches like you that give decent women a bad name, the note read. *Sluts who go around picking up total strangers, taking them home to fuck with no damn condoms deserve whatever they get. It was a bitch like you that burned me, so I'm just returning the favor. Have a happy life, slut!*

Sherita sat there in shock re-reading the letter.

"Oh my God! I don't believe this shit," she said aloud. "What the hell does he mean he got 'burned'? I knew I shouldn't have figured that just because that piece of slime was fine and wearing a designer suit, that he was cool. His ass might have AIDS. I can't believe I exposed myself like that. Now what am I gonna do?" Just then the phone rang and Sherita reluctantly picked it up. "Hello?" she said apprehensively.

"Hey sweet pea, what's up? Do you want me to pick you up or are you gonna drive out to Schaumburg today?" Reggie asked.

"Reggie, I'm not going," Sherita said with a shaky voice.

"Sherita, you never miss a good home cooked meal. What's wrong?"

"Reggie, I'm scared," Sherita cried. "I think I fucked up big time."

"What's going on? What's wrong, Sherita?" Reggie said, alarmed. Sherita continued to cry as she told Reggie about what had just happened.

"Look Sherita, I want you to try to calm down. Go take a couple of aspirins, fix yourself something to eat, and lie down. I have something to take care of then I'll be by there as soon as I'm done."

"No Reggie, you don't have to come by here. I just want to be by myself to think."

"Uh-uh! You're not gonna be alone, and you *are* going to dinner if I have to tie you up and drag you with me," he said. "Now go do what I told you to do."

"Okay," Sherita sniffled.

"By the way, have you spoken to Tara? I tried calling her last night and early this morning, but got her voicemail."

"Oh yeah, she had a date last night with Stan, the son of the man Aunt June used to be married to. I'm sure she's told you about him," Sherita said.

"Yeah, she did; but I thought he was in Louisiana."

"He was, but he's moved back to Chicago. I guess the date must have been hot if she didn't go home last night."

"Well, I'll try her again later," Reggie said. "Do you want me to tell her what happened, or will you?"

"You can tell her. She's gonna know something's wrong anyway when she sees me," Sherita sighed.

"Yeah, you know Tara doesn't miss a thing. Now you get some rest. I'll see you later."

"Okay, Reggie."

"Man, that's messed up," Reggie said as he hung up the phone and walked back into the bedroom.

"What's messed up, baby?" Jackie asked.

"Oh, nothing baby. Just a good friend who's gotten herself into a situation."

"Now that's cold Reggie. You mean to tell me you're gonna get out of bed with me to go call another woman?"

"Look woman, don't start trippin'," Reggie said with annoyance in his voice. "Shouldn't you be heading home now? Isn't your husband coming back home today?"

"Yeah, he's coming home today. But that doesn't mean we don't have time for you to break me off a little sumthin sumthin," Jackie said as she started rubbing Reggie's chest. Reggie, who was 27 years old, stood 5'9, with a medium build, and bore a striking resemblance to the singer Ginuwine. He was definitely a ladies' man who never seemed to be satisfied with just one woman. Jackie, Reggie's current fling, was 35 and was the mother of one of Reggie's 6th grade students.

"Baby, I would love to serve you some more, but I have some things to take care of, so why don't you take your fine ass in there, shower, get dressed and head on home, okay?" Reggie said as he slapped her on her backside.

* * *

"Man! I'm glad she's gone," Reggie said aloud when Jackie had finally left. "I don't know what possessed me to get involved with the mother of one of my students, but I just could not turn down getting some of that." Just then the phone rang.

"Hey cous', what's up?" Tara said when Reggie answered the phone.

"You must be psychic or something. I was just about to call you, like I did last night and this morning but your butt wasn't at home. It must've been one hell of a date."

"I see you've been talking to Sherita."

"Yeah, I have. But we'll get to your date in a minute. First I need to tell you what happened to Sherita." As Reggie pro-ceeded to tell Tara about what had happened, she didn't want to believe it, but she wasn't surprised.

"How is she doing now?" Tara asked. "I guess I should call her."

"Well, she's pretty shaken up, but I told her to go lie down and get some rest and that I would be by there soon. She's prob-ably turned the phone off. But I did convince her to come to dinner, so you can talk to her there," he said.

"So who was the guy?"

"I don't know. I was supposed to go out with Sherita last night, but I hooked up with Jackie instead and I guess Sherita went out by herself."

"Now would that be Jackie, mother of one of your students?"

"Yes, that would be she."

"Reggie! I don't believe you. You know that shit is unethi-cal," I said incredulously.

"Yeah, I know, but I'm about to put an end to that. She's starting to get too attached and that could be some deadly shit," he stated. "But cous', I just couldn't resist her. You know how I am about a sexy older woman."

"You mean sexy older *women,* don't you? Or have you for- gotten about Jolene and Bernice?"

"Naw, I could never forget about my two favorite girls. That's why I have to let Jackie go. If tryna love two ain't easy to do, then tryna juggle three is starting to kill me!" he laughed.

"Oh, it will be killing you if they ever find out how you're playing them."

"Hey, I'm just a young brother out here enjoying myself."

"You know, you never cease to amaze me, Reggie. Here you are a dedicated, hardworking teacher by day, and a big ass whore by night. You are something else, you know that," Tara said.

"Me! What about you? I called you last night and this morning and you weren't at home. Out with Stan the man, huh?"

"Sherita might be in a state of distress," I said, "but I see it doesn't stop her from gossiping."

"So is it a love connection. And when do I get to meet him to check him out and make sure he's good enough for my cousin?"

"No, it's not a love connection, but I do care for him. You'll get a chance to meet him today. I invited him to dinner."

"Whoa! Does Aunt June know who's coming to dinner?"

"I'm calling her as soon as I get off the phone with you. Besides, I know Aunt June won't have a problem with seeing him again."

"As long as he doesn't bring his father along," Reggie said. "Now that would be an interesting family reunion. It might turn into some Jerry Springer kinda shit."

"Yeah, I heard that! Look Reggie, let me get off this phone. Give Sherita a hug for me and tell her I'll talk to her this evening."

"Okay cous', peace out," Reggie said, hanging up.

"Tara! It's good to see you, sis," Denise said when I walked into the kitchen later that day. Since I'm expected on Sundays, that's the only time when I use my key to let myself into the house.

"Something sho' smells good in here, sis," I said, going over to give her a hug.

"Ta Ta, Ta Ta," the twins yelled as they came running in the kitchen, pulling on my dress so I could pick them up. "Where's Aunt June?" I asked.

"She went upstairs to freshen up. She seems to be really nervous about seeing Stan again," Denise said as she brushed flour from her hands. "Reggie and Sherita are in the basement with Houston shooting some pool."

"We wan go in poo," Kyle said as he and Kianna played with my hair while I continued to hold one in each arm.

"No sweetie, it's not warm enough today to get in the pool, but you and your sister go upstairs and play until dinner is ready," Denise said.

"Toss me an apron and I'll help you out," I said.

"Girl, that's not necessary. Everything is under control in here. Besides, something seems to be troubling Sherita. Why don't you go on downstairs?"

"Okay, I will. Call me when Stan gets here." As I headed through the living room, Aunt June came down the stairs.

"Tara. The twins told me you were here," she said as she nervously looked around.

"I got here about ten minutes ago," I said as we hugged one another. "Aunt June, you look like a nervous wreck. What's wrong?"

"I don't know, baby. I guess I'm just nervous about seeing Stan again. When I saw him at your mom's funeral he acted as if I wasn't even there when I spoke to him."

"I didn't know that Aunt June. Why didn't you say some-thing this morning? If I had known you'd be uncomfortable around him, I would have come up with a reason to un-invite him. But when I asked him to come, he seemed excited about seeing you."

"Really?" Aunt June said as her face brightened up.

"Yes, he seemed like he was really looking forward to seeing you. Stan's a grown man now Auntie, I'm sure he's put the past behind him. So why don't you just calm down, take a deep breath and enjoy yourself," I said as I gave her a kiss on the cheek. "I'm going downstairs to see who I can beat in a game of 8-ball."

"What's up with my peeps?" I said when I entered the base-ment.

"Hey, Tara," Houston and Reggie said in unison.

"Hey, girl," Sherita said in a sullen voice.

"You ready to get your butt kicked?" I asked as I went over to hug her. I could see the tension and anxiety written all over her face. I was anxious for the chance to talk to her in private.

"Tara, I beat you the last two times we played," she said. "You don't want none of this."

"Oh girlfriend, it's on now!" I said as Houston and Reggie started cracking up.

"Well, I'm moments away from beating Houston on his own table," Reggie said, winking at me, "so you girls can go next." Just as we were about to start our game, Denise called downstairs. "Tara, Stan's here. And dinner will be ready soon."

"I guess it's time we took this little soiree upstairs," Houston said.

"Yeah, let's go meet Stan the man," Reggie said.

"Looks like I'll have to put off redeeming myself until later," I said to Sherita. I squeezed her hand while we walked upstairs.

"Stan," I said as I walked over to him with outstretched arms. "I'm so glad you made it."

"Thanks for inviting me," he said, embracing me.

"Let me introduce you to everyone. This is my brother-in-law, Houston. My cousin, Reggie, and my girl, Sherita," I said.

"What's up, Stan. Welcome to our home," Houston said as he reached out to shake Stan's hand.

"It's good to finally meet you. I've heard a lot about you," Reggie said.

"Well, well, well. So you're Stan," Sherita said as she em-braced him. The girl might have been distraught from her experience that morning, but it sure didn't seem to stop her from perking up when she saw how fine Stan was. I noticed Aunt June had not come back downstairs yet. *I hope this wasn't a bad idea,* I thought as we headed for the living room. As soon as we'd sat down, she walked in with the twins in tow.

"Stan!" she said, walking over to where he was seated. "It's so good to see you again." As Stan stood up, Aunt June tried to look relaxed, but I could tell she was about to jump out of her skin.

"June!" he said as he bent down and kissed her on the cheek. "It's good to see you again, too. You look just as beautiful now as you did when I was a little boy," he said as he took her hands into his.

"Why, thank you, sweetheart," she said as she seemed to loosen up a little.

"And who are these two little people?" Stan asked as he bent down and picked up the twins.

"That's Kyle and Kianna," I said, "also known as Ren and Stimpy." As they started laughing, Stan put them down and they ran over and hopped in Houston's lap.

"Excuse me everyone, but I'm gonna go help Denise set the table so we can get down to some serious eating," Aunt June said as she headed for the kitchen.

"Is there anything I can help you with?" Stan asked as he stood up.

"No baby, you're company. You just relax and make your- self at home." We sat there for another ten minutes making small talk, inhaling the fragrant aroma of the roast beef, mashed potatoes, baked chicken, beans, and other delicious dishes Denise and Aunt June had prepared, while listening to our stomachs rumble. Finally, Denise called us to the table. After we were seated, with Stan next to me, we said grace and then proceeded to tear into the food like a pack of hungry wolves. After we'd finished dinner, no one thought they'd have room for dessert, but when Aunt June brought out the peach cobbler, vanilla ice cream and banana pudding, we all managed to find a little spot in our stomachs that had yet to be filled. The conversation was great and Stan was so comfortable and at ease, telling jokes and sharing stories about his life in Louisiana, that time seemed to fly by. Everyone seemed to enjoy listening to Stan's stories, even Aunt June. But I noticed Houston seemed to be unusually quiet as he intently watched Stan. I couldn't help but wonder why. As for me, I was getting turned on just watching Stan. Every time he smiled his absolutely charming smile, I melted. Just inhaling his intoxicating aroma was enough to make any woman lose control. *His wife must have been out of her mind,* I thought as I smiled at him. As we were finishing up dessert, we heard a soft splat. When I looked down the table, I saw my poor little nephew had eaten himself into exhaustion and had fallen asleep in his high chair. The splat we heard was his head falling into his mashed potatoes.

"My poor baby," Denise said as she took Kyle out of his mashed potatoes and his high chair.

"Denise, me and Sherita will take care of the dishes," I said. "Why don't you go ahead and get the kids ready for bed."

"I guess us fellas will go shoot some more pool," Houston said.

"Tara, I'll help you and Sherita wash dishes," Aunt June said.

"Oh no you won't!" I said. "You've done enough preparing the meal. You just relax. We've got this covered." While I was sincere in what I'd said to Aunt June, I really wanted to be alone with Sherita so that we could talk. After clearing the table and scraping the dishes, I turned to Sherita, "Sherita, Reggie told me what happened," I said. "Are you gonna be alright?"

"Tara, I don't know. I don't know what to think. I don't know what to do. I just want to crawl in my bed and never get up again," she said with tears in her eyes.

"Look sweetie, I know you're upset but you've got to do something. And the first thing should be to get yourself tested."

"I know Tara, but I'm scared. What if he has AIDS?" she said with a look of fear on her face.

"Sherita," I said, wrapping my arms around her. "I'm here for you, girl. Whatever you need, whatever you want me to do, just let me know. Maybe when he said a woman burned him, he was talking about a woman stole his money and that's why he stole your purse."

"Yeah, I didn't think of that," she said.

"Have you notified your credit card companies?"

"Uh-uh."

"Okay, first thing in the morning call your bank and credit card companies. But first call your doctor for an appointment."

"Tara, thank you for being such a good friend. I'm sorry I didn't listen to you when you told me I should stop picking up men and taking them home."

"Sherita, we all make bad decisions. But what's in the past can't be changed. We just need to deal with this and get past it. Now, when I get home tonight, I'm going to light some extra candles and meditate and chant to every god I can think of on your behalf. You just gotta have faith and learn the lesson that was meant for you to learn from this. You know what they say, 'he who doesn't learn from his mistakes is doomed to repeat them.' So what I want you to do is to take a deep breath, put a smile on that lovely face and enjoy the rest of the evening. Besides, you still got a butt whipping coming when we get down- stairs, so let's go join the guys."

"Tara, I love you, girl. You always know what to say to make me feel better. And I know you just want to get downstairs so you can be near Stan."

"I do not!" I said as I slapped her on the arm.

"Yeah, right. Girl, it's written all over your face. You're sweet on him. I saw the way you kept looking at him and hang-ing on his every word. Not that I can blame you," Sherita said. "Girl, why didn't you tell me he was that fine? The man looks like a Hershey Bar—with nuts!"

"Sherita! You are a damn fool, you know that? But I must admit, he certainly is starting to get under my skin. Every time I look at his fine ass, my nipples get hard," I said as we headed downstairs.

"Reggie, Tara tells me you're a school teacher," Stan said as he casually walked around the pool table, beating Reggie miserably.

"Yes I am, and I love it. It's worth it to see when they grasp something new and that little light bulb goes off in their heads. Then they're eager to learn more."

"Yeah, man, that's great," Stan said as he knocked two more of his balls into the pockets. "We can certainly use more dedicated black men as teachers."

"Amen to that," I said as I plopped down on the sofa. "There are too many kids out here who don't have a positive role model to look up to. And my cous' is one hell of a teacher."

"Why thank you, Tara. And for saying such glowing things about me, I promise to let you win," Reggie said as he gave me the thumbs up.

"*Let* me win! Oh, like you're letting Stan win," I said. No sooner had the words left my mouth than Stan hit the 8-ball into his pocket and the game was over. "Are you next, Houston?" I asked.

"Naw sis, you can go next," he said.

"Well, Stan," I said as he racked the balls, "don't take this whipping I'm about to lay on you as anything personal, but I just need to get through you to get to Miss Thang over there."

"Oh, I got your Miss Thang," Sherita laughed as I broke.

As I proceeded to clear the table, I couldn't help but wonder if Stan was intentionally missing shots. It sure seemed like it. "Well, Sherita," I said after pitifully beating Stan, "come on over here and take this whipping."

"You ain't said nothing but a word, bird," she said as she broke. Needless to say, I was on the receiving end of the ass whipping that time. Again.

"Damn! I can never beat this girl in pool!"

"Ah, could someone bring Tara a bowl of crow?" she called out. "Stan, how 'bout you? You want a piece of this?" she cockily said.

"I'll have to take a rain check on that," Stan said as he stood up, smoothing out his pants. "It's about time I headed for home."

"I'll walk you to your car," I said.

"I just bet you will," Sherita whispered under her breath as I passed by her.

"Rack 'em up, Sherita," Reggie said. "I'll have a piece of that. You know how I hate turning down a good piece."

"Well, goodnight everyone," Stan said, laughing at Reggie's crazy ass. "It was a pleasure meeting all of you and I look forward to seeing you all again."

"Hey man, it was good to finally meet you," Reggie said.

"Yeah," Sherita piped in, "I certainly look forward to see-ing you again."

"Houston, thanks for having me in your home."

"Yeah man, glad you could make it," Houston said dryly.

Now what in the world is up with him? I wondered. *He's been acting funky towards Stan all night.* When we got upstairs, Denise and Aunt June were in the dining room talking.

"Denise," Stan said, as he gave her a hug, "it was wonder-ful to see you again. You have a beautiful home and two of the most adorable little kids. Thanks for having me over."

"Stan, you're welcome in my home any time, so please don't be a stranger," she said.

"June," he said as he took her hands in his, "I've really missed you and I enjoyed being able to see you again. It's good to see you still have that magic touch when it comes to cooking a delicious meal. Thank you, both of you," he said, hugging her.

"Stan," Aunt June said, teary eyed, "you've grown into such a beautiful man. I'm just sorry….."

"Shhhh," he said as he put his finger to her lips, "no need for you to apologize about anything. I'm just glad to see you again. And you can be sure, this won't be the last time."

"I'm gonna walk Stan to his car," I said as we headed out the door with his arm around my waist.

"It's been awhile since I've had a good home-cooked meal, and those two women know they can burn," he said, smiling.

Oh shit, I thought, *there he goes again with that 'make me wanna melt' smile.* "Stan, I'm really glad you came," I said while moving closer to him. "I hope we can do this again, soon."

"Tara," he said as he put his finger beneath my chin and lifted my face up, "I hope we can do a lot of things together, soon." And with that, he pulled me in close to him and softly kissed me. As his scent enveloped me, it seemed as if time stood still. All I wanted was for him to continue kissing me, which he was doing with a passion I had never before experienced. I don't know how long we stood there, but even though it was a brisk night and I was wearing a silk dress, his warm embrace and hot kisses were enough to ward off the chill in the air. *I could really get used to this,* I thought as I grabbed the back of his head, eagerly matching the intensity of his kisses.

FIFTEEN

"Well Tara, I'm glad you were able to take time out of your busy schedule to have lunch with me," Sherita said sarcastically. "I haven't seen much of you these past four or five weeks. Stan seems to be keeping you pretty busy."

"Get out of here, Sherita. I've been doing more than just spending my time with Stan. I am working on my next novel, or did you forget about that?" I said.

"Yeah, whatever," she said. "And I can't believe as much time as the two of you have been spending together, you still haven't given up the panties. Don't tell me he suffers from little dickitis."

"I don't think there's anything wrong with his dick," I responded. "But girl, it has been a challenge! You have no idea how many times I've wanted to rip his clothes off and send him into ecstasy heaven. But we've just been spending time getting reacquainted and enjoying each other's company. We're having so much fun hanging out together. Girl, the man is definitely all that! I can tell by the way he moves on the dance floor that his moves in bed will leave nothing to be desired."

"So when do you plan on finding out what he's really made of?" Sherita asked. "You know, since I've been on this celibacy kick, I have to live vicariously through my friends' sex lives."

"Well, actually, I've invited him over for dinner tonight," I smiled, "and tonight it's on! I'm gonna do things to him that will have him testifying in church tomorrow."

"Ohhh, girl," she laughed, "I heard that! Lay that thang on him."

"And you know it," I said. "But on a serious note, Sherita, how are you doing now?"

"Tara, I'm just taking it one day at a time and not being reckless with my life."

"I heard that, girl." After Sherita's scare with her one night stand, she had herself tested. When she found out it would take five days for the results of her HIV test to come back, she almost went ballistic and pretty much drove me crazy also. Fortunately for both of us, Sherita's doctor was also a client of hers and she pulled a few strings and was able to get the results in three days, sort of as a thank you to Sherita for the money she'd been able to save through tax shelters Sherita had found for her. My girl might have made crazy choices in her personal life, but profess- ionally she was the shit! She was the best damn financial planner I'd ever met and her doctor was a very happy client. Sherita had her own practice and she loved showing people how to create personal wealth and get out of debt. Five years ago, Reggie was in debt up to his eyeballs, with his flamboyant lifestyle which consisted of a Jaguar, an exquisite home, and numerous credit cards. Sherita set him up on a debt management plan where in-stead of being in debt for 30-plus years, he would be totally debt free within almost a third of that time. She then allocated some of the money that had been freed up into a tax-free variable annuity plan with a cash value that he could access at any time. She advised him on wise investments to make, but she made him promise that he wouldn't touch any of the money for at least seven years. At first Reggie cried like a little baby when Sherita told him how he had to discipline himself and follow the rules she laid out for him; but now he was more than happy that he had listened to her because now he was debt free with a nice little nest egg set aside. Sherita certainly had a long list of satisfied clients, with me being at the top of the list.

When the results came back from her tests, I went with her to see her doctor, who informed her that her HIV test was negative, but that she tested positive for gonorrhea. You would have thought the girl had hit the lottery the way she beamed.

"Yes! It's only gonorrhea!" she shouted.

But then Dr. Jensen burst her bubble when she reminded Sherita that the virus could lie dormant for a number of years be-fore becoming detectable. I'm sure Sherita had already thought about that, and surprisingly she took the news much better than I'd thought she would. She did promise to get tested every four or five months for the next three years and to abstain from having casual and unprotected sex. Thank God!

"Well Sherita, I'm so glad we had this time together," I started singing a'la Carol Burnett, and Sherita joined in, "just to have a laugh and sing a song. Seems we just get started and be-fore you know it...." People in the restaurant were looking at us as if we'd lost our minds, but we didn't care. We were just two good friends having fun and enjoying each others' company.

"Be sure to call me tomorrow and give me all the dirty little details," she said as we headed for our cars.

"I don't know," I said as I buckled my seat belt. "It might be too much for your tender ears," I laughed as I sped off to pre- pare for what was to be a glorious night.

* * *

"Why am I so darn nervous?" I said aloud as I looked around to see if anything else needed to be done to the apartment. There wasn't. The place was immaculate—I'd had the cleaning company come in and do a thorough cleaning that morning. The candles were lit, a Herbie Hancock CD was playing, and the standing rib roast I had prepared was smelling so good that if Stan didn't arrive soon, I was certain to start eating without him. Five minutes later when the buzzer sounded, I checked myself in the hall mirror and anxiously waited for him to get upstairs.

"My, aren't you a vision of loveliness," Stan said when I opened the door. I was wearing a red satin mini-dress, and 3- inch red pumps. I had my hair swept up with a few tendrils hanging loose. Stan knew how I loved having my neck kissed and caressed and I didn't want my hair to stand in the way of his sensuous lips. He was dressed casually in a pair of slacks and a polo shirt which accented every muscle in his arms and chest, and I could swear the man had gotten finer since the last time I'd seen him—two days ago.

"This is for you bright eyes," he said as he closed the door behind him, never once taking his eyes off me. I loved when he gave me gifts. They were always unusual or unique. Like the time he had a case of Pay Day candy bars delivered to me with a note that read: *Being with you makes everyday seem like a pay day. I'm just nuts about your sweet, sticky, caramel colored self.*

Needless to say, I wasn't disappointed with the gift he'd just given me—a gorgeous ruby and diamond necklace with matching earrings that went perfect with the outfit I was wearing. "Thank you baby, they're beautiful! How did you know I would wear an outfit these would complement?"

"Because, my dear," he said as he wrapped his arms around my waist, brushed his lips gently across my neck and whispered in my ear, "I make it my business to know everything about you. Your likes," he said as he ran his tongue up and down the side of my neck, "your dislikes. Everything."

"Alright now," I said as I gently pushed him away, "you about to start something up in here."

"So let's get it started," he said as he reached out, grabbed me by the back of my neck and pulled me in close to him.

"We are about to get started—eating. I didn't spend time preparing you a delicious meal to let it go to waste.

Now get over there and sit down while I get us something to drink."

"Yes ma'am, whatever you say," he said, smacking me on the butt.

I went to the bar to pour us some Amaretto and mentally went over my plan of seduction. First the drinks to mellow him out, then a scrumptious dinner, another drink, and then dessert, which would be yours truly. Then I would spend the rest of the night doing things to him that would have him screaming out my name. But Stan, always full of surprises, had his own agenda, and I gotta tell you, the person who ended up doing the scream-ing that night was me. As I walked back into the living room, Stan was standing up and he'd put on my Men of Vizion CD; "Break Me Off" was playing. "Dance with me, baby," he said as I handed him his drink, which he finished in one gulp. He then took my glass, grabbed my hand, stuck my index and middle fingers in my drink and proceeded to lick every drop off my fingers while looking deeply into my eyes. As he pulled me in close, we started swaying to the music with our bodies in tune with one another. As I felt him growing harder, I thought I would cum right then and there. *Damn! He has a lot of nerve throwing a monkey wrench in my game plan,* I thought to myself as I felt him slowly lowering the zipper on my dress. *I'm supposed to be the seducer here! Oh well, when in Rome…* I thought as I started caressing his firm butt. As he eased my dress off my shoulders and let it drop to the floor, I stepped out of it and slowly took a couple of steps backwards so that he could enjoy the view.

"Um, um, um," he said, licking his lips. "Turn around baby, slowly. I want to look at you from all angles."

I raised my arms, slowly turned around, and heard him gasp. I took that to be a sign of total approval. When I was facing him again, I winked at him and seductively walked up close to him, massaging the bulge in his pants.

"What about dinner?" I asked as I continued running my hand over my 'new friend.'

"Don't worry baby, you about to get fed."

"Now that's what I'm talking about," I said as I grabbed his hands and headed for the bedroom. By the time we got there, we had already discarded his shirt, shoes and pants. The only item left was his Joe Boxer briefs which were stretched to the limit. We stood in the middle of the room passionately kissing and I wondered how wrong it would be to thank God for what I was about to receive, but I thanked Him anyway. As he laid me on the bed, he gently started rubbing my clit through my panties, which by now were soaking wet. I reached out to grab his briefs, wanting to unleash the beast, but he grabbed my hand and started licking my fingers, one by one. "Not yet, baby," he said, un-snapping my bra and sucking my breasts like a newborn baby at feeding time. I lay there moaning, enjoying how he would suck one breast while rubbing the nipple of the other one between his fingers, and then switching over to the other one. I started rubbing his firm, tight ass while again trying to remove his briefs, but once again he grabbed my hands. "What's the matter, baby? We got all night and I ain't going nowhere," he said as he straddled me with the family jewels resting on my breasts. I swear, if I could have gotten my hands on my gun at that moment I would have shot him without hesitation for teasing me like this. But I decided to go along with his program. "Okay, baby," I panted, "I'll behave."

"Now that's a good girl," he said as he continued kissing my breasts, working his way down my stomach. I quivered with each kiss as he got closer and closer to the honey pot. He lifted my hips and removed my panties, gently inserting two fingers inside me and slowly going in and out until I was about to cum. Then he took his fingers out and started licking them as if it was the best meal he'd ever tasted. He started kissing my inner thighs and finally worked his way to his target, where he began licking and sucking my clit with such passion that I thought I would scream. But instead I did what any good girl would do, I grabbed his head to make sure he stayed right there. I opened my legs wide and slowly started rotating my hips. "Damn baby, you taste so good," he said as he grabbed my ass and lifted my hips up so that he could better enjoy his meal. "Now you just hold this sweet little pussy right there," he said as again he put his fin- gers inside me. Thank goodness I was in good shape and pretty flexible. I planted my feet firmly on the mattress, kept my hips lifted and moaned with pleasure as he began sucking, licking and finger fucking me with such intensity that I could no longer contain myself. "Oh shit, baby! Keep doing that! Don't stop! Don't stop!" I screamed, grabbing his head as I came with such force that for a moment I was afraid that I would either break his neck or drown him. But Stan was a real trooper. He happily and eagerly stayed right there, enjoying each and every drop of love juice and not letting one drop get away from him. As I collapsed onto the bed panting and moaning, he sat there a moment watch-ing me, smiling so sexily that I came again. "Now for being such a good girl," he said as he leaned forward and kissed me on the forehead, "I have a real treat for you." He stood up and hooked his thumbs in the top of his briefs.

Yes! Yes! Yes! I thought to myself. At that point I was so turned on that I would have begged, turned cartwheels, or pro-mised my firstborn to Satan just to feel Stan inside of me. He teasingly lowered his briefs and out popped 'the beast.' And a lovely beast it was! As he put on a condom and lowered himself back onto the bed, we began kissing then he grabbed my legs and placed my feet on his chest while rubbing 'the beast' against my clit, still teasing me. As he began licking and sucking my toes, he winked at me and then plunged inside of me. The pleasure was so intense that I gasped, wanting him to do it again. As if reading my mind, he pulled back, waited a couple of seconds, then buried himself inside me again. From there it was on! I'm sure you've heard the expression 'bone me like you own me.' Well that's exactly what he did. He screwed me like I was his property, and I loved every minute of it. There were a couple of times when I thought he must have mistaken me for a pretzel because he certainly gave my legs a workout. My feet on his chest, my knees by my ears, my legs crossed while he lifted my hips up, my legs straight up in the air. The man definitely had skills and he worked me that night. He had me to the point where I didn't know whether I was coming or going. But one thing was certain, I was definitely cumming! Hell, I couldn't even remember how many times I came. When we started doing it doggy style, I think that was the highlight of the night—we turned into primitive beasts and were going at it like there was no tomorrow. Ohhh weee, did that feel good!

"Yeah baby, give it to daddy," he said as he continued ramming me. "Give me this sweet little pussy!"

"Stan! Stan! Stan!" I yelled as I matched him stroke for stroke. "Baby, you go' make me cum all over this dick!"

"Come on baby, give daddy what he need," he yelled as I felt him tense up and begin pounding furiously. I don't know how long we both came, but those were the most intense and pleasurable orgasms I'd had in a long time. We both collapsed onto the bed, panting, breathing hard and clinging to each other. I don't remember falling asleep, but I do remember hearing a loud noise which woke us both up.

"Damn, girl," Stan said, rubbing his eyes. "Is that your stomach making that noise?"

"Yeah, it is," I said somewhat embarrassed. "You know we never got around to eating dinner."

"I'll tell you what; you lie here and I'll go fix us something to eat. I'm sure you're in no condition to get up and walk right now anyway. Not after the workout I just put you through."

"Oh, is that so, mister crusty dick?" Stan laughed as he looked down at himself. He'd fallen asleep with the condom on and our juices had dried on his penis. "Yeah, maybe I should take a shower first. Care to join me?"

"No, you go ahead. I'd prefer to take a bubble bath." I didn't want to admit that he was right. I was too exhausted to stand up at that moment.

After we'd eaten a late, late dinner, Stan ran us a bath, which was just what my body needed. We sat there, laid back sipping on champagne, listening to Maxwell and allowing the warm water to soothe our tired bodies. I think the combination of the drink, the music, the intimacy of being close to him and thinking about the unendless pleasure I'd experienced just hours earlier, caused that fire to ignite again inside of me. I made my way over to him, kissing his neck as he started getting hard. "Come on, baby," I said, standing up. We hurriedly made our way to the bed, dripping wet, and spent the next two hours fulfilling each others needs and desires until we drifted off to sleep.

* * *

"Hello," I said sleepily as I reached over, snatching up the ringing phone.

"Tara? Girl, you sound whipped! What's up? Oh, don't tell me. Let me guess. You have an overnight guest there, huh?"

"Reggie, what do you want this early in the morning?" I asked as I ran my hand through my hair.

"Early! Baby girl, it's 12:30! What did that man do to you?" Reggie laughed. I peeked over at the clock, not believing it was so late. It seemed as if we'd only been asleep a couple of minutes instead of hours.

"Look, Miss lady, I'm just calling to make sure you're coming to dinner today. I have some good news I want to share with everyone."

"Yeah, I'll be there. But Reggie, you know how I hate being kept in suspense, so why don't you go ahead and tell your favorite cousin your good news now?" I coerced him.

"Uh-uh. You'll have to wait."

"Well I hope the news is that you're about to stop fooling around with so many different women. Especially married ones."

"Yeah, I know. You're still bent out of shape about Jackie. But you'll be happy to know I'm cutting her loose. In fact, I'm stopping by her place first to share my good news with her and to give her the bad news, that it's time we ended this affair."

"Reggie, why can't you do that over the phone? Do you think it's a good idea to be going over to her house, or have you forgotten about her husband?"

"Aw cous', it's cool. He's out of town on business, and I'll only be there a minute, so chill out. I'll see you later."

"Is everything okay?" Stan asked when I'd hung up.

"Oh yeah," I said, rolling over and giving him a big kiss. "Reggie has some good news he wants to share at dinner today. And by the way, I'd love it if you'd join us."

"Baby, I really wish I could," he said, "but I have a client I need to see today. Besides, I don't think your brother-in-law too much cares for me."

"Don't be ridiculous Stan. You've only met Houston once."

"Okay Tara, maybe I just misread him, but I'll still have to pass on the invite. And as much as I hate to leave you," he said, softly kissing my breasts, "I gotta get out of here so I'm not late for my appointment."

"Well," I said as I began to massage his manhood, "we do have time for a quickie, don't we?"

*   *   *

"Hello Gina," Stan said as he stood in his attic later that day. "It's about time you answered the phone. I've been calling for an hour now."

"Stan, what do you want?"

"I want to talk to my daughter!"

"Well, she's not here. She went to Great America."

"With who!?" Stan demanded.

"With friends of mine. Why!?"

"Look, you bet not have some man around my daughter taking her places when you won't even let me, her father, see her."

"Well Stan, she's my daughter too and I can let my daughter go places with my friends if I choose to. And I've never said you can't see your daughter. *I* don't want to see *you*."

"Are you seeing someone, Gina?"

"That is none of your business! See Stan, that's your problem and that's one of the reasons why I left you. Because of your insecurities. Always seeing affairs where there are none, accusing me of sleeping around, and trying to control every moment of my life. You need to get some help and stop trying to fit back into my life, because it'll never happen. Not after what you've done to me, my friends and family. So leave me the hell alone." Gina said, struggling not to lose control.

"Gina, I don't give a damn about you or what you do. I just want a relationship with my daughter. And if you think I want you back, you can forget that. I have someone in my life and she's a much better woman than you'll ever be. As a matter of fact, I just left her very happy and satisfied."

"Well good for you, Stan. I feel sorry for her and I hope she knows what she's getting herself into. But like me, I'm sure she'll be taken in by your charm and fake sincerity. Then some- where down the road after she's made the mistake of falling in love with you, she'll see you for the sick, dual-personality having motherfucker that you are!" And with that, Gina slammed the phone down.

"Stupid bitch!" Stan yelled as he hurled the paperweight on his desk across the room. As he paced back and forth looking around the room at the various photos of Tara, he gradually regained his composure. He reached into his pants pocket, pulling out the panties Tara had been wearing the night before. As he inhaled deeply, remembering the events from the night before, he found himself getting an erection. He continued to inhale, slowly lowering the zipper on his pants and walking toward the life size photograph of Tara.

SIXTEEN

"Look Jackie, I just stopped by to share my good news with you before heading to my family's for dinner," Reggie explained.

"Good news! I don't see anything good about you moving to Dallas. What about us?"

"Come on now," Reggie said as he stood up. "You're a married woman. And even if I hadn't accepted the teaching job in Dallas, we couldn't continue our relationship. You know it's not ethical for me to be sleeping with the mother of one of my students."

"Oh, so now you got a conscience?" Jackie said as she rubbed Reggie's arm.

"Look baby, don't take this personal. It's a great opportu- nity for me and I'd be a fool to turn down almost doubling my salary. You're a beautiful woman. I enjoyed our times together and I'm certainly going to miss you, but it is what it is. So baby, I'm gonna go on and get out of here. I don't feel comfortable being in another man's home," Reggie said as he headed for the door.

"Relax baby, Andrew won't be back home until tomorrow. Just have one drink with me to celebrate your job offer and to say goodbye, okay?" Jackie said as she headed for the den.

"Alright baby, but I gotta be out of here in fifteen minutes," Reggie said as he sat back down. When Jackie walked back into the living room, she was wearing spiked heels, a leather thong, and a smile. "Aw shit baby, don't do this to me," Reggie said as he felt himself getting harder than a bag of bricks.

"Come on, daddy. Just one more time. Let me give you something to remember me by," she said, lowering her 36 C's into Reggie's face.

Well, I guess one more time can't hurt, Reggie thought as he pulled Jackie down onto his lap.

Unfortunately, Reggie would soon find out how fatal that way of thinking could be. Not only can one more time hurt, sometimes it can kill.

* * *

"Dang! When is Reggie gonna get here? I'm starving."

"Sherita, you're always starving," I said, rolling my eyes at her. "Besides, you know how Reggie is. He's probably being late on purpose, just to keep us in suspense."

"Well he has exactly twenty minutes to get here, then we're starting dinner without him. He'll just have to tell us his news while he's heating his plate up in the microwave," Aunt June said.

"I heard that," Denise said while wiping Kianna's runny nose. "Tara, I know he's already told you what the good news is, so why don't you just go ahead and tell us?"

"Girl, I'm in the dark like everyone else. You know I tried to get it out of him, but he wouldn't talk."

"I hope the good news is that he's finally decided to settle down with one good woman and turn in his playa's card," Houston said. "That man's playing a dangerous game toying with women's emotions. One of these days he's gonna bite off more than he can chew."

We sat around for the next twenty minutes making small talk while Aunt June set the table. "Okay, time's up for Mr. Reggie Martin," she said. "So let's eat."

"Here, here," Sherita shouted.

The dinner was delicious and mouth watering, as always, and the conversation was pleasant, but I kept noticing Sherita looking across the table at me, staring and smiling. "Girl, what on Earth is the matter with you?" I finally asked. "Do I have food on my teeth or something?"

"Or something, girl," she laughed. "Your face is lit up like a Christmas tree. I mean, you are absolutely glowing! In fact, I haven't seen a glow like that since I waxed my kitchen floor."

"Shut up, Sherita," I said, throwing a bean at her.

"Well Tara, I wasn't gonna say nothing," Aunt June said, "but she is right. You look like a woman's who's had an epiphany."

"Oh, is that what they're calling it now?" Sherita laughed.

"Uh-uh. Oh no y'all won't go there. Not at the dinner table with these kids here," Denise said.

As I looked down the table, I noticed Houston's expression had changed.

"So why didn't Stan come to dinner with you?" Sherita asked.

"He had to see a client," I said, looking at Houston. "Besides, he seems to think that Houston doesn't much care for him."

"Tara, don't be silly. We all like Stan very much," Denise said.

"No we all don't," Houston said matter-of-factly.

"And just what do you mean by that!?" I said defensively.

"Look Tara, I love you. You're my family. I respect you and your choices and I want you to be happy. You deserve it. But somethin's not right with that guy. He strikes me as a man with a hidden agenda, and I think you should be careful. But that's just my opinion of the man."

I sat there gripping my glass, fighting the urge to hurl it at my brother-in-law, wondering what in the hell was wrong with him. "Well Houston, dear brother-in-law of mine," I spat at him, slipping into ghetto mode, "that's the thing with opinions; they're just like assholes—everybody has one, and some people are one!"

The room grew so silent you could hear a pin drop—in the neighbor's house. I could tell by the looks on everyone's face that they were as shocked by Houston's remarks as I was, and as equally taken aback by my response. Guess I've been a perfect lady for so long that they'd forgotten about the don't-fuck-with-me-'cause-I-will-get-all-up-in-your-face Tara. The silence in the room was shattered by the ringing of the phone. In contrast to the silence in that room, the ringing seemed extremely loud.

"Houston, just what in the..." But that was as far as I got. I was cut off by the sound of Aunt June crying out, "Oh God, no!"

"What is it? What's wrong?" everyone said as we ran into the kitchen.

"That was Northwestern Hospital!" she gasped. "Something about a shooting, and Reggie, and somebody dead!"

Time seemed to stand still and everything felt surreal as we all ran to the garage and scrambled inside Houston's car. Sherita stayed at the house with the kids, but made me promise I would call her as soon as we were able to get more details. The ride to the hospital was unbearable as we all sat in silence, wondering what had happened and if Reggie was alright. I had a sinking feeling that whatever had happened, somehow had something to do with Reggie's fooling around.

I loved my cousin with all my heart and it was at that moment I realized the void that would be left in my life if I lost him. So I started to pray. I prayed that Reggie would be okay. I prayed that whatever the circumstances were surrounding the shooting would be something everyone involved could deal with without there being any more repercussions. I prayed, most of all, that Aunt June had made a mistake when she said someone was dead.

When we arrived at the hospital, we found out that Reggie's parents had been notified and they were flying in from Texas. A Detective Wyndham, along with the nurse, took us into a conference room to give us the details. Nurse Jenkins started by telling us that Reggie was being prepped for surgery. "Mr. Martin has a bullet lodged in his spine," she informed us with a pained expression on her face.

"Oh my God!" Denise gasped, grabbing Houston's arm.

"I'm sorry," Nurse Jenkins said. "We're doing everything we can, and as soon as I can, I'll give you an update on his con-dition," she said before she left the room. We all turned our attention to Detective Wyndham, bracing ourselves for what he was about to tell us. We listened in horror as he told us how Jackie's husband had walked into the house to find his wife and Reggie on the sofa making love. Without any warning, he pulled out a .45 and started shooting. One bullet caught Reggie in the lower back, another in his leg. He turned the gun on his wife, shooting her three times, killing her. He called the police, told them what he'd done, then took his own life. I sat there in stunned silence and lowered my head into my hands.

"Why Reggie? Why? Why? Why?" I cried. The tears started to fall as I thought about the lives that had been destroyed simply because two people wouldn't control their sexual urges. My heart broke into a million pieces as I thought about Jackie's little boy who would somehow have to be told about this madness.

After what seemed like a lifetime, the doctor came in and told us the devastating news. They were able to remove the bullets, but it was unlikely that Reggie would ever walk again. "Can we see him now?" Aunt June asked through tears.

"Well, he's been heavily sedated and he's in post-op now. Why don't you all go on home and get some rest then come back later?" Doctor Richards suggested. We agreed that would be best. As we prepared to leave, Reggie's parents rushed in. Everyone exchanged hugs as Doctor Richards proceeded to tell the Martins about the surgery, Reggie's current condition, and his prognosis. He left the details of the shooting to us. We told them, regrettably, what the Detective had told us and watched as Reggie's mom broke down, crying uncontrollably as her husband tried to console her, with tears streaming down his own face.

"Do you have someplace to stay while you're here in town?" Aunt June asked when the Martins had been able to regain their composure.

"We came straight here from the airport. We'll check into a hotel later," Mr. Martin said.

"Nonsense! You'll come stay with us," Denise said. "We're family and we need to be together to help each other through this."

"That's right," Houston said, reaching into his pocket for a pen and paper. "Here's our address. When you're ready, call a cab and come on out to the house. We're gonna go on home now since we can't see Reggie just yet."

"Thank you all so much," Mrs. Martin said. "We'll call you when we're on our way."

When we arrived back home, we filled Sherita in then we all just sat around, lost in our own thoughts. "Tara, why don't you go upstairs and lie down?" Aunt June suggested.

"No, I'm okay Aunt June. I'm too tense to go to sleep right now anyway. In fact, I think I'll go drive around for awhile to clear my head. Then I'll go on home, change clothes and head back to the hospital," I said as I stood up and grabbed my purse.

"You be careful, girl," Sherita said, giving me a hug.

I drove aimlessly around for about an hour and finally, without even realizing it, I found myself parked in front of Stan's house. As I sat there debating whether I should go ring the bell or go on home, I saw a light go on in Stan's living room. The front door opened and he came outside. He hurriedly walked over to my car as I got out and fell into his arms, sobbing loudly and uncontrollably. "Shhh, baby," he said as he rubbed my back. "I'm so sorry about Reggie. Come on inside and let me take care of you."

I later found out that Aunt June, worried about me and sus- pecting I might go to Stan's, had called him and told him what had happened, which is why he was up looking out for me. Stan sat me on the couch, gave me a box of tissues and went to fix me some tea. When he came back, he sat down, removed my shoes, and as he began to massage my feet, he encouraged me to talk about Reggie. When I started to cry again, he reached over and took me in his arms. "Come on, baby, you need to get some rest," he said as he picked me up, carrying me upstairs where he proceeded to tenderly and lovingly remove my clothes. At first I was tense, thinking he might try to get intimate. At that moment sex was the farthest thing from my mind. But instead, he removed my clothes, slipped one of his t-shirts over my head, laid me on the bed, pulled the covers over me and climbed in beside me. As he wrapped his arms around me and pulled me in close to him, he started softly singing 'Always and Forever' by Heatwave. I felt so safe and protected in his arms as I drifted off to sleep. I had such a peaceful sleep, full of loving dreams of Momma and Daddy when they were alive, of Reggie at a family reunion, clowning around, of Jeremy, my good friend whom I sorely missed. But mostly I dreamed of Stan. Of us hugging, laughing, kissing and just having fun together. I think it was somewhere in those dreams that I realized I was in love with Stan Bishop.

* * *

The next six months seemed to fly by. Reggie spent two months in the hospital. When he was released, his parents took him home with them so that they could help him with his rehabilitation. He took the news that he would be paralyzed from the waist down, very hard. He took the news of Jackie's murder and her husband's suicide even harder. He allowed the guilt he felt for the part he played in the ordeal to eat away at him. But in time, with the help of his therapist, he was able to accept responsibility and move on. He wanted to talk to Jackie's son, but was advised against it. He was grateful for the investments that Sherita had made for him over the years. He'd managed to accumulate an impressive amount of wealth which was able to pay for his astronomical hospital bill, his ongoing therapy, and a custom made home not far from his parents.

As for me and my boo, (yes, I'd started referring to Stan as my boo) we had managed to grow extremely close in that time. In fact, we were practically inseparable. We pretty much divided our time between staying at each other's place. I was really touched when one day he gave me a beautifully gift wrapped box which contained the keys to his home. I promised myself that I would give him keys to my condo, but it just seemed to keep slipping my mind. Not only was the sex with Stan indescribably good, but I honestly enjoyed being around him. At first I thought having him around while I was trying to write would be a distraction, but it seemed to have the opposite effect. I was able to finish my fifth book, *If You Don't Scream, I Won't Holla*, sooner than I had anticipated. Stan never complained or got upset whenever he called to ask me out to dinner or for a night out on the town and I turned him down so that I could write. He would just come over, prepare dinner and entertain himself while I wrote. He had stopped asking me to come over to his place whenever I told him I was working on the book, because I always declined. It's not that I didn't want to go over to his place, but my thoughts just didn't seem to flow whenever I tried writing at his home. You'd think as much time as I spent there that I would be used to all of the hidden rooms, but I wasn't. In fact, on the few occasions I did try to get some writing done there, it always seemed that Stan would disappear. I knew he was in the house, but I could never seem to find him. *Maybe he has a hidden room here that he likes to play around in that he hasn't told me about,* I thought to myself one day as I searched for him. If so, I certainly had intentions of one day finding it, whenever time permitted. I guess that was just the natural sleuth coming out in me. But aside from that, Stan was perfect for me. There were times when I found myself fantasizing what it would be like to be married to him and have a couple of little Stans. I had voiced my concerns that I had yet to meet Brie. He responded that Gina was refusing to let him take Brie with him, and insisted that he not bring another woman into her life just yet. I was hoping she would come around and not force this to turn into a messy legal matter.

Yeah, it certainly felt good being in love with a man as kind, considerate, and understanding as my boo. Even though I hadn't yet told him what my tour schedule looked like as far as the new book was concerned, I knew he would be understanding and we would be able to work out not being able to see one another as often as we had been. Or so I thought.

Those six months had been very good for Sherita, as it saw her business explode. She was able to hire two financial consultants and the girl was living in the lap of luxury in a condo in the River East community. Unfortunately, being celibate had gotten to be too much for her and she was back to her old games. She did assure me that she kept a supply of Trojans and used them religiously.

She, however, didn't want to hear it when I tried to remind her that condoms couldn't protect you against everything. Especially not some crazy assed man who might decide to do some harm to her.

"Girl, I'm screening these niggas now," she informed me one day at lunch. "I now have a three date minimum waiting period before they can get anywhere near the drawers."

"Sherita, you're hopeless," I said, shaking my head.

"And don't you sit there giving me this sanctimonious bull-shit about condoms, because I know you and Stan don't practice safe sex every time you do it. Not with all the fucking you two do. I ain't even hearing it."

I hated to admit it, but she did have a point. Sometimes we got so caught up in the heat of the moment that we threw caution to the wind. But since we'd made it a point to go to the clinic together and get tested, and neither of us was sleeping around, we felt safe.

"So don't you get tired of having the same dick every day?" she asked with a look of disgust on her face.

"Hell, no! Not when it's the best sex I've ever had. Not when boyfriend's got me walking around in broad daylight with a flashlight looking for his sexy ass. Not when almost every night he got my toes curling and me screaming out his name. Not when......"

"Okay, okay! I get the picture!" Sherita laughed. "Your ass is sprung!"

"Yes my sister, that I am."

"So has Houston finally accepted him?"

"Me and Houston talked and he apologized for what he said that day at dinner, but he still seems to think Stan has some kind of hidden agenda. So I just left it alone and I make it a point to not have them under the same roof at the same time," I said.

"Ohhh, so tell me about your birthday present. How'd you like it?" Sherita excitedly asked.

"Oh, Sherita! A week in St. Lucia. Girl, it was the bomb! We had so much fun; scuba diving, sailing; hang gliding, swim- ming, and lots of hot passionate sex. And look at what else he gave me," I said, holding out my hand to show off the enormous rock on my finger.

"Girl, that's an engagement ring!" Sherita shouted.

"It is?" I sarcastically said. "Thanks for clearing that up for me."

"Tara, you're getting married!"

"Now hold the phone, Miss Thang. Don't start sending out the invitations just yet. We're gonna take it slow and continue to do what we're doing and enjoy ourselves. Besides, somehow during the past six months I managed to finish writing what will certainly be on the next bestseller's list. It will be in bookstores in three weeks," I proudly announced. "I have a lot of things lined up with the book tour and things have been finalized with Tavis's show and Queen Latifah's show, so look for my smiling face kicking it with superfine Tavis and the Queen."

"Tara, I can't believe you're gonna be in the same space with Tavis Smiley. Damn! I'm getting moist just thinking about him."

"I heard that. I hope I don't drool on myself," I laughed.

"I heard Latifah's show is being cancelled," Sherita said.

"Yeah, I heard that too. But the show I'll be on will be shown before it's cancelled."

"So what are the topics gonna be about?"

"Tavis' show is about successful black authors; how we got to where we are and what other aspiring writers can do to succeed in this business. Latifah's show will deal with young inner city girls who think because they're poor and black that they can't rise above their circumstances."

"Well I know from past experience, whenever you go on a book tour you might be away from home for weeks at a time. So what does Stan think about your schedule?"

"I kinda haven't told him about it yet. I mean, he knows I was trying to work out something for the two shows, but I haven't told him about the tour dates and all of the cities I'm scheduled to appear in."

"Uh-huh," Sherita said with a smirk on her face. "Now you know damn well Stan is not gonna be hearing that you'll be out on tour and he might not see you for weeks at a time. No way, no how. Not as much as he likes being all up in your Kool-Aid."

"Don't worry," I said as I reached over and ate a piece of her apple pie. "We'll work something out."

"So when do you plan on telling him? When you're board- ing the plane?"

"No, Miss Smarty Pants. I'm taking him out tonight to make up for the times I neglected him while I was busy writing. I'll discuss it with him then."

"So where are you taking him?" Sherita asked.

"First we're going to dinner, then I'm taking him to that new spot, 'The Gentlemen's Club'."

"*Hold up!*" she exclaimed, throwing up her hands. "You mean to tell me you're gonna take your man to a strip club? Whyyy?"

"Oh woman, get a grip," I said. "You know I like being a little unorthodox every now and then. Besides, he'll be so turned on from seeing so many beautiful, naked women, I know when we get back home—if we make it that far—he's gonna turn my world upside down," I laughed.

"Yeah, you're laughing now, but I wanna see if you'll be laughing when you come home from your tour and find him with one of those girls from the *Club,*" she laughed back at me.

"Ohhh Sherita, that's cold, girl," I said, kicking her under the table.

"Not as cold as you're gonna be when you find your man's dick warming another woman's coochie. But I'm just messing with you, homefries. You know you got Stan so all up in your stuff, I doubt if he even knows other women exist," she said as she kicked me back.

SEVENTEEN

That night as we drove past The Gentlemen's Club on our way to dinner, I noticed Stan trying to nonchalantly glance at the club. *Boy, is he gonna be surprised when he finds out that's where we're going after dinner.*

* * *

"Tara, this is a great restaurant. Cozy and intimate," he winked at me. "And this shrimp scampi is the best I've ever had. You know you take good care of your man."

"Only the best for the best," I said, reaching over to wipe sauce from the corner of his mouth. "Just wait till you see what I have in store for you next."

"I hope it involves you sitting nude on my lap," he said sexily.

Uh-huh, I thought to myself, *I knew he was checking out the club.* "Baby, I have some good news," I said, changing the subject for a moment.

"Oh yeah? Then let's hear it," he said as he put down his fork and caressed my hand.

"Well, I've finalized my tour dates and the dates for the show tapings."

"Hey, that's wonderful. My baby's gonna be on TV, with a Queen. So when's the tapings for the shows?"

"The book release parties will start on the West Coast, two days after the release of the book. The first one will be in Anaheim, from August 3rd to the 5th. Then I have the Tavis Smiley show on the 7th. Then I'm flying out to New York for the Queen Latifah taping, which will be on the 9th. I also have book release parties scheduled for the 9th through the 11th in and around the New York area." As I paused to catch my breath and take a sip of wine, I couldn't help but notice how the expression on Stan's face had changed, not to mention he was no longer caressing my hand. But I'd made up my mind to give it to him straight, so I continued, "I'll come back home on the 12th, then I'm flying down to Atlanta on the 15th for two days, Florida for three days, then I'm coming home to do my Midwest tour."

"Sweetheart, that's all good and fine and you know I'm be- hind you a hundred percent," he said as he strained to maintain his composure, "but you're a soon to be married woman. You're already an established writer and your books are gonna sell regardless, so I don't understand why you need to be gallivanting all over and being away from home for so long."

Okay, I thought to myself as I fought to maintain my composure. *I see this is gonna have to be a 'gimme'. I'll let what he just said about my 'gallavanting' roll off my back and try to understand that he's grown accustomed to us being together. He's just acting like a big spoiled baby, so I'm gonna let that shit fly.*

"Look, baby," I said, "this has nothing to do with you or us, but this not only is my profession, it's my passion. I have to market, promote and sell myself. Besides, I was hoping that you'd go with me to some of the cities when your schedule per- mits. Do you have any idea how lonely I'll be not being able to see or talk to you for days at a time?" I softly smiled at him. Some of the tension seemed to leave his face as he relaxed and smiled back. I was still salty about his comment, but I didn't want to get into some crazy drama because his ego was bruised. I guess if the shoe were on the other foot, I might have initially reacted the same way. And anyway, I didn't want to let anything ruin the rest of the night, as the best was yet to come.

"So, are you ready for your next treat?" I naughtily asked as we left the restaurant.

"I cannot wait to see what you have planned next," he responded. He gave me a passionate kiss before opening the car door for me. When I pulled into the lot of the 'Club,' Stan could barely contain himself, though he tried unsuccessfully to play it off. As we took our seats, I could see he was impressed, as was I, with the club. It was very classy and top-notch, featuring some of the top women in the industry. As we ordered our drinks and sat back to enjoy the show, a tall, leggy sister who called herself Jaguar, was performing. She was wearing black leather chaps, pasties, a Stetson, and unnaturally high stilettoes. How she managed to balance herself on those heels was a feat in and of itself, but the grace and agility with which she moved left me awestruck. Some of the things she did convinced me that either she was triple-jointed or she just didn't have any bones at all. By the third act, Stan was so turned on his entire body was practically pulsating, so I decided to really put the icing on the cake. "Baby," I said, leaning over and whispering in his ear, "for being such a good boy, I have a special treat for you."

"Oh yeah?" he responded in a deep husky voice. "And what might that be?"

"You get to choose any one of the ladies for a private lap dance," I said, running my tongue lightly over his ear.

"I get to choose?" he asked.

"Yeah baby, your choice."

"You know you gonna be in for it when we get back home, don't you?" he said as he massaged the enormous bulge in his pants.

"I can't wait," I said as the announcer came to the stage to announce the next act.

"Coming to the stage now is one of the hottest ladies around. Back from the West Coast, returning to her hometown, Chicago, let's hear it for the brown bombshell, Miss Wendi City!"

I thought I would fall out of my seat as I sat there and watched as Wendi, a woman whom I hadn't seen or spoken to in three years, a woman who was even more beautiful now (if that was even possible) than she was when I last saw her, a woman with whom I'd had a hot and passionate relationship with for seven months, glided onto the stage. The audience went wild and I could tell from the expression on Stan's face that he had found his private dancer. Wendi was wearing a full length, leather coat tied at the waist. As she moved across the stage you could catch glimpses of her long, shapely, chocolate legs. She was sporting a leather fedora under which she'd swept her long thick hair; hair that was her very own. I knew, because I'd had the pleasure of playing with it on countless occasions.

"Damn, she's the spitting image of Kenya Moore," Stan whispered in my ear.

"Yes, she is one beautiful sister," I responded. Wendi had everyone mesmerized as she performed her act, one I'd had the pleasure of seeing her perform many times, mainly in the privacy of her home. The act was even better as she'd added some variations. As she stood center stage with her back to the audience, legs spread apart and head lowered, the music started. She slowly removed her hat, allowing her beautiful long hair to fall out as she loosened the belt on her coat, pirouetted around and let it fall to the ground. It was obvious that her belly dancing and ballet classes had paid off. Her moves were graceful, erotic, and very sensual. Beneath the coat, she wore a black leather garter belt, leather thong, and a leather push up bra which just enhanced the beauty of her already full, erect breasts. As she straddled the chair, which she used as a prop, she slowly bent over, placed her hands on the seat of the chair and proceeded to shake her perfectly rounded butt. She then lowered herself into a squat and slowly, seductively started grinding and moving up and down as if she were riding a penis. The crowd was going wild, but they didn't know the best was yet to come. She came up and sat on the chair, still with her back to the audience, raised her legs up in the air, draping them over the back of the chair and stretched her body out with her hands on the floor, balancing her- self as she looked out at the crowd, upside down. She then brought her legs straight up in the air, opening and closing them in a scissors fashion. She ended by bending her knees as if in an upside down squat, pumping her body up and down, then rolling over and into a perfect split, spinning around to face the crowd. She came up on her hands and knees and stealthily crawled toward the edge of the stage. The lights went lower, smoke came up out of the stage, enveloping her as she seemed to disappear into thin air. Everyone was on their feet applauding, cheering, and making no attempts to cover the tents in their pants. I'm sure there were even some women with wet spots in their panties.

"That was one hell of a performance," Stan said as he continued to clap and cheer.

"So, are you ready for that lap dance now?" I asked him.

"Baby, I just need to get home as fast as we can. I wanna show you how much I appreciate you doing this for me. I'm gonna lay it on you tonight!" he said, rubbing my hand over his rock hard dick.

"Well in that case, let me go to the ladies' room. Then we can go home and I'll show you some of my moves." While I really did have to pee, I was just as turned on by Wendi's performance as everyone else, and I wanted the opportunity to try and catch her to say hello up close and personal.

"Tara! I thought that was you!" I heard as I headed down the hall.

"Wendi! It's so good to see you. That was one hell of a show you put on," I said as we embraced. "How long have you been back in Chicago?"

"Oh, about a month now," she said, adjusting her robe. "Who's the gorgeous man you're with?"

"That's my fiancé, Stan."

"Jeremy! Oh, it's good to hear your voice too!" I excitedly said. "What's been going on?"

"Well first I should apologize for phoning you so late."

"Man, don't be ridiculous. You know you can call me anytime."

"Okay, baby girl. I just wanted you to know I'm coming home. I'll be moving back to Chicago in about a month or two," he informed me.

"Get out of here! Oh I can't wait. We have so much to catch up on."

"Yeah, that's for sure. But look, I'm not gonna keep you. I just wanted to share that with you and thank you for sending me a copy of the new book. I started reading it this morning and I must say, it's got me hooked. So I'll be seeing you soon."

"Bye, Jeremy. Love ya," I said, hanging up the phone, smiling. "That was Jeremy!" I said to Stan as I walked back into the living room. "He's moving back to Chicago."

"So I heard," Stan said unenthusiastically. "I see that con- versation managed to perk you up. You don't seem to be tired anymore."

"Stan, I'm leaving in two days and it seems as if we're not going to resolve this anytime soon, so why don't you just let it go? Besides, this would be a good time for you to be with your daughter. Since Gina has finally agreed to stop playing games with you and let you have a relationship with Brie, you need to focus on that. I would like the chance to get to know her and meet Gina."

"Why do you want to meet Gina? Hell, you can forget meeting either one of them for now. I've found out that they've moved back to Louisiana."

"What! Why in the hell did she do that? I can't understand why she insists on playing these teen-aged bullshit games with you. You really need to pursue this through the courts."

"I am pursuing it," he said annoyed. "Hell, how should I know why she's playing these games. You're a woman, you tell me what her problem is. It seems like women are notorious for doing things that make no sense!"

"Okayyy, that's it. Stan, goodnight," I said as I headed to my bedroom. "Make sure my door is closed when you leave."

* * *

.....Ring. Ring. Ring. *Now who in the world is calling me at this time of morning?* I thought as I looked at the clock. It was 2:30 in the morning. "I guess Mr. Bishop is at home lonely and wants to apologize."

"Hello?" I said sleepily.

"Hey, baby," the voice on the other end said. "You've been on my mind and I needed to hear your voice. I love the way you sound when you're sleepy. Remember how much fun we used to have calling each other in the wee hours of the morning with stimulating, erotic talks?"

"Wendi?"

"Yeah baby, it's me. I hope your man's not there. I'm not disturbing anything, am I?" she asked in a sultry voice.

"No, you're not. And yeah, I do remember."

"Do you remember how I used to make you cum, over and over again?"

"Oh yeah," I said, finding myself getting aroused. "I miss that, baby."

"I miss the silkiness of your skin against mine. I miss the way you would respond when I touched you in all your sensitive spots. I miss the way your breasts felt in my mouth. I'm sucking them right now. Can you feel that baby?"

"Ohhh, yeah, I feel it," I said as I began to caress my breasts.

"Can you feel me kissing your stomach, stroking your pretty little pussy with my fingers? Do you like that, baby?"

"Ohhh yes, I like that," I whispered. "I like that a lot."

"Spread your legs, baby. I want to taste you. Can I suck on your juicy pussy? Is it wet like I like it?"

"Yes baby. Yes, yes, yes."

"Good," she said. "I'm hungry. Wrap your legs around my head and feed me. Can you feel me sucking on this wet, hot, sweet ass pussy? Licking your clit the way you like it."

"Ohhh weee," I moaned in pleasure as I began sliding my fingers in and out of my pussy, remembering, reliving, and recounting how this woman used to drive me crazy as she skill- fully worked my body.

"Come on, Tara, give me what I need. Feed me, baby. I wanna taste it."

"Ohh, ohh, ohhh, yesss," I screamed into the phone. "Oh baby, I'm cummin, I'm cummin," I moaned as my body tensed up and the juices started running over my hand, down my legs.

"That's a good little girl. That's what I want," Wendi whispered. "Goodnight, baby. Sweet dreams."

I lay there a few moments cradling the phone against my breasts, panting and feeling totally relaxed. "Damn, that girl is good!" I said aloud, finally reaching over and hanging up the phone as I slipped off into a pleasant sleep.

The next day was spent preparing for the first leg of the tour. The book was already in stores, and judging from those sales and internet orders so far, I was certain I had another best-seller on my hands. I kept myself busy, hoping I wouldn't notice that I still had yet to hear from Stan; but I did notice. Stubborn- ness kept me from calling him. After all, I was the one about to leave town and he was the one who started this silly argument. So if he wanted to be an asshole about this then I was gonna take the low road and be one too. Besides, I had the memories of that awesome session with Wendi to keep me smiling and moist. But at the same time, I was a little unsettled about it. I mean, my relationship with Wendi had so far been my only affair with another woman and it was a good relationship except for one tiny flaw. Wendi loved beautiful women and she wasn't too big on monogamy. As much as she turned me on and out to women, I still needed me some tube steak, a pipelayer, or put plain and simple, some DICK. So even though our little episode last night was the bomb, I knew we wouldn't be going down that road again.

I was shaken out of my thoughts by the buzzing of my intercom. "Yes," I said, pushing the button.

"Girl, let me up," Sherita yelled. I pressed the button and anxiously waited for her to get upstairs. I hadn't seen my girl in two weeks and I was looking forward to seeing her before I left.

"What's up, homey?" I said, opening the door and embracing her. "I thought you wouldn't be back till next week."

"Well, that's what happens when you go to beautiful Jamaica with a boring ass man. And anyway, I couldn't have my girl leave without wishing you well in person. So, what's been up? Done anything interesting while I was gone?" she asked.

I don't know why, but I just knew she was fishing for something. "Naw, nothing much," I said, putting more dresses into my garment bag. "Just preparing for this tour, that's about all."

"How's Stan?" she asked.

"He's alright, I guess. His brain seems to be stuck in stupid mode, though."

"Uh huh, I told you he would start trippin' about you being out of town, around gorgeous, successful men for weeks at a time. Told ya his fragile ego couldn't handle it," she laughed.

"Girl, this shit ain't funny," I said as I threw a shoe—a hard shoe—at her. "Hell, I had entirely different plans about how I wanted to spend my last two days at home, and they certainly didn't include arguing or having to defend my decisions. Stan must be out of his damn mind!"

"Girlfriend! Calm the fuck down. Save yourself," she said as she put her hands up to her head, mimicking Iyanla Vanzant.

I started laughing, 'saved myself', and fell down on the bed. "You're right, Sherita, I shouldn't let it get to me like this. I think Stan's just pissed off 'cause his ex-wife moved back to Louisiana."

"Wait a minute. She just moved here last year and purchased a home, didn't she?"

"Yeah, she did, but I guess she sold or rented it. Just to hurt Stan and keep him from being with his daughter."

"Uh-uh, Tara. I ain't buying it. I mean that shit just don't add up. She moves here from Louisiana, then Stan moves here. She refuses to let him see his daughter on his terms, then she just pulls up stakes and moves back to Louisiana. It don't make sense to me."

"So what are you saying, Sherita?"

"I'm just saying you've only heard one side of the story. There's something going on there."

"Maybe what's going on is she's just a silly chicken head and she likes playing these juvenile games."

"Yeah, whatever," Sherita said, rolling her eyes at me. "Maybe I'm wrong, but I know if there is something fishy going on, you will certainly find out and deal with it."

"You damn skippy!" I said, jumping up off the bed.

"By the way, you never told me how your little outing to the Gentlemen's Club worked out. See any interesting people there?" Sherita asked.

"You knew!" I screamed at her. "I can't believe you didn't tell me."

"Hold up! Don't start throwing more shoes at me," she laughed. "I didn't know that night that she was back in Chicago and just happened to be working at that club. Go figure. As a matter of fact, I just found out yesterday when I ran into her cousin Najee. You know he's a neighbor of mine," she said defensively. "I bet your ass nearly fell out when you saw her."

"Yeah, you can say that again. But I maintained."

"So, did you introduce your man to your ex-woman?"

"No, I did not."

"Yeah, he probably wouldn't understand his woman being a closet dyke."

"I am not a dyke!" I said, hurling another shoe at her. "Do you see me sniffing up behind your dry-ass pussy?"

"Girl, you know you want some of this," she said as she rubbed herself. "So, did you and Wendi get a chance to talk?"

"We spoke briefly that night. And she called me last night—late last night."

"Oh don't tell me y'all still into that phone sex shit. I'm having a hard enough time trying to figure out how two people of the same sex could possibly be interested in doing each other, let alone what the hell could be stimulating about saying dirty things to someone over the phone. 'Oh Tara, let me suck your clit.' 'Oh Wendi, put those big titties in my face,' " Sherita said, trying to be funny.

"Sherita, you're about two seconds away from me kicking your ass out of here. Maybe it's not fun for you because you and your tired ass lovers have no imagination. Phone sex—good phone sex—takes skills," I informed her.

"Girl, you need God in your life, 'cause you're crazy," she said as she fell back in the chair laughing.

"Naw, heifer, you ain't seen crazy yet," I said as I charged toward her, grabbed her by her blouse and yanked her out of the chair.

"Woman, have you lost your damn mind! This is a $400.00 blouse you just ripped," she said, trying to break my grip on her. She knew what my next move would be; body slamming her on the bed like I used to do to her when we were dorm mates.

"Don't worry about it. I'll buy you two more," I said as I slammed her on the bed, pinning her arms down with my knees. "But first I'm gonna teach you a lesson. Don't fuck with Queen T!" I started tickling her in her sides, something I knew would drive her mad. "So who you calling a dyke?" I said as she cracked up laughing, trying to get away.

"Okay, okay, I'm sorry. You're not a dyke. Even if you are resting your coochie just inches from my face," she screamed out in laughter. I had to laugh at that one myself. "Now let me up," she pouted. "You've torn my blouse and fucked up my hair."

"There, there, baby. I'm sorry," I said, helping her up. "Am I a dyke?" I asked her, faking like I was gonna knock her back down.

"No, you're not a dyke," she said as she straightened out her skirt. "You the man!" she yelled, throwing a shoe at me as she took off running.

"Girl, you are a fool," I laughed as I followed her into the living room.

"Look Miss Lunatic, I gotta get outta here. Do you need me to take you to the airport in the morning?"

"Oh, I can take a cab. Besides, my flight leaves at 7:00 a.m. and I know how much you hate getting up early."

"Don't be ridiculous. I'll see you in the morning at 5:00. Have me some breakfast ready," she said, hugging me as she headed out the door.

As soon as she'd left, the phone rang. *Uh-huh, I knew he would call sooner or later,* I thought as I picked it up.

"Hey sis, we just wanted to call to wish you a safe and fun trip," Denise said with the twins yelling in the background. "We love you Auntie Ta-Ta," they kept saying over and over again. "Alright! Alright! She heard you, Ren and Stimpy."

"Ha ha. Mommy called you Stimpy," I heard Kyle say to Kianna.

"Uh-uh, she called you Stimpy," Kianna responded as I heard their voices fading out. I guess they'd run off to get into some other kind of devilment.

"Girl, these kids are loco," Denise laughed. "They remind me so much of you, Tara."

"Ahhh, then they're definitely destined for greatness," I laughed.

"Yep, all three of you are loco. But look, I'm not gonna keep you. I know you got those last minute things to do, so have a safe and productive trip. Aunt June says to give Tavis a hug for her."

"Okay, tell Aunt June I'll do that; and thanks for calling. I love you guys."

"We love you too, Tara. Call and let us know how things are going."

"Okay Denise, I'll do that. Catch you later," I said, hanging up.

"Well, that should just about do it," I said later that night as I finished packing my things. I glanced at the clock and couldn't believe it was 10:30. I also couldn't believe Stan still had not called. I reached for the phone, but stubbornness kept me from dialing his number. So instead I decided to do a little cleaning before going to bed.

I'd been asleep a couple of hours when the phone rang. I snatched it up, expecting to hear Stan's voice, but instead it was Wendi. "Hey beautiful, I wanted to catch you before you left town," she said in a soft, seductive voice.

"Hi Wendi, thanks for calling, but I can't talk right now," I said, disappointed.

"Oh, I understand. Well, good luck and goodnight. Wish I were there with you." I'm sure she thought I was busy getting my groove on, but at that moment what she thought didn't matter to me because I wasn't in the mood for either her or Stan.

*   *   *

"Tara, why are you so damn quiet?" Sherita said as she drove me to the airport. "You act as if you're on your way to a funeral."

"I'm sorry. I just can't get over Stan not calling or coming to see me off."

"Well, that makes two of us. What the hell is up with him? If he keeps pulling shit like this, I might be inclined to believe that maybe Houston was on to something," she said, pulling up to the airport.

"Well I'm not about to trip over it," I said disgustedly. "He'd better get his shit together before he finds himself on the outside looking in."

"I heard that," Sherita said as she got out to help me with my bags. "Look, just try to put that aside for now and get on out there and do your thang. And please don't forget to give Tavis my number," she said as she hugged me.

"I love you, Sherita. You behave yourself while I'm gone, you hear me?"

"Yeah, yeah, yeah. I'll be a perfect angel. Now get on out of here."

"Bye, girl," I said, heading for my terminal.

* * *

After boarding my flight, I settled into and reclined my seat and put on my headphones to listen to some music. The last thoughts I had before drifting off to sleep were about Stan and how we needed to work this thing out. *That's my baby and I love him. I'm sure by now he's missing me as much as I miss him, so I know it's gonna be alright. We're gonna be alright,* I thought to myself. Boy was I ever wrong!

NINETEEN

"Miss St. Pierre. Your attorney is here," Officer Johnson said as he entered the room I was being held in. Once again, I was snapped out of my stroll down memory lane.

"Well, it's about time," I said, looking at my watch. I was surprised to see only three hours had passed since the time I'd phoned Jeremy. It seemed like days. Just then Jeremy walked into the room, looking like he'd just stepped off the cover of an America's Best Dressed magazine. "Jeremy!" I said, running over to him and wrapping my arms around him. "Thank you for coming."

"Come on baby girl, we're getting out of here," he said, kissing me on the forehead.

"I don't have to stay here and give a statement?" I asked.

"No. You're not giving anything until we've had a chance to talk. Now let's go. You've been here long enough."

"Thank you Officer Johnson for being so kind," I said as I followed Jeremy.

"It was my pleasure, Ms. St. Pierre. I'm certain everything will work out fine for you," he said, squeezing my shoulder.

"Thank you, officer."

As we got into Jeremy's Lexus, I sat back, closed my eyes and sighed deeply. "I am so glad to be out of there."

"Uh-huh," Jeremy said as he reached over, patting my leg. "But before you get all comfy, I think you should start talking and let me know what in the world is going on. I never knew you and Stan were dating. Last I heard he was married and living in Louisiana."

"Well he was—married and living in Louisiana," I said, beginning to tell Jeremy about my running into Stan in the restaurant, renewing our friendship, and how we eventually started dating, fell in love and got engaged. I grew silent and somber as we drove past my old condo. A place that held so many fond memories. A place that I'd called home for so many years. A place that I'd had to move from because of Stan. I could see Ralph, the doorman, opening the door for a couple.

"Are you okay, Tara?" Jeremy asked.

"Yeah, I'm okay. Just being a little nostalgic," I said as I pointed out the building. "I used to live there."

"Very nice, very expensive," he said. "Why'd you move?"

"Stan," I said. For the next fifteen minutes as we continued the ride to my new home, I told Jeremy about how great things had been going between us. I even told him about the fantastic sex.

"But, let me guess," Jeremy said. "He changed."

"Yep. He certainly did."

"What do you think caused him to change?"

"My career. He became jealous of my career."

"Tara," Jeremy said, pulling into my parking garage. "I know you're tired, but I really need for you to tell me everything. So if you'd like, I can come over in the morning and we can talk then. I know this has been a very trying day for you and you look like you could use some rest."

"Actually Jeremy, I would prefer your company and I want to tell you everything now. So if you don't have anyplace you need to be for the next couple of hours, I would really like for you to come upstairs with me."

"It would be my pleasure," he said, getting out to open my door. As soon as we entered my condo, I kicked off my shoes. "Ohhh, it feels so good to be home."

"Boy, this is a nice place you have here," Jeremy said, looking around.

"Thank you," I responded. "Jeremy, I really need to take a shower first. Why don't you make yourself comfortable? The kitchen is that way. Help yourself to some eats and drinks. I'll be out in thirty minutes."

"Take your time, sweetie. I'm not going anywhere," he said, removing his coat.

While I was dying to get in the tub and take a long, hot bath, I instead took a shower so I wouldn't keep Jeremy waiting. Once I'd finished showering and washing my hair, I put on my pajamas and stepped out of my room to the aroma of broiling steaks. "Dag, man, that smells good," I said, holding my growling stomach.

"Well little lady, you just grab a seat. The steaks will be done in a minute and there's a salad in the fridge. I hope you don't mind my taking over your kitchen like this."

"Not when you got it smellin' like this" I laughed. "Damn! I'd almost forgotten what a good cook you are."

"News flash, baby. I've only gotten better with age," he said as he placed the steaks on our plates and got the salad out.

"Tara! Girl you wanna slow down before you hurt your- self?" Jeremy said as he watched me ravenously tearing into my food.

"Man, leave me alone," I said, licking my fingers. "I haven't had a decent meal all day and this steak is the bomb."

"Well if you keep shoveling food in your mouth like that, you go blow up."

"Ha, ha, that's real funny."

Once we'd finished eating and cleaning up the kitchen, we headed for the living room where I turned on the fireplace, fixed us a couple of drinks and got comfortable. "Tara, I hope you don't mind me taping our conversation," Jeremy said, taking his tape recorder from his briefcase.

"Do I have a choice, counselor?"

"Of course you have a choice. You can either choose to let me tape our conversation, or you can choose to let me tape our conversation. The choice is yours."

"Well in that case, I guess I choose to let you tape it," I said, punching him in the arm when he sat back down.

"Okay, now you've told me how you and Stan got involved with one another and how smoothly things were going and that the two of you were looking forward to getting married. So when did things start to change?"

"When I told him about my tour schedule and how much time I'd be spending away from home." I continued to tell Jeremy about the arguments and confrontations we'd had and how I boarded my flight without having heard from Stan.

"I can't believe he would be that selfish as to let you leave town without contacting you," Jeremy said as I got up to refresh our drinks.

"Well believe it, because he did."

"Okay, so when was the next time you heard from him?"

"It was during my first night in California when I next heard from him....."

TWENTY

MY STALKER

"Man, what a day," I said aloud as I soaked my tired body that night in the Jacuzzi in my suite. My fingers were sore from autographing so many copies of the book and shaking so many hands. But it was well worth it. This was the first stop on the tour, and day one of the three day expo here. So far, more than three hundred copies had been sold. I was looking forward to seeing what the next two days would be like. I'd also met a very interesting man, Marc Chenault, a publisher who was at the expo doing a seminar. He'd asked me out to dinner for tomorrow night. I told him I'd give him a call as soon as I saw how my day was shaping up. I wasn't interested in anything romantic, just a little friendly companionship. As I laid back and closed my eyes, my cell phone rang. "Hello."

"Tara baby, I'm sorry. I miss you so much. Please tell me you're not mad at me."

"Stan? What's up," I said, trying to sound nonchalant and not let my voice betray the fact that I really missed him too. I wanted him to beg my forgiveness. "I have no reason to be mad at you. Your actions have spoken loud and clear and I can accept that."

"Tara, I know I should have talked to you before now and worked this out, but you know how stubborn and pigheaded I can be at times. I'm begging for your forgiveness. Please. I love you so much and I miss you. Can we work this out, baby?"

He sounded so sincere that my heart just melted. No matter how much I wanted to be mad at him, I couldn't. So I gave in. "Stan, I'm sorry too," I said. "I shouldn't have left without talk-ing to you, and I miss you too. As soon as I get back we'll get together and work everything out."

"Why can't we work it out now?" he said seductively.

"Yeah, alright," I said, not really understanding what he meant.

"Well then, if we're gonna work it out now, shouldn't you let me in?"

"What do you mean?" I asked curiously. Just then I heard a knock on my door.

"Let me in, baby."

"Stan! You're here?" I said incredulously as I jumped out the tub, grabbed a towel and headed for the door.

"In the flesh," he said as I snatched open the door.

"What are you doing here? How did you know where I was staying?" I breathlessly asked, hugging and pulling him in the room.

"Well, I bribed your Aunt into telling me where you were staying," he said, putting down his bags.

"Where are you staying? Do you have a room here in the hotel?"

"No, I don't have a room. Actually, I was hoping you'd let me stay here with you," he said as he played with the towel I'd tied around me.

"Of course you can stay here," I said. But for some reason I wasn't totally comfortable with that. I mean, I didn't really mind sharing my room with him. It was his presumptuousness that I was having a problem with. But I quickly dismissed that thought. I decided to make the best of it and use this time to reconnect and get back to where we were before all of this silly arguing.

"So, have you been a good little girl and behaved yourself?" he asked, loosening my towel and letting it drop to the floor.

"Uh-uh, I've been very bad," I said as I ran my finger over my hardened nipple.

"Well in that case, I guess Daddy's gonna have to teach you a little lesson," he said as he picked me up, laid me on the bed and started doing magical things with his tongue and hands. When he'd gotten me right where he wanted me—which was trembling and begging for more—he got up and started removing his clothes. "Now, I'm gonna take a quick shower and I want you to lay right there and don't you even think about moving. I'm not through with you," he said as he headed for the shower with a rock hard dick. I lay there running my hands over my body, anticipating what would happen when he returned, but I guess the long and strenuous days I'd had, had caught up with me because before I knew it, I'd fallen asleep. The next thing I remember was hearing the phone ringing for my wake up call.

"Ahhh," I let out a gasp as I rolled over. There was Stan, sitting up in bed watching me. I'd forgotten he was there.

"What's the matter, baby. Did you forget I was here?"

"I'm sorry, baby," I said, kissing him. "Why didn't you wake me up last night when you finished showering?"

"You were sleeping so peacefully and snoring so loudly, I didn't have the heart to disturb you. Besides, I know how much you like it in the morning, and I'm ready to give it to you," he said as he began to massage my friend, 'Russell the love muscle.'

"Ohhh baby, you're talking my talk. But it'll have to be a quickie," I said, glancing at the clock. "When I asked for a wake up call, I hadn't factored in a love session and I'm kinda pressed for time," I said apologetically.

"Oh, so now all I get is a complimentary fuck."

"Come on baby, you know it's not even like that. Look, I promise I'll make it up to you tonight. We can have a nice dinner then spend the night seeing who can make whom scream the loudest," I said, running my tongue over his stomach.

"Well, if I have to wait until tonight to get some lovin', what are we gonna do to entertain ourselves during the day?"

"Stan, my day is already planned. I may not make it back to the hotel until 7:00," I said. "Why don't you do a little sight- seeing? You could also come out to the expo and keep me company."

"Tara, I didn't come all the way out here to be alone. I came to be with you."

What the fuck, I thought to myself, *I guess he must have forgotten that I didn't ask his ass to come out here in the first place!* I rolled my eyes at him as I got out of the bed and headed for the bathroom.

"Oh, so now I can't even get a quickie," he said.

"Stick it in the blender," I said as I closed the bathroom door.

* * *

"Stan, here's an extra keycard for the door," I said after I'd finished dressing. "Why don't you go out and entertain yourself? I'll see you later on," I said as I gently kissed him on the cheek and headed out the door.

* * *

"Well hello, Ms. St. Pierre. How're things going for you today?"

"Marc! Hi. Things are going great," I said as I autographed another book. "In fact, today's sales have been better than yesterday's, and yesterday was a good day. I can't wait to see what happens tomorrow."

"Judging from what I've read of the book so far, you certainly have another hit on your hands. The only reason I put the book down today was so that I could come out to see you again," he said with a twinkle in his eye.

"Thank you so much, Marc. I'm kinda sorry that I won't be able to join you for dinner tonight. My fiancé surprised me and flew out here last night."

"Now that's too bad," he said. "At least it is for me."

"Are you having another seminar here today?" I asked, trying to change the subject.

"No. I only came out to see how things were working out for you."

"Why, that was sweet of you. Look, why don't you have a seat here and keep me company for a little while? I'd really enjoy your company."

"Okay, you've twisted my arm. I'll stay," he laughed as he sat down.

Between giving autographs, talking with my fans and with Marc, the day seemed to fly by. We were sharing a laugh when I looked around and there was Stan, standing at my booth.

"Well it looks like you two are having a Kodak moment," he said, looking intently at me.

"Hey baby, I'm glad you decided to come out," I said, ignoring his snide remark. "Stan, this is Marc Chenault. He's a publisher doing a seminar here at the expo. Marc, this is my fiancé, Stan Bishop," I said as Marc stood up to shake Stan's hand.

"That's funny, I don't see your name on the program for a seminar today," Stan said, ignoring Marc's outstretched hand.

"Actually, my seminar was yesterday. I'm here today speaking to some of the authors here."

"Well, you've been at this booth for quite a while now. I'm sure there are lesser known authors here who might want some of your time," Stan smiled.

"Ms. St. Pierre, it was a pleasure to meet you. I'll be sure to post my comments on the book on your website. I hope you enjoy your stay here in California," he said as we shook hands.

"Thank you, Marc. It was good talking to you."

"I cannot believe how rude you were!" I said to Stan once Marc was out of earshot.

"I can't believe that after blowing me off this morning—and I don't mean that literally—that you would have the nerve to be here all chummed up with some clown who didn't get the memo that Jheri curls had played out. I've watched the two of you for the past twenty minutes over here laughing and talking like you've known each other forever."

"Oh, so are you spying on me now, Stan?" I said, trying hard not to raise my voice.

"Do I need to spy on you, Tara? Is there something you're trying to hide from me?"

"Stan, the only thing I'm trying to do right now, is to not lose my temper and act unprofessional here."

"Well we wouldn't want that to happen, now would we? I guess I'll see you tonight at the hotel," he said, walking off.

"God, give me strength and send me a sign. Is this man losing his damn mind, or what?" I said through clenched teeth. Somehow, I managed to regain my composure, put on my game face and make it through the remaining three hours without exploding. As I got in my rental car and headed for the hotel, I found myself dreading going there. "Uh-uh," I said aloud as I pulled into the parking garage. "There's no way in hell I'm gonna allow this man, or any man, to have me so upset where I'm dreading going back to a hotel room that I'm paying for. Hell, naw! We're gonna settle this tonight and if he has a problem with what's going on, then he can take his insecure ass back to Chicago." Having said that and ignoring the looks I was getting from people in the lobby who were looking at me, wondering who in the hell I was talking to, you would have thought I would be pumped up and ready to walk into that room and tell Stan to take a hike. But I wasn't. In fact, I was bone tired. I wasn't up to a fight. I only wanted to go in my room and have a nice, relaxed night. *Oh well, gotta do what I gotta do,* I thought as I opened the door.

"Oh, oh, I must be in the wrong room," I said as I stopped in my tracks. There were scented candles everywhere. A table had been set up in the middle of the room, a bottle of wine was chilling and Grover Washington's melodic voice was coming from the stereo. The aroma coming from the covered trays was so delectable that I wanted to rush over, snatch off both covers and dig in. But what stopped me was the delectable sight next to the table—Stan. He was standing there wearing a loin cloth with his chocolate body oiled and glistening. Tarzan himself would have been envious. A little voice in my head was telling me that there was a battle to be fought, harsh words to be exchanged, ultimatums to be made. But that little voice was drowned out when Stan slowly started walking over to me. After gently closing the door and taking my briefcase and other bags from my hands, he took both my hands in his and got down on one knee.

"Tara, I am so sorry for all the negative things I've done and said lately. You are the last person I should be lashing out at. Let me spend this night showing you how much you mean to me. I promise you things are gonna change and we'll be like we were before," he said with a tear in his eye as he got up, carried me to the bed, removed my shoes and gave my feet a much needed massage.

"So, my queen, would you like to eat first, or would you prefer me to bathe you first?" Before I could say anything, my stomach answered for me. "Well I guess that settles it then," he laughed. "But I want you to know that this is a clothing optional dinner, and I opt for you to remove your clothes."

"Your wish is my command," I said, undressing.

After finishing a delicious, mouth watering meal consisting of smothered short ribs, mashed potatoes, broccoli with cheese sauce, and pie a`la mode for dessert, we went into the bathroom where he'd already prepared the bath. After soaking for about thirty minutes and Stan tenderly washing and drying my body, we went into the bedroom where he had oil warming. As he massaged and caressed every inch of my body, I felt sooo good. I just wanted to drift off and sleep like a baby. But Stan wasn't having any of that; not after last night. So he turned me over on my back, pushed my legs back, and with the skill of a highly paid gigolo, sucked and licked me until I had his face covered with my juices. Now maybe it was the stress and long hours of the past couple of days that had taken a toll on me, but for some reason I wasn't enjoying making love with Stan as much as I had in the past. Even though he made me cum, I was not feeling him. (No pun intended.) I found myself doing everything I could to make him cum so that we could get it over with. *I'm just tired, that's all,* I thought to myself as I drifted off to sleep in his arms.

* * *

I'd asked for a wake up call the next morning thirty minutes earlier than what I'd asked for the day before so that I could spend that time getting me a little morning sumthin' sumthin'. I also wanted to see if my response would be different than last night. And it was. It was just like old times and I was glad Stan hadn't noticed that I wasn't really into him last night. If he did, he didn't say anything.

"Can I take a shower with you?" he asked when we'd finished our little quickie session.

"Of course you can," I said, grabbing hold of his limp dick and leading him to the bathroom.

"Well baby, I've decided to spend the day doing some sightseeing and a little shopping," he said while soaping up my body. "So I'll see you when you get back."

"Okay, that sounds like a good idea. I don't have anything scheduled for tomorrow until it's time for Tavis' show, so we can spend the day together."

"Alright baby," he said, caressing my breasts.

* * *

If there's any truth to the saying, 'the third time's a charm,' then it proved to be true that day. The third and final day of the expo, sales far exceeded those for the two previous days. I was also a panelist at a writers' seminar which was scheduled for that day. My agent and publicist, Renee, was also there. She'd flown out to see how things were going and to inform me how well internet sales were going. By the end of the day I felt as if I was floating on a cloud. It had been a wonderful day and I was looking forward to having a wonderful night. I hoped Stan was sincere about what he'd said last night and we could put all the bullshit behind us. By the time I'd gotten to the hotel, I was still soaring and extremely horny. When I walked into the room there were five or six gift wrapped boxes of various sizes on the floor.

"Surprise, ba..." Stan said as he got off the bed. But before he could finish his sentence, I dropped my bags, grabbed him by his wrists and pulled him to me, passionately kissing and caressing him. "Hey lady, cut that out," he said, gently pushing me away. "My fiancée will be here soon."

"Well, can your fiancée do this?" I said, pulling down his briefs as I dropped to my knees.

"Ohhh, shit girl," he said as I took him in my mouth and he started singing D'Angelo's "How Does It Feel." I had no idea what was in those gift wrapped boxes we were next to, but as far as I was concerned, I was unwrapping the best gift of all. We spent that night and part of the next day wrapped in each other's arms, talking and enjoying each other's company. It was just like old times. The first thing I did when we woke up the next morning was to open my presents. "Oh Stan, thank you, thank you!" I said, planting kisses on him. He'd bought me a leather suit which I'd been eyeing back in Chicago, some sexy lingerie, a handbag with matching shoes, body oils and a diamond necklace with matching earrings. "Baby, you didn't have to buy me all of this," I exclaimed.

"Oh, okay," he said, getting up. "I'll take it all back."

"The hell you will!" I yelled, pulling him back on the bed and jumping on top of him, ready for another session. We finally decided around 2:00 to get out and enjoy the beautiful weather. We visited the zoo and took the bus tour of the stars' homes. After the tour we decided to have an early dinner then go back to the hotel and relax before going to the studio.

"You are coming with me, aren't you?" I asked that night as we showered.

"I don't know, baby. Will I be allowed inside the studio?"

"Of course. Besides, knowing you're there will keep me from being nervous and making a fool of myself on national TV," I laughed.

"Woman, don't be silly. You'll do just fine. But I'll be there to give my baby emotional support if that's what you want," he said.

"Oh thank you, sweetie."

After showering and putting on my makeup, I laid four different outfits on the bed, trying to decide which one to wear. "Stan, help me out here. Which one do you think I should wear?" I asked as I tried on each one.

"Are those the only outfits you brought?" he asked.

"Why? What's wrong with these?"

"Nothing, baby. If you're going out clubbing. I just don't think any of those are appropriate for tonight. The first outfit was too short and the last one shows too much skin," he said as he put on his suit.

"Welll," I whistled, trying not to let his comments get next to me. "I guess I'll just have to decide on my own," I said, picking up the last outfit I'd tried on. The one that showed 'too much skin.' It was a 3-piece silk, royal blue, formfitting, knee length skirt and top with spaghetti straps and a matching shrug. It was the very same outfit I'd worn a couple of months ago when we'd gone out and Stan had spent the evening complimenting me on how good I looked wearing it. But now all of a sudden there was a problem with it. Go figure. I was determined not to let him cause me to lose my focus. As it was, I already had butterflies in my stomach, so I certainly didn't need any distractions. I decided to ignore him. I turned up the music, fixed myself a drink and finished dressing. As we drove to the studio, Stan made attempts at conversation and when he saw I was being non- responsive, he asked if anything was wrong. "I guess you're nervous about the interview. Don't worry baby, you'll be fine," he said as he reached over and rubbed my leg.

Once we'd arrived at the studio, Stan was seated and I was taken to the dressing room where the other two guests (both men) were waiting. I'd never met either of them before, but I'd read some of their books. Once introductions had been made, we sat around laughing and talking until the man himself, Tavis Smiley, came in to say hello and welcome us. *Ohhh weee, this man is even finer in person,* I thought as I stood up to shake his hand. He told us the show would be starting in about fifteen minutes. After we'd been seated in the studio and the show had begun, I immediately forgot about my butterflies and my nervousness. Tavis was such a great host. I made a mental note that if his show was ever cancelled, I would personally hunt down and kill anyone responsible. We had a wonderful time discussing our books, telling our stories of how we got started, and answering the callers' questions. I thoroughly enjoyed myself and couldn't believe an hour had passed.

Once the cameras stopped rolling, everyone got up and Tavis congratulated us on a great show. I gave him a hug and thanked him for having me on the show. Stan came over and I introduced him to everyone. After a few minutes of exchanging pleasantries, it was time to go so I told my new friends how much I enjoyed being on the show with them. I wished them the best of luck and success and gave them both a hug. I thanked Tavis again, gave him a big hug and we left. I was so excited and hyped up that I was a regular chatter- box on the way back to the hotel. "That was great! I had such a good time!" I said excitedly. "Did I seem nervous? And isn't Tavis a wonderful person?"

"Naw Tara, you didn't seem nervous. In fact, it was pretty obvious you were enjoying yourself. Touching this man's hand, rubbing that man's arm, hugging everybody. I thought that was so unprofessional and disrespectful to me."

"What! Stan, what in the hell are you talking about? Have you lost your damn mind?" I exploded.

"Tara, don't raise your voice at me. Hell, I was watching how you were carrying on. For a while there I thought it was a taping for the Dating Game."

I was so hurt and shocked by what he'd said that I sat there fighting back the stinging tears welling up in my eyes. I couldn't believe he could be so cold and callous. Not to mention stupid. By the time we arrived at the hotel, I'd managed to fight back the tears. I was determined not to let him see me cry.

"Tara, I'm gonna drive around for awhile to clear my head. I'll see you in an hour or so," he said, pulling up in front of the hotel. Without a word, I got out of the car, closed the door, and went inside. As soon as I was in the room, I sat on the bed and started to cry.

"Fuck this!" I said after ten minutes of shedding crocodile tears. "There is no way in hell I'm gonna let this insecure mother-fucker mess with my head." So I got up, washed my face and packed my bags. I thought about leaving him a note, but decided against it. "Fuck him! He don't deserve a note," I said as I kicked one of his shoes out of my way. I called the front desk to settle my bill, letting them know my fiancé would be turning in his key when he returned, then I checked out. I drove to a Comfort Inn near the airport so I could get a few hours sleep before my flight left for Chicago, hoping that Stan wouldn't be on the same flight. He wasn't. I flew back to Chicago with my mind firmly made up that I wasn't taking any more of his bullshit.

* * *

"Tara, I'm sorry you had to go through that," Jeremy said as he reached over and gave me a hug. "I suspect it didn't end there."

"Oh no, not by a long shot," I said, continuing my story.

TWENTY ONE

"Home, sweet home," I said as I walked in my house and headed for the bedroom with my bags. I'd had time to do a lot of thinking on the plane and I knew what I had to do would be the best thing for me. I'd only been in the house about fifteen minutes when the phone rang. "Hello?"

"Hey, Tara. How's my favorite cousin?"

"Reggie! I'm great. How's my favorite cousin doing?"

"As well as can be expected. You looked real good on the show. How did everything go out in California?"

"Thank you. Everything went well, for the most part."

"What do you mean 'for the most part'?" he asked.

"Reggie, I don't know what's going on. I mean, the book signings went well, and getting to meet Tavis was awesome."

"Yeah girl, you were a natural. You looked like you were having a good time."

"Yeah, I was. It was a wonderful experience."

"So what's the problem then?"

"Stan. That's the problem."

"Uh-oh, trouble in paradise, huh?"

"That's an understatement. I don't know what's wrong with that man. First he starts trippin' about my schedule and how long I'll be away from home. Then he surprises me and flies out to Cali unexpectedly, telling me how sorry he was. Then he starts trippin' about my clothes and my *behavior*, like I'm a child or something."

"Man, Tara, that's messed up."

"He had the audacity to accuse me of flirting with Tavis and the other guests."

"No he didn't, cous."

"The hell he didn't," I said, starting to get angry again.

"Damn! So where is he now?"

"Don't know. Don't care. After the way his ass acted last night, I checked out of the hotel while he was out driving around to 'clear his head', and came home."

"You didn't tell him you were leaving?" Reggie asked.

"Hell naw!"

"Girl, you something else. He should know better than to mess with you," Reggie laughed. "But I don't mean to make light of your situation. I know how much you care for Stan. On a lighter note though, let me give you some good news."

"Ohhh, what is it?" I excitedly asked.

"I was accepted for the teaching job I applied for here!"

"Reggie! That's great, man! I'm so happy for you."

"Hold on, now. There's more."

"What, what, what? Tell me."

"Okay, okay, slow down girl. I've met someone. Her name is Margo and she's my physical therapist. Tara, I think I'm in love."

I could hear the happiness in his voice. "So how long have you two been dating?"

"About three months now. At first, I wouldn't let myself get close to her and I fought my feelings. I mean, I didn't want her pitying me and I didn't want to get my feelings hurt. But she made me feel so at ease and comfortable with her. She's really a special woman."

"Well I'll have to get down there and meet this special woman. Sounds like she's really got your nose open."

"She wants to meet you too. She couldn't believe you're my cousin."

"Well tell her I'm looking forward to meeting her," I said.

"I will. I know you have things to do, so I'll let you go. I just wanted to share my good news with you. I'm sorry about the way things are going with you and Stan. I'm sure everything'll be alright. If you need someone to talk to, give me a call, okay?"

"Okay Reggie, I will. Thanks for calling. I'll catch you later, sweetie."

I'm so happy for Reggie, I thought after hanging up the phone. As I grabbed my garment bag and started unpacking it, I suddenly felt very lonely. I felt tears starting to well up in my eyes and I refused to give in to them. "I know what I need," I said, picking up my purse and heading for the door. "Family". I knew going out to Momma's would help me get centered. Even if no one was home, just being there would help to calm and soothe me.

* * *

"Tara! No one told me you were coming out here today. Give me a hug and get on in here."

"Hey Houston," I said, hugging him. "No one knew I was coming. In fact, I just got back in town today."

"Denise and June took the kids to the mall. They should be back shortly," Houston said as I kicked off my shoes and sat on the sofa. "So how was Cali?"

"Oh, it was definitely going on," I responded.

"Then why do you sound so down?"

"Houston," I said, taking a deep breath, "what was it about Stan that rubbed you the wrong way?"

"Whoa! I thought we had put that behind us. I apologized for my comments and agreed to stay out of your personal life."

"Yeah, I know. But that was then. Now I'm really interested to know what you meant."

"Tara, is everything alright?" Houston asked as he sat next to me.

"I don't know, Houston. Stan's changing."

"How so?"

"Well, one day he's all sweet telling me how much he loves me, and then he's accusing me of flirting with other men and all sorts of crazy shit. He has a problem with me being away from him, and he's so insecure and suspicious," I said.

"Tara, the first time I met Stan he struck me as being kinda phony. He was trying so hard to make everybody like him. Now I know sometimes a person is nervous when they meet someone's family, even though he already knew Denise and June, but he came across to me as being insincere. For instance, he was acting all charming and nice to June, telling her how much he missed her and was happy to see her again. Yet, when he thought no one was watching him, I caught him giving her a look that was so intense and ugly, for a moment I thought he was gonna attack her. Of course, that would have been a big mistake on his part, but still, that's how he looked. Then he snapped out of it and was back to his phony, charming ways."

"Are you serious, Houston?"

"Very. I decided to let it go since you all seemed to think so highly of him."

"Wow," I said as the front door opened and Denise, Aunt June and the twins came in.

"Tara!" Denise said as she hugged me. "Why didn't you tell us you were coming out here? We would have waited for you. How was your trip? We saw you on Tavis' show."

"Of course we taped it for you," Aunt June said, kissing me on the cheek.

"I got back this morning," I said as the twins hopped up on the couch. "I just wanted to see my favorite people."

"So what did you two get at the mall?" Houston asked the twins.

"We got clothes and toys," Kyle said.

"Cool. Why don't we go upstairs and you can show Daddy what you got," Houston said, picking them up. "We'll let the big girls have a chance to talk."

"Tara, is everything alright?" Aunt June asked as she and Denise sat down.

"No Auntie, everything's not alright."

"What's wrong, sis?" Denise asked.

"Stan," I said, rubbing my hands together. "I'm starting to see a different side of him."

"What do you mean?" Aunt June asked.

So I recounted to her and Denise everything that had happened, starting with the night I told Stan about my schedule and ending with my packing my bags and leaving him in California.

"Tara, that's so unfair. I can't believe Stan would be so insensitive," Denise said. "Maybe he just needs time to adjust to your hectic schedule. If he really loves you, and I'm sure he does, then the two of you should be able to work things out. I mean, there's no such thing as a problem-free relationship. There are certainly going to be problems and arguments, and things are not always gonna happen the way you'd like them to."

"I don't know, Denise. I hear what you're saying and I can accept having disagreements and a difference of opinion, but I don't think a relationship should be like a rollercoaster, full of ups and downs. It should pretty much stay on an even keel and be about understanding and acceptance," I said.

"I agree with Tara, Denise," Aunt June said. "Look at you and Houston. You have a great relationship. Houston always encourages you. He would never berate you about your clothes. Whenever his buddies come over he never accuses you of flirting with them when you're simply being friendly and sociable. Houston is secure with himself and he accepts you for who you are."

"Thanks Aunt June," Denise said. "Houston is a special man, but so is Stan. He's just had a lot of challenges in his life; especially with women. No offense Auntie."

"No, Denise. You're right. I have to accept and own up to what I did to Stan as a little boy. His mother hurt him, I hurt him, and so did his wife. He's bound to have some kind of issues with women behind that."

"But hell, I didn't do anything to him," I said, getting upset.

"I know, baby," Aunt June said. "You have always been there for Stan and the one constant thing in his life. You'd think you would be the last person he would hurt, wouldn't you?"

"Yeah, I certainly would," I said.

"But I don't think he realizes what he's doing. I think he's afraid of losing you and that's why he's reacting the way he is."

"Losing me! I just went out of town. I've never given him any reason to feel like he's losing me. And I understand what you're saying, Aunt June, but I'm not a psychotherapist. I don't have the time or the patience to try and heal him of past wrongs."

"So Tara, what are you going to do?" Denise asked.

I sat there a moment in silence before answering. "I quit. I'm going by Stan's when I leave here and I'm ending this relationship. I think we're better off being just friends."

TWENTY TWO

When I arrived at Stan's, out of habit I took his house keys out, then decided against using them and rang the bell instead.

"Well since you're ringing the bell and not using your key, I guess that means you're still mad," Stan said, opening the door. "Come on in."

"Thank you," I said, walking into the living room and sitting down.

"You know that was pretty juvenile how you packed up and left without telling me. Just because your feelings were hurt from me saying you were flirting. I wasn't trying to hurt you and I apologize if I did."

"Stan, first of all, I am not juvenile. And I accept your apology. But your apology doesn't change things. It doesn't change the fact that even though we've known each other practically all our lives, you really don't know me at all."

"And what's that supposed to mean?" he asked.

"You've accused me of flirting with other men. You're not supportive of my career. One day you're loving me and being Prince Charming, then the next day you're being insulting, suspicious and controlling."

"Tara, I love you. No one is happier than I am about your success, but I feel a woman's place is with her man, not off here, there and everywhere. I have money, you have money, so I don't see why it's necessary for you to be gone so much. I need you here with me."

"Stan, I love you too, but I am not your property and I can't handle a rollercoaster relationship. Happy one day, crying the next. This isn't love and support, it's controlling and smothering and I'm sick of it. I'm not trying to shut you out of my life. I wanted you to go with me out of town sometimes so that we could be together, but look at what happened in California," I said as I stood up and walked around the living room.

"What happened in California was I commented on your clothes and your behavior, you got upset and left," he said, coming over to me. "But now I'm ready to put that behind us."

"You just don't get it, do you?" I said incredulously.

"Baby, all I know is that I want to leave what happened in California, in California. What do you want?"

"Stan," I said, as I removed my engagement ring, "I want the man I fell in love with. The man who I thought understood me and had my back. But obviously he ain't here." I handed him the ring. "Here!"

"Tara, put the ring back on your finger, where it belongs."

"No!" I said defiantly.

"What in the hell is wrong with you? I love you. I have never felt about anyone the way I feel about you, and now you want to throw it all away because I hurt your feelings? You just wanna throw in the towel? Is that what you want? Because it's not gonna happen. Not now, not ever!" he said as he stormed out of the living room.

"Shit! Shit! Shit!" I said as I sat on the couch and waited for him to return. I could have left, but I waited for him to come back so that I could let him know that I did love him. But I would never be totally happy in a relationship where I felt I was being treated as less than an equal. I wanted him to know that he would forever remain my friend. After twenty minutes, he still had not returned so I got up to find him. I called out to him, but he didn't answer. The doors concealing the master bedroom and the staircase were closed, but he'd shown me where the controls were and had given me the codes, which I entered and then waited as the doors opened. I looked in the bedroom, but he wasn't there. Then I went upstairs to check the bedrooms up there, but he wasn't there either. "Now I know this man didn't just up and leave," I said aloud as I went back downstairs to check the garage. The car was still there, so I went back inside the house and called out again. Still no answer. I went back into the master bedroom and sat on the bed. The door to the walk-in closet was open and I saw a couple of my dresses in there. *Well, I might as well take those with me,* I thought, walking over to the closet. I'd grabbed the dresses and was walking away when a light caught my eye. "What in the world..." I said as I got closer and saw the light was coming from a crack in the wall. I reached out and stuck my fingers in the crack. That's when I found out there was a sliding door in the back of the closet. I pushed the door back and saw there was a staircase leading upstairs. I cautiously walked up the stairs and came to another sliding door.

"I'll just be damn!" I said as I pushed the door back and saw I was standing in the closet of the guest bedroom. The same bedroom I'd slept in the first time I'd spent the night. "I'm getting the hell out of here." I said as I walked out of the bedroom into the hallway. As I headed toward the staircase, I passed the bathroom, stopping in front of the wall next to the bathroom, which had a full length mirror on it. As I glanced at the mirror, I heard a crash and a muffled noise which seemed to come from behind the mirror, but a little higher up. "What the....!" I said aloud, looking in the bathroom, thinking maybe something had fallen. But I knew that couldn't be the case because the noise had come from the left of the bathroom and above my head. "I knew it!" I said to myself. I'd often thought there were other hidden rooms in the house, but now I was certain of it. "Stan!" I called out. "I don't know where you are, but I'm leaving!"

I headed downstairs for the front door. I was about to leave when I remembered the ring, which I still held in my hand. I placed it on the table in the foyer along with Stan's house keys, closed the door, got in my car and left.

"I can't believe this shit!" I said as I pulled off. "This is like some kind of bad dream." Little did I know that this 'bad dream' was about to become a fucking nightmare.

TWENTY THREE

"Girl, I ain't even believing this shit!" Sherita laughed as she stuffed popcorn in her mouth. "You mean to tell me he got hidden rooms and staircases in his house?"

"Yep, he sure does," I said. After leaving Stan's, I came home, did some cleaning and unpacking, made some phone calls, then called Sherita and asked her to come over and kick it with me. We decided to have a pajama party, pig out and watch movies. When I phoned her, I didn't tell her about the events that had happened in California or at Stan's. I wanted to tell her in person and see her expression.

"Tara, this is too wild! So are you really through with him?"

"Girl, I don't have time for his crazy ass."

"So here you are again, dickless in Chicago," she laughed.

"Screw you, Sherita," I said. As we sat around eating, talking and enjoying ourselves, the intercom buzzed.

"I wonder who the heck that is," I said as I went to answer it. "It's 1:30 in the morning."

"Yes?"

"Ms. St. Pierre, it's Ralph. Your pizzas are here. Are you having a party or something?"

"No I'm not having a party or something. And I haven't ordered any pizzas. There must be some mistake."

"The guy is standing here with ten pizzas and the ticket has your name on it," he said.

"Well Ralph, I'm sorry about the mistake, but I haven't ordered any pizzas."

"Okay, Ms. St. Pierre. I'll tell him. I'm sorry for disturbing you."

"What was that about?" Sherita asked.

"The hell if I know. There's a delivery guy downstairs with ten pizzas that he claims I ordered."

"What! Girl, what you trying to do, replace sex with food?"

"Sherita, why are you so dense? I didn't order any pizzas."

"Had they already been paid for? I got a taste for some pizza," she said.

"I don't know. And what in the hell are you gonna do with ten pizzas?"

"We coulda ate some and used the rest as torpedoes to drop out the window on people's heads."

"I got a better idea. Why don't I open the window and drop your ass out?"

We sat around for another hour or so, kicking it until we both fell asleep. I awoke the next morning to the wonderful smells of breakfast cooking.

"Good morning," Sherita said as I walked in the kitchen. "Damn, girl! You still look like a gremlin when you wake up in the morning. But that's okay. You still my girl and I'm fixing you a delicious breakfast. So why don't you please go clean yourself up while I finish up in here?" she said as I swiped a piece of bacon.

"So what time does your flight leave?" Sherita asked as we sat down to a delicious breakfast of grits, eggs, hash browns, bacon, and buttermilk biscuits.

"Three o'clock," I mumbled while stuffing my mouth.

"What you wanna do it's time for you to go?" she asked.

"I need to go to the mall and pick up a few things."

"Okay, well let's finish up in here and go charge it!"

After cleaning the kitchen and getting dressed, we left for the mall.

"Let's take my car," Sherita said as we got on the elevator.

"Okay, that works for me," I said. As we headed down the street, laughing and talking, Sherita suddenly stopped dead in her tracks, gasping.

"What the fuck happened to my car!?"

"Oh my God!" I said as we walked up to it. The windshield had been completely shattered, all four tires had been slashed and white paint had been splashed inside. I pulled out my phone and dialed 911 as Sherita stood there shaking with rage. "What sick motherfucker would do some shit like this?" she screamed.

It took about five minutes for the police to arrive. By that time I'd managed to get Sherita to calm down—somewhat. While the police made out a report and talked with her, I phoned AAA and asked to have a tow truck sent out. After the police left, we went back upstairs where Sherita promptly fixed herself a drink.

"Sherita, that didn't look like a random thing. You don't have any idea who might have done that?" I asked.

"Hell naw!" I don't know anybody who would do some scandalous shit like that. And anyway, if somebody had a beef with me, why would they fuck with my car by your house? No one knew I was over here last night. What, do you think some- body followed me here and waited until the middle of the night to destroy my car? Uh-uh. I think it was just some sick asshole and my car happened to be in the wrong place at the wrong time." she said.

"Sherita, I don't know. I mean, the windshield and the tires could have been a random thing, but the paint? That seems pretty deliberate."

"Deliberate or random, I don't know. But if I ever find out who did that shit I'm gonna break, splatter, and slash something on their ass!"

"I feel you, girl," I said as I fixed myself a drink. "Just save a piece of their ass for me."

"Look Tara, I'm gonna get a cab and go on home."

"Girl, don't be silly. Why don't you relax and get your- self together. I'll pack my things, then we'll take my car to the airport and you can keep the car until I get back. Just please put my car in the garage," I said, heading for the bedroom.

* * *

After arriving in New York and picking up my rental car, I went to my hotel and checked in. There were two messages waiting for me. The first was from Connie Wesley. I'd met Connie when I first started out in the business. She owned two Afrocentric bookstores in New York, and since she'd been instrumental in helping me establish a customer base in New York with my first book, I always made it a point to make her stores one of the first stops on my tours. *Tara,* the note read, *Trust you had a safe flight. Good luck with the show tomorrow. You'll love the Queen. She's a beautiful sister. Give me a call in the morning and we'll get together after the taping for lunch. Am looking forward to seeing you again and to having the stores filled with your loyal fans.*

I smiled as I read her note while on the elevator heading up to my room. The next message wiped that smile from my face. It read: *Tara, we have invested too much into this relationship to just throw it away. We are going to work this out. I refuse to let you walk out of my life. Love, Stan.*

I don't believe this shit! How in the hell did he know where I'm staying. I never told him I'd be staying in this hotel and I know Aunt June didn't tell him, I thought as I walked into the room and double-bolted the door. *Okay, Tara, calm down. Don't let him get you all upset.* I was determined to put Stan out of my mind, so I tried to keep myself busy. First I unpacked my bags, then I made some phone calls. The first one was to Sherita to make sure she was alright, and to make sure my car was alright. We talked for twenty five minutes about the car incident, and I told her about Stan's message.

"Girl, that man is determined to keep you. So what are you gonna do about him?"

"I'm gonna ignore his ass," I said. But I was about to find out that that would be easier said than done.

* * *

When I arrived at the studio the next day, I found out Connie was right. Queen Latifah was one of the most down to earth and personable people I'd ever met. I'd followed her career since she'd started out as a rapper then branched off into other ventures. I'd always been impressed with her, but to meet her in person left me awestruck. The show we were taping was very touching. There were five young ladies who were totally out of control and being reckless with their lives. They all came from the projects or poor neighborhoods and they all lacked self esteem. They had pretty much resigned themselves to believe that where they were now was where they would always be, so why even bother trying to do anything productive with their lives. Myself, along with the two other guests, had come from similar backgrounds, but we had become successful and hadn't used the fact that we were poor as an excuse to throw in the towel before we'd even gotten our feet wet. I was feeling pretty good about the show. It seemed as if we were making an impact on them and they were giving some thought to what was being said. I was talking to one of the young ladies seated next to me when Latifah went to take a comment from someone in the audience. "Yes sir, do you have a question or comment for one of our guests?"

"Yes, this is addressed to Ms. St. Pierre."

I stopped talking, immediately recognizing the voice. The room seemed to stand still as I turned and stared directly at Stan. I don't remember what the question or comment was, nor my response. All I remember was fighting not to lose my composure and praying to God to let me make it through the rest of the show without snapping. After the show was over, I hugged each girl, encouraging them to set goals and believe in themselves. I thanked Latifah for having me on her show and told her how much I admired her. Then I left and headed for my car.

"Tara, can we talk?" I heard as I was about to get in my car.

"Stan! What in the hell is wrong with you? What are you doing here? Stalking me?" I yelled.

"No, I'm not stalking you. I'd already planned on surprising you by coming out here when you first told me about the show. Surprise! And what's wrong with a man fighting to get his woman back?" he said, walking closer to me.

"Stan, it's over. Now leave me alone, alright? Go back to Chicago, or Louisiana, or west hell, or wherever. Just leave me the hell alone! No wonder Gina keeps moving from state to state. It's to get away from your ass!" I said as I got in the car, slammed the door and promptly locked it. As I pulled off I saw a look on Stan's face that I'd never seen before. One that left me chilled to the bone.

After driving a couple of blocks, I pulled over to give myself a moment to calm down. I was on my way to the restaurant to meet Connie and I didn't want her to see me upset. When I arrived at the restaurant, I drove around the block three times, making sure Stan hadn't followed me. When I was certain he hadn't, I parked the car and went inside. Connie was seated and waiting for me. When she saw me she stood up and hugged me.

"It's so good to see you again, Connie," I said as we embraced.

"You too, Tara. Sit down and tell me how the show went."

"It went well. Latifah is a great person; charming and sooo funny. I hope she invites me back again before the show is cancelled."

"Yeah, you know how it is. All the good shows get cancelled before they should."

"Are you ladies ready to order?" the waitress asked.

"Yes, I'll have the baby back ribs with macaroni and cheese, and cole slaw; and I'll have a sprite," Connie said.

"I'll have the chef's salad with bleu cheese dressing, and a Coke," I said.

"Tara, are you okay?" Connie asked when the waitress walked away. "You look nervous, and I've never known you to be a light eater."

"I'm alright, Connie. It's just my ex-fiancé. He doesn't want to let go and he's started hassling me. He had the nerve to come all the way here to New York and was even at the show today. But it'll be alright. Once he realizes I'm serious about ending this relationship, then he'll move on."

"Um, that sounds pretty deep. I hope you're right. You know how some guys are. They just can't accept being dismissed, so you should watch your back girl."

"Yeah, I heard that. But I'll be okay."

While we enjoyed our meals, we brought each other up to date on what had been going on in our lives. We then discussed the book signings I would be doing the next day at Connie's stores. After finishing our meals, we left the restaurant and Connie walked me to my car. "I'll see you tomorrow," she said. "Be careful."

"I will," I said, starting the car. "Thanks for lunch."

When I got back to the hotel, I'd made up my mind that I would not let Stan get me upset and I would focus on enjoying my stay in New York. So I spent the evening sightseeing.

The next morning I awoke feeling refreshed and ready for a great day. I decided to do some shopping before going to the first signing, which would be from 1:00 to 3:00.

The next one would be from 5:00 to 7:00 at Connie's other store. By the time I'd arrived for the 1:00 signing, I had pretty much managed to put Stan out of my mind and I was able to relax and enjoy talking with my fans. The signing went great. There was a steady flow of customers and both Connie and I were ecstatic with the turnout.

"Well, I must say this was a success," Connie said when it was over. "I need to stay here and take care of some things, then I'll be over around 6:00 to see how things are working out."

It was 4:45 when I arrived at the other store and there were already about twenty people waiting. "Well, if this is any indication of what the next two hours will be like, I'd better stretch my fingers and get ready to do a lot of signing," I said to the clerk.

"Your book is one of our bestsellers," she said.

"I'm certainly glad to hear that," I said, walking over to greet the customers.

Things were going well until around 6:30 when I looked around and saw someone who I thought was Stan. I peeked through the crowd to get a better look, but he was gone. *Maybe I'm just imagining things,* I thought to myself.

"Hey Tara, looks like today is your day," Connie said. "Sorry I couldn't get here sooner."

"Oh, that's okay," I said. "But yeah, things are going beautifully. I'll have to give this day two thumbs up."

"I heard that! Hey, when you're done here why don't you go change and we can go out and check out the clubs? I've been practicing and I'm sure I can out-step you now," she said with her hands on her hips.

"Oh no you're not gonna challenge me! Don't you know ain't no stepper like a Chi-Town stepper?" I said as some of the ladies nearby started laughing.

"Uh-oh, we go' have a step-off, y'all," one of them yelled out. "New York vs. Chicago!"

"We'll pick you up at 11:30," Connie said as she headed for her office.

"We'll?"

"Why, of course. We do need steppin' partners, you know. Don't worry. I'll make sure our partners are some of New York's finest."

I didn't know if she meant 'finest' as in handsome, or as in policemen. But either way, I was looking forward to it.

Back at the hotel, I was in the parking garage headed for the elevator, when I caught a glimpse of a car pulling into a spot. I thought the car looked somewhat familiar, but quickly dismissed it. When I got inside my room, I ordered room service, took off my clothes and ran myself a bath. After I'd eaten and poured myself a glass of champagne, I hopped in the tub. I was exhausted, but I knew the hot, swirling waters would take care of that. After thirty minutes of soaking, I felt totally revived. I stretched out on the bed to watch a little TV until it was time to get dressed. At 11:20 the phone rang. It was Connie calling to let me know she was in the lobby waiting for me. "Okay, I'll be right down," I said, turning off the TV.

"Yeah, well hurry up before I have to curse this jerk out who keeps staring at me," she said.

"Maybe he's just working up the nerve to push up on you."

"Actually Tara, I think he's a well-dressed, fine-as-wine nutcase. I mean, he's just standing off to the side staring at me with this look on his face like I stole his mamma's purse or something," she whispered into the phone. "Wearing an Armani suit, looking good enough to eat, and crazier than Charles Manson. Girl, you better hurry and get down here."

"I'm on the elevator right now," I said. I was thinking about the car I'd caught a glimpse of when I was leaving the garage earlier. What triggered that memory was when Connie mentioned the Armani suit. Stan loved Armani suits.

When I got to the lobby and stepped off the elevator, I anxiously looked all around. "Where is he?" I asked as I briskly walked over to Connie.

"What? Don't tell me you're into good-looking, well-dressed psychos," Connie said, giving me that sister-girl look. "But if you are, he just headed toward the parking garage."

"I'll be right back," I said, heading in the direction of the garage, with Connie looking at me as if I'd lost my damn mind. When I got to the garage, the car I'd noticed earlier was gone. I went back inside to the registration desk. "Hi," I said to the young lady behind the counter.

"Hi," she said as her eyes lit up when she recognized me. "Ms. St. Pierre, welcome to New York. It's a pleasure to meet you. I have all of your books. I wanted to make it to your book signing to get my copy of *If You Don't Scream...* signed, but I'm stuck here working today and tomorrow."

"I'll tell you what. If you do me a favor, I'll gladly auto-graph it for you now."

"Oh, you will? Thanks," she said, pulling her copy from beneath the counter. "What's the favor?"

"Could you tell me if there's a guest staying here named Stan Bishop?"

"Okay, that's not a problem," she said checking the computer. "Oh, Mr. Bishop checked out this morning."

"Thank you, Christine," I said as I signed her book. "If you bring your other copies to work with you tomorrow, then I'll sign those as well."

"Girl, what the hell is going on?" Connie asked, pulling me aside.

"That nutcase who was staring you down was my ex, Stan."

"Are you serious? How would he know that I know you? And why is he hating on me?" she said as she nervously looked around. "I guess he has nothing better to do than to follow you around. Well, if he likes lurking around spying on you, then he's about to get his feelings hurt when he sees the gorgeous brother who's your date for tonight," she said as we headed out the door for the Escalade that was parked out front.

"Tara, this is Detective Jerome Nelson," she said, intro-ducing me to the brother behind the wheel. "And this is Detective Dennis Wiley. "Gentlemen, this is Tara St. Pierre." As we exchanged greetings, I wanted to reach up and hug Connie. When she said 'two of New York's finest,' I had no idea in what context she meant. But it didn't matter because it applied in both instances. These were two very, very, very, very, handsome brothers. VERY! I made a mental note that the next time I was in New York, I would have to commit a serious crime so that I could see what else New York's law enforcement had to offer. As we headed to the club, Jerome and Dennis shared stories with us about their job. Not anything gory or extremely violent, just the amusing and positive things.

"Tara, Jerome and Dennis are good friends of mine. Maybe they can give you some advice about what to do about your 'little problem'."

"Umm, I don't know…." I hesitated.

"Hey, it's cool," Dennis said, "you're among friends here."

"Well, it's just an ex. He's having a problem understand-ing the 'ex' concept."

"A problem! Hell, he had the nerve to follow her here to New York, show up at the Latifah show, and even stay at the same hotel as Tara. He was in the lobby just now when I went in to meet her. Looking at me all crazy like I'd done something to him, and I've never even met the dude!" Connie said.

"Is he threatening you or doing anything to make you feel uncomfortable or intimidated? Are you afraid for your safety?" Dennis asked.

"No. He hasn't done anything to make me afraid. He's just being a nuisance, that's all. I'm not worried about him, though."

"Well, keep your eye on him," Jerome said. "Don't take him for granted. We see this kind of thing all the time. Before you know it, it'll escalate into something bigger. So be careful, and if necessary get a restraining order."

"Okay, if I think it's necessary, then I'll do that. Thanks guys."

"Hey, it looks like this place is jumping tonight," Connie said as we pulled up to the club.

"Well lets get in there so I can show you how we do it Chicago style."

There was a table reserved for us near both the dance floor and the bar. It was a very cozy club, lots of ambience. Full of exotic plants, a waterfall, wonderful murals and a live crowd. I saw quite a few celebrities, a couple of professional athletes, some rappers, and an up-and-coming film star. The DJ was blowing the place up. "This place is tight!" I said, looking around. We'd ordered our first round of drinks and the waitress had just returned with them.

"You like it?" Dennis said as he leaned closer to me. Or maybe I leaned closer to him. The brother definitely had a magnetic quality about him.

"Yes!" I said enthusiastically. "I love it. It's so beautiful and intimate."

"Well thank you. I'm part owner," he said proudly.

"Get out of here! Well it certainly looks like a very happenin' place. How long have you had it, and who's the other owner or owners?"

"We've had it almost two years now; and you're sitting across from the other proud parent of this baby—Jerome."

"Well congratulations on the job you've done with it," I said, rubbing Dennis' arm and giving Jerome the thumbs up as he and Connie headed for the dance floor. "So who manages the place for you guys while you're out serving and protecting?"

"Fortunately, we were both blessed with family members who are intelligent, business-minded and most importantly, trust- worthy," he laughed. "You know ain't nothing worse than having an Uncle who's robbing you blind, or a crackhead sister playing on your sympathies."

"Ohhh, you are so bad," I laughed, "but true. I feel for anybody who's got family members that can't be trusted as far as you can throw 'em."

"You know, Tara, you're alright. I've never read any of your books, and I'm sure it's my loss. I don't get much time for pleasure reading and when I do, it's usually..."

"Players, Hustler," I interjected.

"Ha, ha, ha," Dennis laughed. "I was gonna say 18th century history. I have a fascination for that period in time. So, are we gonna dance or sit here and talk all night?"

"Oh, is my conversation not engaging enough for you?" I asked mockingly.

"Au contraire, your conversation is very engaging. You're very engaging. But I wanna see your moves on the dance floor," he said, grabbing my arm and pulling me out of my seat.

"Hey! Watch the rough stuff," I said as I playfully punched him in the arm and strutted my sexiest strut out to the dance floor where we started getting our groove on. When we started feeling the music, we really got into it. I could see women throwing daggers my way as they ate their hearts out with envy while I seductively danced with Dennis. The brother had some smooth moves and we were definitely in sync with one another. As he teased me with his body, pulling me in close to him, I could see guys looking our way. A couple of them gave him an approving nod, and some looked like they were wishing they could be in his shoes. The DJ decided to slow it down a bit with three slow jams in a row. The first one was "I Get Off On You" by the Rose Brothers. I wrapped my arms around Dennis' neck as he pulled me closer. We started swaying and slowly moving in rhythm with one another. I thought he might have to pry my arms away to get me to let him go. He certainly rated a 10 as far as blind dates went. We danced through all three slow cuts and then the DJ played some steppin' tunes. I looked around for Connie and Jerome and saw them headed back to the dance floor. Connie was anxious to show me what she'd learned in her steppers class, and I must admit she'd gotten pretty good, but she was still no match for me. Once Dennis got a feel for my style, he had no problem leading me and we were on the dance floor clowning. All eyes were on the four of us as we put on our steppin' faces and glided around the floor.

"So, how you like me now?" Connie said. "Girl, you doing it! You got some smooth moves there, but watch this," I said as Dennis spun me and we went at it like we were in a million dollar competition.

The four of us had a great time that night and I didn't want it to end, but I had a signing to do the next day before going home. We left at 3:00a.m., with me and Dennis hugging and teasing each other as if we'd been friends for years instead of a few hours. "So what time is the signing tomorrow?" he asked as we headed for my hotel.

"It's from 12:00 to 2:30, then my plane leaves for Chicago at 6:00."

"Well I'm certainly gonna hate seeing you leave," he said as we arrived at the hotel.

Damn! I thought to myself. *Why does it seem like it only took five minutes to get here?* I was in no way ready to depart this man's company. Dennis got out and came around to open my door. Jerome and Connie also got out.

"I'm glad I got a chance to meet you and hang out with you, Tara," Jerome said, hugging me. "You take care of yourself and don't forget what we told you about your ex."

"Thanks, Jerome. I'm glad I met you too. I had a lot of fun tonight."

"Tara, you know it's always a pleasure seeing you and doing business with you," Connie said as we hugged. "Don't let Stan get next to you. And I don't wanna brag, but I out-stepped you tonight."

"Yeah, okay Miss Thang, you held your own," I laughed. "I'll give you a call when I get back home."

"Hey man, don't have me waiting here all night," Jerome said to Dennis.

"I don't know," Connie said under her breath. "Looks like we might have a love connection here."

As Dennis and I slowly made our way to the elevator holding hands, I could sense he didn't want to leave me any more than I wanted him to leave. "Tara, I really enjoyed being with you tonight. You are such an interesting woman. Smart, funny, talented, a great dancer, and sexy as hell!"

"Thank you, Dennis. Being with you has certainly been the highlight of my visit to New York."

"Even better than all the money I'm sure you must have made?" he laughed.

"Oh, okay. Then you have been the *second* best highlight," I laughed back. "I want you to feel free to call me anytime. And if you're ever in Chicago, be sure to look me up," I said as we stood in front of my door.

"You can bet on it," he said as he looked into my eyes and gently kissed me with those sweet, sexy lips of his. I wasn't having a short, quick kiss, so I wrapped my arms around him and kissed him with a passion that would keep him up all night long—and I mean that literally.

"Wow!" he said. "You certainly make it hard for a brother to say goodnight, but if I don't leave now…." he trailed off.

"Yeah, I know," I said, smiling at him. "Goodnight, Dennis. I'm certainly going to miss you."

Once I was in my room, I kicked off my shoes and fell on the bed. "Why! Why! Why!" I said aloud, punching the pillow. "Why couldn't I be the kind of sister who can sleep with a man on the first date? Why did I have to be cursed with morals? Damn these morals!" In order to take my mind off the fire that was burning inside me, I decided to pack my things and get some sleep.

* * *

"I have all of your books, and I can't wait to read this one," the woman standing in front of me said as I started signing the six books she'd purchased. "Some of the women in my book club couldn't make it out for the signing, so I offered to pick up copies for them."

"I appreciate your support. I hope you and your book club enjoy this one," I said, shaking her hand. The day had been going pretty well. It was 1:30 and I was looking forward to going home—kinda. I had managed to think about Dennis only about a thousand times; and Stan, none.

"Would you sign my book? I'm one of your biggest fans," I heard from behind me.

"Dennis!" I said as I turned around. "I'm surprised to see you here."

"Hope it's a pleasant surprise," he said, holding out his book.

"Oh, most definitely."

"So, how are things going?"

"Very well, thank you. I'm glad you decided to stop by."

"I wanted to see you again before you went back home. If you don't have any other plans, I'd like to come back and pick you up when you're done here. Then we can go have an early dinner and I'll take you to the airport."

"No, I don't have any other plans, so you're on. I just need to take my rental car back and freshen up a little. You can follow me to the rental agency then we'll go to the hotel and I can get my things and check out."

"Okay, then I'll see you at 2:30," he said, giving me a quick peck on the cheek.

Dennis returned promptly at 2:30 and as agreed, he followed me in his car to the rental agency then we went to my hotel. "Would you like for me to wait down here in the lobby?" he asked.

"Of course not. You can come up. I won't be long." After freshening up, we grabbed my bags and headed out to enjoy each other's company for the next couple of hours. We decided to go to a bar and grill near the airport. During the ride, we talked about our families. Dennis was from a large family with three sisters and two brothers, two of whom were also in law enforcement. We had both lost our fathers at an early age. When we arrived at the bar and grill, we ordered our food and drinks and continued our conversation, practically non-stop, for the next two hours. We talked about everything from politics, to celebrity scandals, to relationships. When I looked at my watch and saw it was 5:15, neither of us could believe it. "I can't believe so much time has passed," he said, signaling for the waitress. "Woman, you sure do talk a lot."

"Is that right?" I said, kicking him underneath the table.

"Yes you do. And I loved every minute of it. I'm gonna really miss you. I've enjoyed spending what little time I have with you and I'm hoping we can spend some time together again. But you don't have to respond to that right now. Just know that being with you again is something I'll be looking forward to."

"Dennis," I said as we got in the car for the short ride to the airport, "I'm glad I met you and I've had such a good time with you. And now I'm mad as hell at you."

"What for?" he asked, puzzled.

"Because I want to spend more time with you now, and getting on that plane is gonna be damn hard to do," I said as I placed my hand on top of his. "But right now I have a lot on my plate, with the tour. And I need to clear up things with Stan so that he can get on with his life and get out of mine. So I know it'll be a while before we can see each other again. But we will definitely see each other again," I said, leaning over and kissing him near his ear.

"Don't play with me, girl," he said, pulling into a parking spot. "That's a very sensitive spot for me. I know you got to handle your business," he said as he pulled me over to him. "I just want you to know...." he said as he placed those magical lips of his on mine, "...whenever, wherever, just let me know, baby."

"Nothing would bring me greater pleasure," I said as I pulled him even closer and took full advantage of his lips for the next couple of minutes until it was time to catch my flight.

TWENTY FOUR

Sherita was waiting for me outside the airport. When I spotted her, I quickened my pace and hurried over to greet her. I hadn't seen my girl in a couple of days and I missed her. Oh, alright, I confess, the real reason I hurried over was to make sure my car was still in the same condition it was in when I left.

"What's up, homefries?" she said as she popped the trunk and helped me with my bags. "How was things in New York?"

"Things were fabulous. The signings went well. Queen Latifah is all that. And Connie introduced me to my baby's daddy," I laughed.

"Ohhh, weee, you met a man! I want details."

"Okay, okay, I'll fill you in on everything on the way home," I said as we got in the car. On the ride home, I told her about the book signings, Dennis, and of course, Stan.

"Girl, you betta watch that man. He's turning into looney bin material."

"He better back up off me 'cause I am not the one," I said as we pulled into my parking garage. "So what's going on with your car?"

"It should be ready next week. In the meantime, they've given me a rental."

"I'm glad to hear that," I said as we got off the elevator and headed for my apartment. I don't know why, but I could sense something was wrong before I even opened the door. But as soon as I did, it was quite obvious.

"Damn! What is that smell?" Sherita said as she covered her nose. "Did something die in here? And why is it so freaking hot in here?"

I walked in, dropped my bags and immediately went to turn up the air conditioner, but nothing happened, so I opened the windows and the patio door.

"Girl, you don't have any electricity!" Sherita exclaimed. "And that smell is coming from your refrigerator."

"What do you mean I don't have any electricity?" I said, flicking switches. I found out she was right. "What the hell is going on?" I said as I picked up the phone, only to discover that it wasn't working either. I pulled out my cell phone and phoned downstairs. "Ralph, I just got home and discovered I have no electricity, nor is my phone working. Do you have any idea what's going on?"

"No, Ms. St. Pierre, I have no idea. No one else has reported any problems. Let me call Manny to watch things down here and I'll be right up," he said. After talking to him, I dialed my home number and got a recording saying the number had been temporarily disconnected.

"Whew! Smells like something died in here," Ralph said when I opened the door for him.

"You mean that's not your cologne?" Sherita said. "Hell, we know it stinks in here."

"Well there doesn't seem to be any problem with the fuse box," Ralph said. "You're just gonna have to wait until the morning and call the light and phone companies. Maybe you should go spend the night with your friend here."

"Thanks Ralph, but I'll be alright here."

"Tara, don't be crazy. It's about to get dark, you can't stay here," Sherita said.

"Yes I can. I live here. Besides, I need to clean out the fridge. I'll be okay, girl."

"Okay, how are you gonna clean or do anything else with no lights?" she asked.

"Now you know my Momma taught me to always be pre- pared. I have plenty of candles, flashlights, and those cute little tap lights we picked up at Walgreens. I have batteries for my radio and my portable TV. I'm straight."

"Then I'm staying here with you," she said.

"Girl, that's not necessary. I'll be alright, I promise."

"Okay, but call me if you need me."

"I will."

"I'll be here until 10:00," Ralph said, "so if you need any-thing, just call."

"Thanks. Both of you. Ralph, would you get a cab for my friend?" I said as I gave Sherita a hug and Ralph $20.00.

"I certainly will. Goodnight, Ms. St. Pierre."

As soon as they left, I put on some shorts and a t-shirt, got my candles and lights situated, turned on the radio, and went in the kitchen and got busy throwing out spoiled food. After finishing with that, I unpacked my bags and ran myself a bath. I decided to do a little reading and turn in early. I wanted to be fully refreshed and rested in the morning. There were a couple of utility companies that would be receiving a phone call from a very irate customer.

* * *

"I don't know what to tell you Ms. St. Pierre, but our computers show a request being made for service disconnection. All the required information was given—your mother's maiden name, your date of birth, your social security number," the operator for the light company told me.

"Well I'm telling you I never requested to have my service shut off! I spent last night throwing away rotted food by candle- light!"

"I'm sorry and we apologize for any inconvenience you may have experienced, but I don't know what else to tell you."

I could tell she was sincere in her apologies, so I decided to let her off the hook. I had spent the last five minutes venting and I felt a little better. Besides, I still had the phone company to call. "Well what assurances do I have that this won't happen again?"

"You can choose a PIN number that no one else knows. That way, if for any reason you decide to have your service disconnected or transferred, that number would be required in addition to the other information. But in the meantime, we'll have your service restored within the hour. And again, I apologize."

"Thank you," I said, hanging up. Next I called the phone company and pretty much had the same conversation. As soon as I'd finished talking, my cell phone rang.

"Miss Thang, weren't you supposed to call me when you got home? And what's up with your phone?"

"I'm sorry, Connie. I had a little problem here," I said, telling Connie what had happened and what the utility companies had told me.

"Get out of here!" she said. "That man is crazy and childish."

"What are you talking about?"

"Stan. Don't tell me you don't think he did this."

"Why would he? I mean, what would he gain by doing this?"

"Come on now, Tara. The man follows you to another state, lurks around your hotel, stares me down, and you don't think he would do some silly shit like this? Who else would know your social security number? And what he would gain would be aggravating you, pissing you off, and inconveniencing you; all of which he succeeded in doing. I'm telling you, he did it."

"I don't know, Connie. You may be right. I'll start documenting every strange or suspicious thing that happens from now on."

"Yeah, I think that's a good idea. Now moving on to the lighter side of the news; girl, what did you do to Dennis? Jerome told me after he dropped you off at the airport, he stopped by Jerome's and talked about you half the night. And this is a man who has two playa's cards!"

"Oh, so he's a dog?"

"Uh-uh. I'm not saying that. I've known Dennis two years and he's one of the nicest men I know. He just does his fair share of dating. But he's open and honest. I've never known him to try and hurt or disrespect a woman," she said.

"Yeah, well I was digging on him too," I said. "I'll give him a call when I get a chance, but right now I got too much on my mind."

"Yeah, I know what you mean. But look, I'm not gonna keep you. I just wanted to share that with you. Now you be careful with Mr. Pretty-Ass-Psycho. Call me if you need me."

"Okay. Thanks Connie." After talking with Connie, I sat for a moment thinking about what she'd said. Maybe Stan was responsible for my lights and phone. It just seemed like a silly, childish thing to do. It didn't seem like something he would do. But then again, I never would have thought he would have a secret staircase in his house that he would use to spy on me. "Well, I'm not even gonna worry about it for now," I said aloud as the phone rang. "Hello."

"Hey girl, what's up? I see the phone company got your phone back on," Sherita said. "Did you find out what was going on?"

"Hey, Sherita. Yeah, I found out someone called and requested to have my service disconnected." I told Sherita about my conversation with Connie to see what see thought about it.

"You know, I was thinking about that last night. I think he did it. I also think he was the one who ordered those pizzas that night. And if I ever find out his ass was the one who fucked up my car, I'm gonna personally put a bullet in his ass."

"But why would he mess with your car? Why not mine?"

"Maybe he was jealous because I was with you and he wasn't. Maybe he couldn't get to your car. Hell, I don't know, I'm just speculating. But enough about that nut. What are you gonna get into today?"

"I think I'll spend the day relaxing. My flight to Atlanta leaves at 9:00 in the morning."

"Girl, I don't know how you do it. That's too much traveling for me."

"It's tiring, but I've gotten used to it, and I enjoy it. At least this time I'm not staying at a hotel. I'm staying with my Uncle Sammy. That's my father's older brother."

"Well, enjoy yourself. I know you got things to do, so I'll catch you later, alligator."

"Yeah, I'm starving and there's nothing here to eat."

Now that I knew my phone was back on, I decided to turn the ringer off. Otherwise, I wouldn't get much done. I threw on some jeans and a T-shirt, grabbed the clothes needing to go to the cleaners, and headed out the door. I first stopped at the IHOP and had a big breakfast before going to the grocery store. I'd gone grocery shopping on an empty stomach before and ended up buying things I knew I would never eat. I spent an hour at IHOP's then headed for the store, picked up a few items and went home. I'd been home about fifteen minutes when the buzzer sounded. "Yes."

"Miss St. Pierre, someone left an envelope down at the desk for you," Manny said. "I'll bring it up for you."

"Thanks Manny," I said when he finally made it upstairs. "Who dropped this off?" I asked as he handed me a large manila envelope.

"I don't know. I stepped away from the desk for a moment and when I came back it was lying on the counter."

"Okay, thanks," I said, closing the door. There was no return address or name other than mine on the envelope. I sat on the couch and opened it. Inside were five 8x10 photos and a note. "What the fuck?" I said as I spread them out. The pictures were of me and Dennis; outside the club in New York, outside of my hotel, in the lobby of the hotel, and in Dennis' car at the airport. In all of the photos a picture of a dagger had been drawn over my heart. Dennis' face had been replaced with the face of what appeared to be a corpse. I picked up the letter and began to read: *So this is what it's come to. You hurt me for this piece of shit and I'm supposed to accept it? I've known and loved you most of my life and you repay me with betrayal. I thought you were different, but you're no better than that whore of an aunt of yours. You've made your bed. Now, I hope you enjoy it!*

"You sick motherfucker!" I yelled while ripping up the letter. "Who in the hell do you think you're fucking with?" I grabbed the pictures and ripped them up also. As soon as I'd finished, I realized my mistake. "Damn! I shouldn't have done that," I said as I looked at the ripped up pieces. I should have kept them. I picked up the phone and dialed Stan's number. I got his voicemail. "Look you simple motherfucker, I don't know what your problem is and I don't give a damn, but stay the hell away from me. Keep your little silly ass pictures, notes, and anything else you might have, to yourself. I'm not only sorry I ever got involved with you, I'm sorry I ever met you!" I hung up the phone and sat on the couch, breathing hard and seeing red. "I am not gonna let his crazy ass upset me," I said over and over again until I had calmed down. I couldn't understand how a man I once loved and thought I wanted as a husband, could turn into someone I hated with every fiber of my being. I was determined to stay focused and not allow Stan to get next to me. I refused to give him that power, so I busied myself. I called Aunt June and Denise. I didn't want them to worry so I didn't tell them about the pictures. I did tell them about his coming to New York. Aunt June thought he was just trying to win me back, so I left it at that. After talking with them, I called my Uncle Sammy to confirm that I would be coming to Atlanta the following day. I felt somewhat calmed after my phone calls, and I did a little cleaning then took a walk along the lakefront to enjoy the beautiful weather.

When I returned home that evening, I was feeling relaxed and upbeat. Since I was in a good mood, I gave Dennis a call but he wasn't home. I left him a brief message letting him know I was thinking of him and looking forward to seeing him again.

"Well, might as well get my packing done," I said as I put on a couple of CD's, and threw some salmon steaks on the grill. Once I'd gotten my packing done, I fixed my plate and went into the study to eat and read my e-mails. I was busy eating and not paying close attention to whom the e-mails were from. After the first three, which were from fans, I clicked on the next message and immediately knew who it was from. The letter consisted of two pages with one word printed over and over again; SLUT. As I sat there shaking my head, I calmly clicked 'print' and continued my dinner.

TWENTY FIVE

"Hey, baby girl," Uncle Sammy said as he hugged me. "How's my favorite niece?"

"Uncle Sammy, you tell all your nieces and nephews they're your favorite," I said, giving him a big kiss on the cheek.

"Yeah, but I was lying to them. You're number one! You're number one!" he said mimicking Eddie Murphy in the Nutty Professor. "Come on, girl. Let's get back to the house. I have a surprise for you."

"Ohhh, I love surprises!" I said, getting in the car. "So Uncle Sammy, how have you been doing since your divorce?"

"Happier than an 18-year-old boy at the Playboy Mansion."

"I wish I could have gotten a chance to meet her before you sent her packing."

"Honey, you wasn't missing nothing. I shoulda known better than to marry a woman with two grown, unemployed sons living with her in an apartment. Hell, them two Negroes had voices deeper than mine. The first time I met them I was sitting on her lumpy ass sofa and they came and sat down next to me and said, "Is you go be our new daddy? 'Cause we needs some new shoes."

"Uncle Sammy! You need to quit it. Stop lying on them people like that," I laughed.

"If I'm lying, I'm flying. Hell, if they had met you, they woulda been all over you like flies on shit. Them boys and they Momma were scandalous. Didn't wanna leave my house when I told they asses to get to steppin'. But a double-barreled shotgun will make any nigga see the light."

"Uncle Sammy," I said while wiping tears from my eyes, "why did you marry a woman you'd known only six months, anyway?"

"Good pussy, girl! Hell, good pussy and a bottle of Viagra will turn any man into a damn fool." My Uncle Sammy was a riot. I could tell the next five days were gonna be a lot of fun. When we pulled in the driveway there was a custom van already parked.

"That's a nice van you got there Uncle Sammy."

"Yeah, she's a beauty. But it ain't mine."

"Don't tell me it belongs to your new girlfriend who's got a vanload of kids."

"Girl, don't even play like that," he laughed as he got out and grabbed my bags. When we walked in the house my mouth flew open and I dropped my purse when I saw who was sitting in the living room.

"Reggie!" I screamed, running over to him. "What are you doing here?"

"Surprise!" he said as he hugged and kissed me.

"I've missed you so much," I cried.

"Uh-uh, I don't believe it. Tough Tara, crying," Uncle Sammy said, shaking his head. "Girl, you done gone soft on me."

"Leave me alone Uncle Sammy. I'm just happy to see my cousin. Why didn't you tell me you'd be here?" I said to Reggie. "How long are you staying?"

"I'm here as long as you're here." Just then a very attractive woman walked into the living room. "Tara, this is my fiancée, Margo. Margo, this is my cousin, Tara."

"When Reggie told me you were cousins, at first I didn't believe him," Margo said.

"Oh, so now you're calling me a liar," Reggie said, faking a hurt look.

"Naw, pookie-bear, not a liar, just an embellisher of the truth," she laughed, giving him a kiss.

"I'm glad to meet you too," I said. "Reggie has told me a lot of good things about you. I'm glad the two of you are here. I can tell I'm really gonna enjoy being here in Hotlanta. Hey Margo, why don't you help me upstairs with my bags? That way we can get a little 'girl talk' done. I have a signing at 3:00 and another one at 6:00, so I want to get a chance to sit around and kick it before it's time for me to leave."

"Hey Tara," Reggie called as we headed upstairs, "I don't want you telling my girl bad things about me, you hear?"

"Well Margo, I guess there won't be anything to talk about then," I laughed, winking at Reggie. While I unpacked, I got a chance to check Margo out. I could see why Reggie was attracted to her. Not only was she gorgeous, but she was smart and had a crazy sense of humor.

When we went back downstairs, Uncle Sammy and Reggie were sitting on the porch. It felt so good to be with family, listening to Uncle Sammy's crazy stories, that time seemed to fly by. "Oh man, I got to get ready to roll," I said as I looked at my watch.

"Tara, do you mind if I come with you?" Margo asked.

"Girl, no, I don't mind. But I want you to know sometimes these signings can get boring."

"Well then, we'll just have to make sure that doesn't happen," she said as she went over to Reggie. "Do you need anything before we leave, baby?"

"Yeah, I do, but I don't think Tara can wait on you for two hours," Reggie said, pulling her onto his lap. Well, I guess that answered the questions I had about his sex life.

After we'd gotten dressed and were on our way out, I asked Uncle Sammy if he wanted us to bring something back for dinner.

"Heck naw, girl. I'm gonna fix us a nice dinner of possum, turnip greens and fatback."

"He's kidding, isn't he?" Margo asked as we got in the van.

"Girl, yeah," I said, putting on my seat belt. "At least I hope he is."

The first signing was kinda slow and I was glad Margo was with me. It helped make the time go faster. The next signing was much better, but I was still anxious for it to be over with. I wanted to get back to the house and spend time with Reggie. Fortunately, Uncle Sammy had been kidding about the possum. He'd cooked fried chicken, mashed potatoes, corn on the cob, and a peach cobbler. Yeah, this was much better than staying at a hotel.

* * *

"Damn, girl! You got some kinda magic wand or something that makes time fly?" Uncle Sammy said. "I can't believe five days have passed by."

"If anything, I would have made time slow down," I said. "Uncle Sammy, I've had so much fun being here with you guys. I don't want to go."

"Then don't. Hell, I've got enough room here for you."

"Thanks unc', but you know how much I love Chicago."

"Naw, I don't think it's Chicago you missing. It must be a man," he said, helping me with my suitcase. Although I had told Reggie and Margo about what was going on with Stan, I'd made it a point not to tell Uncle Sammy. The man would have been in his car headed for Chicago with his shotgun across his lap.

"Uncle Sammy, I love you. Thanks for letting me stay here."

"Girl, don't be silly. You my favorite niece."

"Yeah, Uncle Sammy, I know."

"So, are you ready to roll?" Reggie asked when we got downstairs.

"Yeah, I guess so," I said as me, Uncle Sammy, and Margo started taking our bags out to the van. Margo and Reggie were going to drop me off at the airport on their way home.

"So Tara, are you gonna be alright when you get home?" Reggie asked.

"Yeah Reggie, I'll be okay. I can handle Mr. Bishop.

"He sounds kinda creepy to me," Margo said.

"Oh, but you don't know Tara," Reggie said. "She can get pretty creepy too."

"Reggie!" Margo said, rolling her eyes at him. "Don't make jokes. This is some really serious stuff. There's no telling what he might do next."

"Aw baby, I'm not trying to make light of the situation. I know from personal experience how deadly things can turn. I just know that no matter what the situation, Tara always lands on her feet."

"Yeah Margo, it's okay. I'm not gonna let him intimidate me. But let's change the subject to something positive."

"Okay, let's talk about me then," Reggie said. For the rest of the ride, we kept the conversation light and upbeat.

"Well guys, it was a lot of fun being with you two. Margo, I'm glad we finally met," I said as we arrived at the airport. "Reggie, I love you. You take care of yourself and this beautiful woman here."

"Oh, you can bet on it cous'," he said as we hugged and kissed. "Give Sherita a hug and kiss for me."

"Here, let me help you with your bags," Margo said as she got out. "Tara, I can see why Reggie talks about you so much. You are off the chain girl. I hope we see you again soon," she said as we embraced.

"You can count on it, cousin-in-law," I said as I headed for the terminal.

On the flight home, I closed my eyes and thought about the wonderful time I'd had. It was so refreshing being around people I loved, and who loved me. With the exception of when I told Reggie and Margo about Stan, and the ride to the airport, I'd managed to put him out of my mind for the past five days. I hoped he had managed to do the same for me and was done with his stupid games. Wishful thinking.

* * *

"Hey home! I'm home," I said as I walked in and headed for the bedroom with my bags. "Damn, I'm gonna have to do a better job of making up my bed," I said, glancing at the bed and what appeared to be a lump in the middle. I wasn't really focusing on the bed though as something else had caught my attention when I walked in the house and I needed to check it out. I never closed my study door, but it appeared to be closed when I came in. As I got close, I saw I was right; the door was closed. I slowly backed up to the bedroom and got my gun. When I got back to the study, I stood outside the door listening for any sounds. When I heard none, I quickly turned the knob and pushed the door back. What I saw made me gasp as if I'd been sucker punched. My study had been totally destroyed. My com- puter had been smashed; all of my books had been ripped to shreds, along with my articles and awards. My pictures had been destroyed and the plants overturned. I stood there for what felt like an eternity, staring in disbelief. I was finally able to will myself to move. I needed to call the police. I went back to the bedroom and dialed 911. "I would like to report a break-in," I said to the operator. After giving the information, I was about to hang up when I saw I had an incoming call.

"Hey girl! I didn't think you'd made it back yet. I was gonna leave you an obscene message," Sherita laughed.

"Sherita," I said. My voice caught in my throat while I struggled not to cry. "He was in my house and he destroyed my study."

"What! Tara, please tell me you're joking."

"I wish I was girl," I said as I sat on the bed. " I just called the police and they're on their way now." It was at that moment that I noticed the lump under my blanket again. I slowly got off the bed as Sherita started asking me questions. "Hold on a moment, Sherita," I said as I grabbed the blanket and pulled it back. I could feel the scream as it started in the back of my throat as a low mewling and grew louder and louder. I dropped the phone.

"Tara! Tara! What's wrong?" I could hear Sherita scream- ing, but I couldn't answer her. All I could do was stare at the bed, screaming until I felt my stomach lurch. I turned and ran into the bathroom, vomiting so violently it made my stomach ache. I sat on the bathroom floor crying as I heard the police pounding on the door. But I was unable to move. Finally I heard Ralph calling my name as he unlocked the door for the police.

"Ms. St. Pierre! It's the police. Where are you?"

"I'm in the master bathroom," I managed to get out. I heard them coming down the hallway.

"Holy shit!" I heard one of the officers exclaim when they'd entered the bedroom. That's when I finally got the courage and strength to get up and leave the bathroom. "Ms. St. Pierre, I'm Officer Younger, and this is Officer Banks, are you alright?" After you called reporting a break-in, we received another call from a friend of yours reporting you screaming."

"Yes officer, I'm okay, I think. It was after I placed my 911 call and I was talking with my friend Sherita when I saw that," I said pointing to the bed. "That's when I started screaming."

"I can see why," Officer Banks said. "Those are two of the biggest rats I've ever seen."

"Ms. St. Pierre," officer Younger said, "why don't we go in the living room and talk? There's no need to stay in here looking at this. I can see how upset you are. But first let's take a look at the other damage."

"Okay," I said as I led them to the study. Just then Sherita burst into the apartment. She hadn't bothered ringing the buzzer, instead she used the key I'd given her.

"Tara, girl, are you alright?" she said as she ran over and hugged me. "What happened?"

"Officers, the study is through there," I said as I went to the couch with Sherita close behind. "I need to sit down."

"Yes, by all means. We'll take a look at the study. Give you a chance to compose yourself, then we'll take your statement."

"Tara, would you please tell me what happened? You scared the shit out of me, screaming like that."

"Sherita, that crazy motherfucker put two dead rats in my bed."

"What!" she said as she got up and headed for the bedroom.

"Sherita, I don't think you wanna go in there." But she was already headed that way and I didn't have the strength to stop her. At least she'd been prepared for the sight.

"That's one sick bastard," she said when she came back. "Where in the hell did he find rats that damn big? Them fuckers look like they've been on steroids. And to arrange them to look like they were fucking? Now that's sick! Why do you think he put them in dry ice?"

"So the smell wouldn't alert me first. He wanted me to see them," I answered as the officers came back.

"Ms. St. Pierre, do you have any idea who may have done this?"

"Yes. It was my ex-fiancé, Stan Bishop. I ended our relationship and now he's trying to make my life miserable. He's followed me, sent me pictures he's secretly taken of me, and sent me obnoxious e-mail."

"Do you have any idea how he could have gotten in? This is a pretty secure building and there's no sign of a break-in."

"No, I don't. The door was locked when I got back. I've been out of town for five days."

"Did he have a key?"

"No. Never."

"Well, I think you should have the locks changed, just to be safe. We'll write up our report and a detective will go by Mr. Bishop's and talk with him. But since you have no idea when it may have happened, I'm sure he'll have an alibi. A technician will come out and dust for prints. In the meantime, do you have an instant camera? If so, I'll take pictures of the little 'package' in the bedroom then dispose of it and your linens," Officer Banks said. "Maybe you'll be more comfortable staying somewhere else tonight."

"Yes, I think I'll go home with my friend here."

"That's a good idea. Good luck," they said.

Sherita hadn't had a chance to see the study yet, so she got up to take a look. "Shit!" I heard her say. "That punk has got to pay for this shit!"

I walked in behind her and once again looked around in bewilderment. "Why would he do this to me? I thought he loved me."

"Well obviously his idea of love differs a hell of a lot from us normal people. Come on girl, let's get you some clothes and go to my place. We can come back tomorrow to clean up."

I headed for the bedroom, but as I got closer I hesitated. "It's alright, Tara. The policemen removed Stan's relatives. Come on," Sherita said as she took my hand.

I called down to the front desk to let Ralph know that I would be gone overnight. "I'm so sorry for what happened," he said. "I have no idea how anyone could have gotten into your apartment. The police said a detective will come and pick up the surveillance tapes to look them over. I'll keep my eyes open and if I see anything suspicious I'll call the cops, ok?"

"Okay, Ralph. Thanks."

After throwing some clothes in an overnight bag, we headed out the door. "Oh, wait a minute. I forgot something," I said as I headed back to the bedroom. I felt it would be best if from now on I kept my gun with me. I didn't intend on continuing to be anybody's victim.

* * *

"Damn, girl!" I said when we walked into Sherita's house. "Did someone break in and trash your house too?"

"You know, I can take your ass back home," she said as she started grabbing glasses off the cocktail table. "I just haven't been in much of a cleaning mood lately."

"Lately! Looks like you haven't cleaned up since the Commodores had their last hit."

"Ha, ha, ha," she laughed. "That's a good one Tara. It's good to see that you still have a sense of humor."

"I'm sorry, boo-boo. I shouldn't make fun of your pen; I mean your place. Since I need something to do to keep my mind off murder, I'll help you clean up."

"Great! But you'll have to start without me. I hate leaving you here alone, but I have a client I need to see. She's a close friend of my receptionist, Mona, and I've promised Mona that I would sit down with her and go over some investment options with her. Seems she just got a very large settlement from her ex-husband. I promise I'll be back as soon as possible. But if you're not comfortable being alone, I can phone Mona and tell her to re-schedule the appointment."

"No, you go on. I'll be fine. Besides, I'm not alone. I coulda sworn I just saw something moving underneath that pile of clothes over there."

"Girl, you crack me up," she laughed, giving me a big hug.

Once she'd left, I went in the kitchen and poured myself a glass of juice in the only clean glass in the house. I now knew what I would give Sherita for Christmas; a year's worth of cleaning services. That is if I could find an agency willing to take the job. Since I was in the kitchen, I decided to start cleaning in there first.

After an hour of nonstop cleaning, I had managed to get the place to the point where the Board of Health wouldn't give her a citation. As I was dusting, the phone rang. I had no intention of answering it, but when I looked at the caller ID, I saw it was coming from Sherita's office so I picked up. "Girl, I told you I would be alright," I said.

"Tara! We need to talk," she said excitedly. "You know the client I had to see today?"

"Yeah. What about it?"

"Well, I hadn't asked Mona her name beforehand. So I get here and she's waiting for me; her and her daughter, a beautiful little girl. Mona introduces us, and guess who she is?"

"Juanita Jordan?" I said. "Girl, I don't know. Who is she?"

"Her name's Regina Bishop! Stan's ex-wife!"

"You're kidding me, right? Stan's ex-wife moved back to Louisiana. Or at least that's what he said."

"Girl, obviously Stan says a lot of shit that ain't true, as you'll find out when we get there."

"What? Get where? We who?"

"Tara, get a grip and don't be so dense. I know you want to talk to this woman, and she wants to talk to you. So we'll be there in half an hour. Try to have the place cleaned up," Sherita's crazy ass said as she hung up. I sat there stunned, but intrigued. I was certainly interested in finding out about her relationship with Stan and what the circumstances were surrounding their divorce.

TWENTY SIX

"Wow!" was all I could manage to say when Regina and Brie arrived with Sherita. I couldn't believe how much Regina and I resembled one another.

"Mommy, she looks like you," Brie said to her mother.

"Yes, she certainly does," Regina said in amazement.

"Honey, why don't we go into my game room," Sherita said as she took Brie by the hand. "You can play some games and watch movies while we grown-ups talk."

"Is it okay Mommy?" Brie politely asked.

"Of course, sweetheart. Enjoy yourself."

"Why don't we go sit down," I said, leading Regina into the living room. As we sat there in an uncomfortable silence waiting for Sherita to return, I again noticed the resemblance. We were about the same height and weight, the same complexion, and similar facial features. The only difference was Regina wore glasses and her hair was short and close cropped.

"Well, I guess you ladies have noticed that Stan's taste in women is pretty consistent," Sherita said, walking into the living room carrying pops and chips.

"I had no idea you and Stan were dating," Regina said. "I knew the two of you knew one another as kids before he moved to Louisiana after his mother's death."

"Stan's mother isn't dead," I said. "Well, not as far as any-one knows. She walked out on Stan and his father when Stan was only five years old. Stan's father then married my aunt."

"What! He told me his mother died in a fire. He never mentioned anything about your aunt. He said the two of you were neighbors and occasionally played together. But I'm not surprised to hear he lied about that," Regina said, shaking her head.

"What happened between you two? Why did you divorce?" I asked, certain the story Stan had given me would not be the same as Regina's.

"Well, I met him when he moved to Louisiana. His family and mine were friends. We didn't start dating until high school and we married when I was in college. By that time Stan had started his own construction business. At first everything was great. We were inseparable and very much in love. Stan was so attentive and caring, he catered to my every need. I worked in the office part-time, helping him out until I got pregnant; then Stan thought I should stay at home. I didn't have a problem with that. I think I started to notice a change in him when I was working there though. He would get upset and suspicious of me talking with the men who worked for him, when our conversations were perfectly innocent. At first I thought his jealousy was kinda cute, but then it started getting on my nerves, so I was glad to be at home when I became pregnant. From the moment he found out I was pregnant, all he would talk about was his 'son' and all the things they would do together. Whenever I would remind him that it might be a girl, he didn't want to hear it. When Brie was born, I could tell he was unhappy that he hadn't gotten a son. He practically ignored her. I can't remember him ever changing a Pamper or getting up with her during the night. When she got older and he did start spending time with her, he would take her only to sporting events."

"Man, that's jacked up," Sherita said.

"Yeah, tell me about it," Regina said. "But as time went on he seemed to warm up to her and started acting like a father. I guess he finally forgave her for being a girl. In the meantime, I was getting bored being cooped up at home all the time. So I decided to get a job; but not with Stan's company."

"Let me guess," I said. "He didn't take too kindly to that."

"Honey, he went ballistic! He berated me, called me an uncaring mother and accused me of wanting to be around other men. He carried on so much that I just said forget it. Do you know I actually ended up apologizing to him for upsetting him?" Regina said, taking a sip of pop.

"Um, um, um," Sherita said, shaking her head.

"Yeah ladies, I had it bad. But that's because Stan was so good. One minute he would belittle and insult me, then once he got his way, he was loving and caring. Since he was the only man I'd ever been with sexually, he knew once he worked his magic in the bedroom, I was putty in his hands and he would have no problem out of me. So I gave up the idea of working and justified it by saying we were doing okay financially anyway. But after about four or five months, I started getting bored again and I decided to take a stand and put my foot down."

"So what did you do?" I asked.

"I went and got a job and I didn't give a damn what he had to say about it."

"Good for you, girl!" Sherita high-fived Regina.

"So what was Stan's reaction to that?" I asked.

"Well since I finally managed to grow a spine and had made up my mind to stand up to him and not give in, I was ready for his temper tantrum. But he surprised me. He took another approach. He told me since I was so determined to do this, then he would give me his blessings if after two months I showed him that I was able to work, take care of him, the house, and Brie without any problems. But guess what he did."

"What, girl?" I said intrigued.

"Every single night he was all over me; sometimes for two or three hours. And a lot of times early in the morning, too. I mean, we had always had a healthy sex life, but he really turned it up. Needless to say, I ended up getting pregnant and since I was constantly late for work due to our late night and early morning sessions, my job terminated me. So he ended up getting his way anyhow, and he was once again happy. I was home where he wanted me. Well, anyway, one day when I was about eight months pregnant, I was going down the stairs and Brie had left one of her toys on the stairs. I didn't see it and I tripped and fell. I lost the baby. It was a boy."

"Oh my God. I'm sorry to hear that," I said with tears in my eyes.

"Me too, Regina," Sherita said, wiping her eyes.

"Thanks," Regina said, "but everything happens for a reason. It was all a part of God's plan, I guess. But Stan didn't see it that way. He blamed me and Brie; said we murdered his son. That was the final straw for me. Once I recovered from the miscarriage, I packed my bags and went home to my family. Of course, he started begging me to come back home, but I'd had enough of him so I told him I was filing for divorce. I found another job and had all of one month of peace and happiness before I found out just how crazy that man was."

"Uh-oh," Sherita said as she looked over at me. "What did he do?"

"First, he started constantly calling my job, which was something management didn't care for. Then one day my super- visor calls me and tells me I have a delivery. It was from a Chinese restaurant we always ordered from. The order was for $120.00 worth of food and they gave me hell when I tried to explain that I hadn't placed an order."

"See girl, I told you," Sherita said. "He did the same thing to Tara."

"Yeah, well he was just getting warmed up," Regina continued. "I had become friends with a woman from my previous job, and we would hang out sometimes. Well one night we went bowling and she was driving her Lincoln Town Car..."

"I don't think I want to hear this," I said, looking at Sherita.

"We leave the bowling alley and find her car with all four tires slashed and BITCH carved into the hood."

"I knew it!" Sherita screamed. "I knew that motherfucker was the one who fucked up my car!"

"Sherita! Please! You're gonna scare Brie," I said as I tried to get her to calm down. "I think I need something stronger than this Sprite," I said as I headed to the bar to pour me a shot of Martell. I poured one for Sherita as well.

"I think I'll have one of those too," Regina said. "I guess he did the same thing to your car also," she said to Sherita.

"At first we didn't even think about him having anything to do with it. I mean, it coulda been some crazy ass man I'd been seeing," Sherita said as she tossed back her drink. "But after some of the other things he did to Tara, we kinda figured he may have been behind it."

"Well I'm not surprised," Regina continued. "See, the thing with Stan is he wants you all to himself, so he has no problem doing things to your friends or even your family to get back at you. I guess he thinks that by messing with people around you, that'll make them afraid to be with you and they'll stay away from you. In his twisted way of thinking, you'll come back to him when everyone else wants to stay away from you."

"Well he's about to find out he picked the wrong friend to fuck with this time!" Sherita said as she got up to pour herself another drink.

"Something tells me he didn't stop there," I said.

"Stan Bishop? Not by a long shot," she said. "About a week after the car incident my mom's dog, Rerun, died of poisoning. My mom and dad refused to believe Stan had anything to do with Rerun's death or Amy's car. That's because he always presented the charming, happy-go-lucky Stan to them. They had no choice but to believe me when one day my father gets some pictures in the mail. They were nude pictures I had stupidly allowed him to take of me. He sent them to my father! How's that for sick?"

I sat there and said a silent prayer of thanks that I had never allowed him to photograph me nude, even though he'd asked numerous times.

"That's when I decided to leave Louisiana. I wanted to get as far away from that man as I could. But somehow he found out where I was and he moved here. At that point I was prepared to do whatever it took to keep him out of my life, even if it meant killing him. But except for his annoying phone calls saying he wanted to see Brie, he pretty much left me alone," she said with a sigh.

"Yeah, that's because by that time we had become involved and he had himself a new victim," I said.

"Unfortunately for you, I think you're right," Regina said.

"Well I guess I should tell you about my experiences with him," I said. "But first let me clear up some lies he told you about his mother, his childhood, and how we first met." I proceeded to tell Regina everything I knew about Stan, from the first time we met up to the present incident that caused me to stay the night with Sherita. When I'd finished, the three of us sat there in silence looking at one another.

"Tara, I'm sorry we had to meet under these circumstances, but I'm glad we did. You've answered so many questions I had about him. And now knowing his history, I feel sorry for him. But you really need to watch out for him. I think he's gone over the edge now. If you need me to give a statement to the police or anything, you call me, okay," she said, giving me her number. "I'd better get Brie home now."

"You be careful too," I said. "I can't imagine him being too happy about the divorce settlement you received."

"Let me get Brie for you," Sherita said as she headed for the den and came back carrying the sleeping child. She was a beautiful little girl and I felt sorry that she was being cheated out of having the type of relationship with her father that she was entitled to.

"Tara, I'm gonna see Regina to her car," Sherita said. "I'll be right back."

"Okay," I said as I got up to give Regina a hug. "Thanks for coming by and sharing your story with us."

"Thank you," she smiled at me. "You're much stronger than I was. I'm sure you'll be just fine."

When Sherita came back inside, I was standing at the bar pouring myself another drink. She quietly walked over and poured one for herself. We sat down staring off into space, thinking and drinking. "That bastard destroyed my car!" she suddenly burst out.

"That bastard destroyed my house!" I yelled back.

"Now I know we're not gonna let this shit ride," she said.

"Oh, hell naw. Obviously he don't know who he fucking with."

"So what's the plan?"

I looked at the clock and saw it was 11:45. "The plan is to go by his house and confront his despicable ass," I said, grabbing my purse and taking out my gun.

"I heard that!" Sherita said, heading for her bedroom and coming back with her piece tucked into the waistband of her jeans. "Should we kill him?" she asked as we got in her car.

"If we have to," I said as we both let the combination of anger and alcohol overtake us.

* * *

"So, should we kick in the door gangsta style?" Sherita asked when we pulled up in front of Stan's house.

"No. We'll act like ladies, ring the bell, and when he answers we'll commence to whupping his ass."

"Good plan," Sherita slurred. It's amazing how liquor can have you thinking, talking, and acting stupid. When we got to the door, Sherita rang the bell like a crazed woman.

"I see a light," I said. We heard the lock being turned and the door slowly opened.

"Motherfucker! You fucked with...." was all Sherita man-aged to get out.

"Who are you?" I said as I stared at the young man stand- ing on the other side of the door.

"Wh, wh, who are you?" he managed to get out, trying to look brave.

"We asked you first!" Sherita said as she got up in his face. He took a couple of steps back. I don't know if it was from fear or from the booze on Sherita's breath.

"Where is Stan?"

"I don't know," the young man stammered. "I'm just house sitting for him. He said he'd be back in a couple of weeks. Hey, aren't you that writer friend of his?" he asked, lookly closely at me.

"Naw, I'm not a writer. I can't even read. And I'm certainly no friend of his," I said as I grabbed Sherita by the arm and headed down the stairs.

On the ride back to Sherita's, neither of us said a word. I guess since the alcohol had started to wear off, we were both reflecting on what we'd just done and what we might have done if Stan had been there. God certainly does watch over fools and babies.

* * *

"I'm going to bed," I said as I headed for the guestroom at Sherita's.

"Yeah, me too. I'll see you in the morning, Batman."

"Goodnight, Robin."

TWENTY SEVEN

"I wish he would hurry up," Sherita said as we sat in my kitchen sipping coffee while waiting for the fingerprint technician to finish up in the study.

"I don't know about you, but I'm not really looking forward to going in there."

"I know you're not Tara, and I'm sorry. I know how much that room meant to you, but the sooner we get in there the sooner we can see what can be salvaged."

"Yeah, I know. Once we're done here, I'm going to Wickes to buy a new bedroom suite."

"Tara, how do you think Stan got in here?"

"He probably swiped my spare keys and had a set made."

"Ms. St. Pierre, I'm finished here," the technician said. "If a match comes up, Detective Barnes will be contacting you. Unfortunately, it can sometimes take up to six weeks or longer before the prints come back, and even then they might not produce anything."

"I understand," I said, getting up to see him out. "Thank you."

"Well, I'm ready," I said, heading for the study with Sherita close behind. After about twenty minutes, it was quite obvious that not much was salvageable. Stan had done a pretty thorough job. The garbage can was full with torn and ripped articles and pictures. My books had all been destroyed and the computer was history. All at once, the magnitude of what he'd done hit me and I sat in the middle of the floor and started sobbing.

"Hey Tara, here's a picture that hasn't been ripped up. It's of you and the twins at…." Sherita was saying before she noticed me sitting on the floor crying. "Oh sweetheart," she said as she rushed over and sat next to me cradling me in her arms. "I'm sorry this happened to you. Somehow we'll manage to get past this, I promise you."

"I know," I sniffled. "It's just so hard to believe that he would do this to me."

"Yeah, I know. Look, I can finish up in here. Why don't you take a break and relax?"

"Okay, that sounds like a good idea. I think I'll walk down to Popeye's and get some chicken," I said, getting up dusting off my pants. "I'll be right back." As I was heading out the door, the phone rang. I looked at the caller ID and saw it was Dennis. "Sherita, that's Dennis. I really don't feel like talking to him right now. Answer it for me and tell him I'll give him a call tomorrow. And don't tell him about what happened," I said, certain Sherita would spill the beans as soon as I was gone.

* * *

"Hello."

"Hey, bright eyes. How's the prettiest woman in Chicago doing?"

"Well, I'm doing great. Thanks for the compliment," Sherita said. "But I don't think Tara will take too kindly to you talking to me like this."

"Oh, excuse me," Dennis said apologetically. "I thought this was Tara. I'm sorry."

"No need to apologize," Sherita laughed. "I'm Sherita, Tara's gorgeous friend."

"Oh yeah," Dennis laughed back. "Tara's spoken of you. Is she there?"

"She needed to get some fresh air. Things have pretty much gotten out of control around here. I've never seen my girl this upset."

"What's wrong?" Dennis asked, alarmed. Sherita spent the next ten minutes filling him in on the latest events. "Thanks for sharing that with me, Sherita. The more I hear about this dude the more I despise him. Something needs to be done about him."

"Well take a number and get in line, 'cause if I could find him I'd do some serious harm to him."

"I feel you. Look, one of the reasons I called was to tell Tara I'm coming to Chicago Monday regarding a case I'm working on. I wanted to see her while I'm there."

"You know, she would really like that, but I just want to say this to you and I hope you don't take offense," Sherita said. "Tara is my dearest friend and Stan has done some shit to really hurt her. I just hope that you're on the up and up and you have her best interests at heart, because the next time I have to see my girl crying over some shit some sadistic motherfucker has done to her..."

"Whew! I get the picture," Dennis interrupted. "Let me assure you I would never do anything to physically or emotionally harm Tara or any other woman. My Momma raised me better than that and Sadie don't play that disrespecting women shit. I'm just glad to know Tara has a friend like you who's got her back."

"Yeah, that's my girl and I just want to let you know where I stand. But I have an idea. Why don't you surprise her Monday? When she comes back from the store I'll tell her you called, but I won't tell her about Monday. When you get in town give me a call and we'll meet up, then I'll bring you by here."

"Okay," Dennis agreed, "that sounds like a plan. Give me your number and I'll see you Monday."

After hanging up, Sherita went back in the study to finish cleaning. As she was cleaning up the dirt from an overturned plant, she found a set of keys. "I wonder what these go to?" she said aloud. *I'll give them to Tara when she gets back,* she thought as she dropped them in the pocket of her jeans.

"So what did Dennis say?" I asked when I got back. I'd been gone about forty minutes and the walk had cleared my head.

* * *

"Oh, he just called to say hi and see how things were going with you. He said he's going out of town for a couple of days and he'll talk to you when he gets back."

"Okay, so what did you tell him?"

"I told him Stan is a rotten son of a bitch and a poor excuse for a man. I also told him that if he ever does anything to make you cry, I'll be in New York and on his ass like a pit bull with a bone."

"Sherita! No you didn't!"

"Well, those weren't my exact words, but he got my meaning."

"I knew you were gonna tell him what Stan had done."

"I knew you wanted me to tell him."

"So what did he say?"

"He wants to take a number and get in the bust-a-cap-in-Stan's-ass line."

"I would really like to hear Dennis' voice," I said, heading for the kitchen with the chicken, "but I don't think I would be a good conversationalist right about now."

"Well, I'm sure he would understand," Sherita said, grabbing a piece of chicken. "So are we going to pick out a new bed today?"

"Yeah, soon as we finish eating. But first I need to call the locksmith."

"Oh yeah, that reminds me," she said while licking her fingers, "I found these keys in the study."

"These are the keys to Stan's house," I said puzzled. "I'm certain I left these on his table."

"Maybe he accidentally dropped them while he was in the study destroying it. Are you going to tell the police about them?"

"Yeah, I guess I should," I said, dropping them in my purse. "Well, let's go bed shopping."

* * *

When I got back home, I was exhausted. It had been a long, tiring day. Sherita had done a pretty good job of cleaning up the study, but as I stood there looking around, I was aware of each and every piece that was missing. I shook my head as I closed the door to the study and walked away.

I curled up on the couch to watch a movie until I was ready to go to bed, then I would go sleep in the guestroom. I was watching "The Bone Collector" with fine-ass Denzel, who exuded sex appeal even as a paraplegic, and Queen Latifah as his nurse. As I laid there with my arm draped over the edge of the couch running my fingers through the carpet, I felt something forcefully brush against my hand. I looked down and started screaming when I saw two rats larger than the ones Stan had left in my bed, gnawing at my hand. I yanked my hand away and saw that three fingers were missing. I was still screaming when I felt a sharp pain in my leg. That's when I realized I'd been having a nightmare. The pain in my leg was from me hitting it on the coffee table when I fell off the couch. I sat on the floor breathing hard, sweating and rubbing my sore leg with one hand, counting the fingers on my other, just to be sure. I wasn't sure if my nightmare was caused by Stan or from the movie I'd been watching, but one thing was certain, and that was my hatred for Stan and my desire for him to feel what I was feeling. I didn't know what I was going to do, but I knew I had to do something. I thought about what Regina had said about Stan poisoning her parents' dog and decided I should tell my family everything so they'd be aware and careful. Especially Aunt June.

* * *

"Hey, Tara," Denise and Houston said in unison when I walked in the house the next day. "We didn't expect to see you here so early," Denise said. "You must really miss our good cooking."

"Yes, that I do," I said as I sat at the kitchen table and removed my shades. "But I also need to talk to all of you."

"Tara, are you alright?" Denise asked as she walked over to me and lifted my face up. "You look terrible. What's wrong sis?"

"There's just been a lot of crazy things going on with Stan. I also got a chance to meet his ex-wife who told me some very interesting things about him. I wanted to make you all aware of what's been going on because he's really getting out of control."

"What is it?" Houston asked. "What's going on?"

"Well, I'd rather tell you all at once. Where's Aunt June?"

"She went to Jewel to pick up a few things for dinner," Denise said, looking at her watch. "I don't know what's taking her so long. She should have been back long before now."

"Oh my God!" I gasped, jumping up. "I'm going to look for her."

"Tara, what's wrong?" Denise said alarmed.

"Houston, come go with me," I said, grabbing his arm. I just had a bad feeling when Denise said Aunt June was gone longer than expected. As Denise and Houston looked questioningly at me, the phone rang.

"Hello," Denise said, snatching it up. I could tell from the expression on her face that it was not good news. I clutched Houston's arm, praying when I saw tears streaming down Denise's face.

"Baby, what is it?" Houston said.

"Aunt June was in a car crash!" she cried.

"Oh God!" I said, sinking into a chair.

"What?" Houston said. "Is she alright? What happened?"

"They said she's fine. Cuts, bruises and a broken leg. I don't know what happened."

"Look, I'll get the kids ready and take them next door," Houston said. "Baby, you and Tara try to calm down now. Turn off the food, lock up and meet me at the car."

We rushed to the hospital. It was like déjà vu as I remembered the night we'd received the phone call about Reggie. Fortunately, this time the ride to the hospital was a short one and we didn't have time to let our imaginations drive us crazy wondering what had happened. When we arrived, Aunt June was in the process of having a cast put on her leg. Once that was done, she was taken to a room where she would be kept overnight. The nurse told us we could go in to see her.

"Auntie, what happened?"

"I have no idea," she began. "Everything was fine on the way to the store, but when I was headed home I got on the expressway and my brakes wouldn't work. The car wouldn't stop and I was scared to death. I just thank God there wasn't much traffic. I was able to pull over on the shoulder and I drove up on the grass."

"How did you get the car to stop?" Denise asked.

"I ran it into a tree."

I sat there in stunned silence as I listened to her tell of her ordeal. Finally, I started sobbing. "I'm so sorry, Auntie. It's all my fault. I should have warned you all before now."

"Tara baby, what are you talking about?" Aunt June asked. "You had nothing to do with this; it was an accident."

I took a deep breath, poured myself a glass of water and began to tell my family everything that had been going on. I ended by voicing my suspicions that Stan may have tampered with the brakes on Aunt June's car.

"Oh baby," Aunt June said, patting my hand. "I'm sorry he destroyed your things. I know how much they meant to you. But none of this is your fault and don't you go around carrying this guilt, you hear me?"

"Yes ma'am," I sniffled.

"What are we gonna do?" Denise said with a fearful look on her face.

"I know what I'm gonna do," Houston said, clenching his jaw. "There's no way in hell I'm gonna sit back and let that sorry excuse for a man terrorize my family."

"Houston, don't do anything crazy," Denise said. "I know you're as upset about this as everyone else, but I think we should let the police handle this. I don't want to see anyone else in this family hurt."

"The only person who's gonna be hurtin' is not in this family," he said with tears welling up in his eyes. "I'm gonna go call and check on the kids."

"You don't think…." Denise said, alarmed.

"Naw baby, I'm sure the kids are fine," he said, kissing her on the cheek. "I would track that motherfucker to the ends of the Earth if I even thought he was *thinking* of doing something to my kids. You have my word on that."

In all the time I'd known Houston, that was the first time I'd heard him curse. I knew something had to be done and soon. Stan was beginning to destroy my family. When Houston returned, he'd managed to calm down. He told us the kids were fine. We sat with Aunt June for about an hour then hugged and kissed her, told her we'd see her tomorrow, then headed home.

* * *

"Tara, why don't you spend the night here?" Denise said after we'd gotten back home.

"Thanks Sis, but I need to get home. I'm having my bed delivered tomorrow and the locksmith is coming to change my locks. I'll just spend a little time here with Beavis and Butt-head," I said, tickling the twins, "then I'll head home."

"Alright then, but please be careful."

"I will. I promise."

Once I'd gotten in my car, after carefully looking it over, I took the side streets for a while to test out my brakes. There was no telling what Stan's next move might be. When I felt confident that everything was alright, I got on the expressway. And wouldn't you know it, my car just seemed to have a mind of its own, because before I knew it, I was parked a block away from Stan's. As I walked toward his house, I saw someone coming out. It was the same young man who had been there the other night. I quickened my pace and caught up with him.

"Excuse me, do you remember me from the other night?" I asked him.

"Oh yeah, I certainly do remember you. I told Mr. Bishop that you and another lady was by here looking for him."

"Is he home now?"

"Nope. He phoned this morning to check on things."

"Oh, I see," I said. "You must be having a heck of a time adjusting to all the hidden rooms in there."

"Not really. Mr. Bishop left the doors open and cleared the codes so they wouldn't lock, so I'm not having any problems."

"Did he tell you where he's staying or when he'll be back?"

"He's in Louisiana and he expects to be back next Wednesday. Well, I gotta go. My parents are expecting me."

"Oh, alright. What's your name?"

"Todd."

"Okay, Todd. It was nice talking to you," I said as he headed for his car. I stood there and waited until he pulled off and was out of sight, then I reached in my purse and pulled out the keys Sherita had found in my study. I was a little fearful and apprehensive about going inside since I didn't believe Stan was really in Louisiana. Either Todd was lying or was being lied to, but I was determined to do whatever I could to get Stan to leave me and my friends and family alone. Maybe I could find some- thing to take to the police to prove that he was the one responsible for the things that had happened to me, Aunt June and Sherita.

As I entered the house, I stood still and listened for any sounds. When I heard nothing, I carefully made my way down the hall. I saw Todd was right, all of the doors were open. I went into Stan's bedroom and immediately started going through his drawers, finding nothing. I then looked in his closet, but there was nothing there either. "Damn!" I said, heading upstairs to the guest bedrooms. I passed the room Todd was occupying but I didn't go inside. I doubted if there would be anything in there. "Oh great," I said as I looked down the hall and saw the door to the other guestroom had been replaced with a sliding door like the ones downstairs, but this one was closed.

I made my way back downstairs, remembering the hidden staircase in Stan's closet. I quickly went inside the closet and made my way up the stairs. Even though I knew Todd probably wouldn't be back for awhile, I wanted to hurry up. I felt kinda creepy sneaking around Stan's house, even though he'd had no problem doing it to me. I was totally caught off guard when I entered the guestroom and found it completely empty. Everything had been removed, even the pictures on the walls, walls which had been painted black. Even the ceiling was black. I had no idea what the meaning was behind that. I guess I would have had to be as crazy as Stan to figure that one out. I was certain, though, that whatever he had planned for that room wouldn't be something positive. I made my way back down the stairs to Stan's room, disappointed that I was unable to find anything. Then I thought about the noise I'd heard the last time I was in the house. A noise I was certain had come from a hidden room that he hadn't told me about. Since there were no stairs leading up to where the attic should have been, I knew there had to be another hidden staircase. I ran upstairs to where I'd been standing when I heard the noise; next to the bathroom in front of the mirror. I stood there looking closely at the mirror and noticed it was crooked. I grabbed the top of it to straighten it out and that's when I felt a little latch. "Bingo!" I said aloud as I pulled it and watched the wall slide back to reveal a staircase. I took off one of my shoes and propped it in the door opening to prevent it from sliding back, then I cautiously went up the stairs.

When I got to the top I found myself standing in front of a wall which I knew led to his secret room. I felt around for a latch or something that would give me entry, but I couldn't find anything. "Shit!" I said, slamming my fist into the wall. I went back down the stairs, grabbing my shoe as I headed for the garage to the control box for the doors. I stood there trying to make sense of it. There were five green lights which were lit up. I figured those were for the rooms which Stan had left opened. There were two lights, which were red. Those had to be for the doors leading to the guest bedroom and the attic.

Now I just needed to figure out the codes, so I started randomly putting in four digit numbers, but nothing happened. I stood there trying to think of what codes Stan might use. I wondered if they would be numbers having some relevance to me, so I started entering dates that were of importance to me: my birth date, the last four digits of my social security number, my address, my phone number; all to no avail. Finally, I tried the date when we ran into each other at the restaurant and *voila!*, the light for the bedroom turned green. “Yes! Yes! Yes!” I cried out ecstatically. I ran upstairs, and sure enough, the door to the bedroom was open. The room, in all of its blackness, looked even more sinister and ominous from down the hall than it did when I’d entered it earlier.

I ran back to the garage, reentering the code and watched as the light turned red again. I looked at my watch, surprised to see that I had been in the house for over an hour. I badly wanted to stay there and figure out the code for the attic, but I knew I couldn’t risk being caught. Besides, I had the key. I could always come back some other time. I reluctantly headed for the front door, opening it a crack and cautiously peeking outside. No one was in sight so I stepped out, locked the door and headed for my car, determined to make a return visit in the very near future.

TWENTY EIGHT

"Oh, that must be the delivery people with my bed," I said aloud as my buzzer sounded. "Hello."

"Hey homefries, it's me."

"Sherita, I thought you were the delivery people. Come on up." I opened the door a crack and went in the kitchen to pour myself a glass of tea. I heard the door close as I headed back to the living room. "Sherita, what are you…." I stopped midsentence, shocked, when I saw who was standing in my living room. "Dennis!" I exclaimed. "What are you doing here?"

"Giving you a pleasant surprise, I hope."

"Surprise!" Sherita said.

"What's going on here? I thought you said he was leaving town for a few days."

"Duh, Tara. He is out of town."

"You know what I mean," I said, standing there unable to take my eyes off him.

"Sherita, I don't think she's glad to see me. Maybe I should go back to my hotel," Dennis said as he faked like he was heading for the door.

"Touch that doorknob and I'll be forced to do you bodily harm," I said as I grabbed him from the back, wrapping my arms tightly around him.

"Oh, so you are happy to see me," he said, turning around and hugging me.

"You and Sherita set me up!"

"Yep, we certainly did. I've missed you," he said softly as he gave me a soft peck on the lips. It's a good thing Sherita was standing there, otherwise I probably would have ravished him right then and there.

"Well, it looks like my work here is done," Sherita said, smiling at us. "I'm outta here. I'll call you later, Miss Thang."

"Okay Sherita," I said as I winked at her and mouthed a silent 'thank you'.

"What are you doing here in Chicago?" I asked, once Sherita had left.

"I'm here for three days working on a case and there was no way I was coming to Chicago without seeing you."

"Well let me show you around," I said, grabbing his hand and giving him a tour of my home. When I got to the study, I hesitated, reluctant to open the door.

"Tara, Sherita told me about what happened. I understand if you don't want to go in there."

"No, it's okay," I said as I opened the door. "It's just hard to see so many of my personal things gone. They really meant a lot to me."

"I know they did," he said as he stood close behind me with his strong hands on my shoulders. I stood there with my eyes closed, inhaling his scent while a sense of calm and serenity overtook me. I felt safe and protected and without even realizing what I was doing, I slowly turned around to face him, hugging him tightly with my face buried against his chest. "I'm so glad you're here," I whispered against his chest.

"I'm glad I'm here too, and I promise you I'll do everything I can to make things right."

"Thank you, Dennis," I said as I wiped a tear from my eye. As we stood there hugging, the buzzer sounded. "That must be the furniture company with my new bedroom set," I said as we left the study. "Why don't you make yourself comfortable while I take care of this?"

The Salvation Army had come by the day before to pick up my old bedroom set. I could have kept it and disposed of the mattresses, but I knew the sight of it would always remind me of Stan and his little 'gift', so I had the mattresses trashed and donated the set. While the men were busy setting it up, I went to sit with Dennis. "So where are you staying?" I asked him.

"I'm at the Westin on Michigan."

"Oh good, you're not too far from here."

"Yeah, I know. I wanted to be as close to you as possible."

Boy! He had no idea how I wanted him to be much closer, but these damn morals kept me from insisting that he stay with me while he was in town. "So what kind of case are you working on?"

"A triple homicide. All of the victims had recently moved to New York from Chicago and they were all heavy into drug trafficking."

"Whew! Sorry I asked."

"That's alright. But, sweetie, I really need to get back to the hotel and go handle my business. I'll come back and pick you up at 5:00, then we can spend the rest of the evening together."

"Oh, so you're not going to ask me if I already had plans for the evening?" I said, placing my hands on my hips.

"No," he said as he stood his fine chocolate self up and put his hands on his hips. "I'm telling you your plans for this evening are with me. So if you had something else planned, I guess you'll just have to cancel them or include me in them."

"My, my, my, aren't we the aggressive one?" I said, smiling at him. "I guess I'll have to call Roy Jones, Jr. and inform him of a change in plans 'cause there's a new sheriff in town."

"Roy wouldn't stand a chance against me," Dennis said, pulling me close to him. "But seriously Tara, I would very much love to spend some time with you. But if you already have plans, I'll understand."

"Five o'clock, sharp," I said, kissing him gently on the lips, "Or it's me and Roy."

"Gotcha, pretty lady."

"Boy, aren't you prompt?" I said when Dennis showed back up that evening at exactly 5:00.

"You have no idea the hurdles I had to jump over to make it here on time, but I make it a point to never a keep a pretty lady waiting. At least I try not to."

"Something tells me in your line of work, you must keep a lot of women hanging."

"Well, I wouldn't say 'a lot', but I have found out that law enforcement and relationships are not a good match. It takes a very special woman to be able to tolerate a man who's always working. But I love what I do, so what can I say?"

"I understand completely," I said, giving him a hug. "Let me show you my new bedroom set."

"Is this your way of luring me into your bed?" he laughed.

"When I'm ready for you to be in my bed, I won't need a lure."

"Ohhh, 'when'. Now that sounds promising," he said as he ran his finger lightly down my neck. "This is nice," he said, looking around the bedroom. "I see you have a thing for mirrors. Any particular reason why you have so many in your bedroom?"

"No. No particular reason. I just like mirrors," I said, eyeing him up and down.

"So what are we going to do with ourselves for the rest of the evening, and night?" he asked while looking longingly from me to the bed.

"Well," I said as I turned him around and steered him out of the bedroom, "I need to go check on my aunt first. I had planned on doing it earlier today, but time got away from me."

"Oh, okay. Is there something wrong with her?"

"Yeah," I said. "I'll tell you about it on the way there. Afterwards, we can go have a nice, intimate dinner."

"I know what I want on my menu," he said as he wrapped his arms around me, kissing me so softly, so sexily, so passionately, I almost changed my plans.

"Did you have any trouble finding a place to park?" I asked as we rode down on the elevator.

"Of course not. That's one of the perks of being a detective. You can park practically anywhere."

"Well, excuse me, Mr. Detective," I said as we walked hand in hand out of the building, laughing and talking.

* * *

Neither Tara nor Dennis noticed the figure standing in the shadows a few doors down, intently watching them. Nor did they see him as he briskly walked to Tara's building, entered, and started talking to Manny, the doorman who was on duty that night. As he headed for the elevator, Manny stood behind the desk and smiled as he counted the ten $100 dollar bills the man had given him. Manny felt bad allowing the man access to Tara's apartment, but the weight of the money in his pocket quickly cancelled out that feeling.

* * *

"So pretty lady, tell me about your aunt," Dennis said as we headed for the expressway.

"She was in a car crash yesterday."

"Wha... Is she alright? What happened?"

"Well, she has a broken leg, cuts, bruises and scrapes, but other than that, she's okay. She was released from the hospital this morning. As for what happened," I said looking directly at him, "I strongly suspect that Stan tampered with her brakes."

"What makes you say that? Why would he want to harm her?"

So I began to tell Dennis about how I first met Stan; about his relationship with my Aunt and what caused him to hate her. I also told him of my meeting with Regina and the things she had shared with me and Sherita about her marriage and the things Stan had done to her family and friends. As Dennis drove, he listened intently and asked direct and specific questions. When I told him about sneaking into Stan's home, he looked at me with raised eyebrows, shaking his head.

"Now why am I not surprised by that? You do realize that was a pretty dangerous thing to do, not to mention illegal. But I do like your style," he said as we pulled up in front of the house. "I want to hear more about this house and the hidden rooms, okay?"

"Yeah, alright," I said as we headed up the stairs. Since it was warm outside, the front door was open and the screen door unlocked. "Hey, isn't that Sherita's voice I hear?" Dennis asked.

"Yep, that's her alright," I said, hesitating before opening the door. We could hear her in there talking to Denise and Aunt June. "Yeah, the brother is fine. I met him this morning, and Tara is definitely digging him. I know she's gonna make the most of his visit here," she was saying. I opened the door, walked in and gave her an 'I'm gonna kill you' look.

"Sherita, it's good to see you again," Dennis said, smiling at her.

"Denise, Auntie, this is a dear friend of mine, Detective Dennis Wiley. Dennis, this is my sister Denise, and my Aunt June," I said as he shook their hands.

"It's a pleasure to meet you both. I'm sorry about your accident."

"Tara doesn't seem to think it was an accident," Aunt June said.

"Yeah, she told me, and considering all the other things she told me about this guy, I think she may be right."

"Detective Barnes was out here earlier to talk to me about the accident and he says the car will be examined tomorrow to see if there are any signs of foul play," Aunt June told Dennis.

"Now is this the same detective who's handling your case, Tara?" he asked.

"Yeah, it's the same guy. I called him last night and told him what happened and of my suspicions."

"Well everyone, it's time for me to bounce," Sherita said. "I have a client to see."

"I guess your work here is done," I smiled at her, referring to her gossip about me and Dennis. She ignored me and walked over to Aunt June.

"I'm glad you're alright Auntie J. If you need me for any- thing, give me a call."

"Okay, baby. Thanks for coming by."

As Sherita headed out the door, Houston and the twins were coming in. "Mommy! Mommy! We went to the park!" Kianna loudly announced.

"That's good, baby. Did you guys have a good time?"

"Yesss," they both sang out.

"Dennis, this is my brother-in-law, Houston Kingsley, and my niece and nephew, Kianna and Kyle. This is my good friend, Dennis Wiley," I said to Houston and the kids.

"Come on, kids. Let's go upstairs and get cleaned up," Denise said to the twins.

"Had you been here earlier when Sherita was here, Houston, she would have informed you that Dennis is a detective from New York," I said. "He's here working on a case."

"Oh, yeah? That's great. I'm sure that must be a very challenging job," Houston said as he and Dennis shook hands.

"Yeah, it certainly is. But right now I'm concerned about the things Tara has been telling me about this Stan character."

"Yeah, now that's someone I would like to reach out and touch," Houston angrily said.

"Will you two be staying for dinner?" Aunt June asked.

"Well, actually, we had planned on going out to dinner."

"Child, don't be ridiculous!" Aunt June said. "You mean to tell me you're gonna pass up a good home cooked meal for something out of a restaurant!"

"Well Auntie, I didn't think you'd be up to cooking today."

"Tara, now you know nothing would stop me from getting in that kitchen and cooking up something. I know you two want to spend time alone, but that's no reason to turn down a good home-cooked meal, so y'all stay for dinner then get on out of here."

"Okay Auntie, we'll do that. Thanks."

"You shoot pool, Dennis?" Houston asked.

"Yeah man, I do."

"Then let's go downstairs and play a couple of games until dinner's ready."

"Girl, that man know he fine," Aunt June said once Dennis and Houston were out of earshot. "Are you two officially dating?"

"Naw Auntie, we're just friends for now. But you are right, he definitely is easy on the eyes, and he's such a sweetie-pie," I said as we headed for the kitchen to make dinner. Once Denise was finished bathing the twins, she came in to join us. After dinner was ready and the table had been set, I went downstairs to get Houston and Dennis. They were sitting on the sofa facing one another, very deep into their conversation. Since they were talking in such low tones, I was unable to make out what they were saying.

Once they saw me, their postures changed and so did their conversation. I glanced over at the pool table and noticed that it hadn't been touched. I didn't know what they'd been doing down there, but it certainly didn't involve shooting pool. I was pretty certain it did have something to do with Stan.

"Hey pretty lady," Dennis said as he stood up, wrapping his arms around me.

"Hey yourself. Dinner is ready, so if you guys are through with your whispered conversation, come on up."

"Ladies, this looks and smells delicious," Dennis said as he sat down at the table to a meal consisting of pot roast, mashed potatoes with gravy, macaroni & cheese, and green beans. "Is dinner like this every night?" Dennis asked Houston.

"Yeah man, it's a wonder we're all not big as a house with the way these ladies cook."

"You know you love it," Denise laughed as she sat down next to Houston. We all said grace then started to chow down. Houston was quiet throughout dinner and seemed preoccupied. I felt the only reason Dennis was talking was because Aunt June and Denise were asking him questions, but otherwise, he too seemed to be deep in thought, like his mind was elsewhere. I noticed he and Houston would occasionally glance at each other with a knowing look. It was killing me to know what they'd been discussing downstairs. Once we'd finished eating and cleared the table, I offered to clean up the kitchen.

"No," Aunt June said, "you and Dennis get on out of here and go spend some time together."

"Yeah, I'll clean the kitchen," Houston volunteered.

"Well okay, if you insist," I said.

"It was a pleasure meeting all of you," Dennis said. "I hope I can get a chance to see you all again before I leave Chicago, but if not, I'm sure I'll see you all again in the future. Thanks for the delicious meal."

"We enjoyed having you here Dennis. You're welcome here any time," Denise said.

"Yeah man," Houston said as he gave Dennis some dap, "I'm glad we met and got a chance to talk."

"No problem, bro'. Miss June, again, I'm sorry about your accident and I'd be interested to know what the inspection of your car turns up," Dennis said. "But I do have one very important question."

"What's that?" Aunt June asked.

"Does good cooks run in your family?" he laughed.

"Boy, you crazy!" Aunt June laughed, "But I'm gonna let you find that out on your own."

"So, what do you think of my family?" I asked Dennis on the drive back to my place.

"I like them. They're good people."

"Yeah, they are. Houston's a good man; really smart and great to talk to."

"We were talking about your ex, okay?"

"Wha.... what are you talking about?" I innocently said.

"Tara, I know it's killing you to know what we were talking about in the basement, so stop trying to be slick with me," he laughed.

"I'm not trying to be slick. I just want details. Exactly what were you discussing about Stan?"

"Nothing specific, just talking about what he's done and what can be done legally to stop his little sick antics."

"Oh, okay," I said, not really satisfied with his answer. My intuition told me there was something he wasn't sharing with me.

"So tell me more about when you snuck into his house. That place sounds kinda fascinating with the hidden rooms and stuff."

So I told him everything I knew about Stan's house; the hidden rooms and staircases, and how I managed to figure out the code for the bedroom. Dennis listened intently, occasionally interrupting me with questions, which I gladly answered.

"Why don't you pull around to the parking garage?" I said when we arrived at my building. "Unless you're in a hurry to get back to your empty, lonely hotel room."

"As a matter of fact, I am. So I'm just gonna slow down a bit and you can jump out," he said as he looked at me, trying to keep a straight face. I was cracking up as I pointed to the entrance for the garage. I noticed Manny standing in front of the building. He smiled and nodded when he recognized me.

* * *

"Well, get comfortable and make yourself at home," I said to Dennis once we were inside the apartment. "Would you…." I trailed off as I looked around, sniffing the air.

"What's wrong Tara?"

"Nothing," I slowly said. "I thought I smelled something," I said, shaking my head, almost certain I'd smelled the faint aroma of Stan's cologne. *You're bugging out, Tara,* I thought to myself as I turned on the television and sat on the sofa.

"You mind if I kick my shoes off?" Dennis asked as we sat talking.

"Of course not. I told you to make yourself comfortable," I said as he began removing his shoes and socks. "Dag man, you've got some pretty feet," I said, marveling at his well manicured, perfectly shaped feet.

"Yeah, I'm just pretty from head to toe," he said, stretching out and resting his feet in my lap.

"And you're crazy, too!" I said. I started massaging his feet while he closed his eyes, sighing.

"Ummm, that feels good. You have really strong hands."

"You're not falling asleep on me, are you?"

"Well, I gotta confess. If you keep massaging my feet like that, I will be."

"In that case," I said, lifting his feet off my lap and placing them on the sofa, "I think you'd better put your shoes back on."

"Aw, come on, baby. Don't treat a brother like that."

"A brother is not about to lay here and fall asleep on a sister. Now I'm gonna fix us a couple of drinks. You pick out a movie to watch."

"Okay, little miss party-pooper."

"Here you are, big baby," I said, handing him his drink. "So what movie did you choose?"

"Love & Basketball. I know it's old, and I'm probably one of a few black people who hasn't yet seen it, but if you'd like to watch something else, I don't mind."

"No, this is cool. I don't mind watching it again. Why don't you stretch out on the sofa? I'll get comfortable right here on the floor," I said as I sat down with my back rested against the sofa.

"Can I take my shirt off?"

"Oh, please do," I said in anticipation as he removed his shirt, placed it on the arm of the sofa and laid back. We sat watching the movie, laughing and commenting on certain scenes as Dennis played with my hair while I rested my head against his chest. It was so soothing and relaxing that I found myself dozing off. I woke up when I noticed that he'd stopped stroking my hair. I was about to complain when I discovered why he'd stopped; he was sound asleep. I went in the bedroom and got him a blanket and pillow. As I slid the pillow beneath his head, I couldn't resist the urge to kiss him. I sat on the floor again, watching him as he slept, running my fingers over his face and down his chest. I was beginning to get aroused, wanting badly to awaken him and make love to him, but instead I placed the blanket over him, kissed him again on his chest and lips, then went to bed to spend my first night in my new bed, alone.

* * *

"Good morning, sleepy-head," Dennis said the next morning as I rolled over to find him sitting on the bed watching me.

"Good morning," I said. "How long have you been sitting here?"

"Not too long. About fifteen minutes or so. You look so cute when you're sleeping."

"I hope you don't mind my not waking you up last night. You were sleeping so soundly, I didn't have the heart to wake you up."

"No, that's alright. I should apologize for falling asleep on you. One minute I was watching the movie and the next thing I know, I wake up and it's daylight. You didn't put anything in my drink, did you?"

"No, of course not!"

"You didn't take advantage of me while I was sleeping, did you?"

"No, I did not."

"Damn! Why not?"

"Well excuse me. Next time I'll jump on the opportunity."

"So," he said, scooting closer to me, "what are you wearing underneath that blanket?"

"This," I said, sticking my bare leg out.

"Can I see more?"

"You certainly can," I said as I began lowering the blanket.

"Wait!" he said, putting his hand up. "Don't do that, Tara."

"Why, what's wrong?"

"Stop teasing me girl. You know if you come from beneath that blanket, I won't be able to control myself, and I've got a busy day ahead of me."

"Chicken."

"Naw baby, there's no chicken here," he said as he slowly ran his hand up my leg. "I'm not a hit it and quit it kind of guy. I believe in putting in a full day's work, and with you," he said as he grabbed my hair, pulling me closer, "I plan on putting in some overtime."

"Ohhh shit!" I said, wrapping my arms around him and kissing him passionately, not giving a damn about morning breath. I hoped he couldn't feel me shudder. His words had aroused me so much that I was cumming and could feel the warm juices wetting my inner thighs. But he knew exactly what he'd done. I felt his fingers going up my leg, then he started slowly stroking my clit. I came again, drenching his fingers with my juices.

"Now what was that you called me a minute ago?" he said as he stood up rubbing his wet fingers across his chest. "I'm gonna take a quick shower, then I must be on my way, lovely lady."

"You sexy motherfucker," I said under my breath as I watched him head into the bathroom.

* * *

"So, what time can I come over this evening?" he asked as he stood in the living room buttoning up his shirt. "Or is Roy coming over tonight?"

"Roy who?" I laughed.

After Dennis left, I was in a very upbeat mood, not to mention I was horny as hell! I decided to take a long, leisurely bubble bath, oil my body down and spend the day walking around totally nude. I spent the morning working on my website and familiarizing myself with my new computer. I also had numerous business calls I needed to make. My Midwest tour was scheduled to start in two weeks and I needed to finalize my arrangements.

All in all, I had a productive and pleasant morning. I worked until 2:00, then began cleaning the house and preparing dinner. I wanted to show Dennis that, yes, good cooks did run in my family. I also planned to prove to him that, no, I'm no chicken either.

* * *

"Hey baby," Dennis said, arriving promptly at 5:30. "Do I score points for being on time again?"

"You certainly do," I said, giving him a peck on the lips.

"You've been on my mind all day."

"I'm glad to hear that. I've been thinking of you, too."

"You look so sexy," he said while admiring me. I was wearing a strapless, black, spandex dress, which accentuated every curve on my body.

"Thank you," I said as I led him to the living room.

"Something certainly smells good."

"Thanks. We're having lasagna and shrimp salad. Can I get you a drink?"

"Yeah, I'll have whatever you're drinking."

"Okay. Two margaritas coming right up," I said, heading for the bar.

"Tara."

"Yes," I said as I stopped to see what he wanted.

"Would you just stand there for a moment? I want to look at you. It's been a long, crazy day and looking at you puts my mind at ease." So I quietly stood there, smiling at him as he sat there looking at me. I could see him loosening up as the tension left his body. Finally, he got up and walked over to me, holding me by the waist. "Thank you, baby. You're gonna make it hard for me to go back home Thursday."

"Shhh," I said, placing my fingers on his lips. "Let's not even talk about Thursday. Let's just enjoy the time we have left together. So, loosen up your tie, kick off your shoes, and we're gonna eat, drink, and be merry."

"How merry are we gonna be?"

"How much merry can you handle?"

"Hey, I'm all yours," he said, removing his tie and shoes. "Use me, baby."

"You are so bad."

We sat at the dining room table sipping our margaritas, talking, while we waited for the lasagna to warm up. As we sat there enjoying our meal, I couldn't help but laugh at how Dennis was wolfing down his food.

"I know you're not over there laughing at me," he said.

"I'm sorry, but yes, I am. You're eating like a man who hasn't had a meal in a long time."

"Yeah, well you'll have to excuse me, but this lasagna is the bomb. And I thought you couldn't cook."

"Well, I'll have you to know that I'm a woman of many skills and talents." Boy did that remark cause him to slow down. He paused with his fork in midair, eyebrows raised. "Prove it," he said.

"Oh, I intend to do just that," I said, wiping my mouth. "You finish up your dinner, I'll get our dessert." I couldn't wait for him to see how dessert was going to be served. I went into the kitchen and hurriedly prepared our baked cinnamon apples, then I ducked into the bedroom, putting my hair up in a ponytail with a bang. I changed into my costume. It was and I Dream of Jeanie outfit that I'd picked up at a costume shop.] Barbara Eden would have been proud, because I looked just like a black Jeanie. I giggled as I ran my hand over my stomach and did a couple of gyrations before going back to the kitchen to get our desserts. I waltzed into the dining room with the serving platter in one hand and my other arm waving seductively in the air, clicking my castanets. Dennis was floored, to say the least!

"Your dessert, Master," I said, placing the platter on the table as I proceeded to do my Jeanie dance, keeping my eyes on him through my veil. I did a pirouette, walked over to him with my hands in prayer fashion, and bowed. "May I?" I asked as I eyed my chair.

"Do that pirouette thing again, then you may have a seat."

"Yes, Master."

I could barely keep from laughing as I sat silently and slowly eating my dessert, while Dennis tried to control himself. He was shoveling his dessert in his mouth faster than he'd done with his dinner. I guess he wanted to hurry up and finish so he could find out what I had in store for him next.

Once I'd finished eating, I danced my way over to him, pulling his chair away from the table. "Would you like more dessert, Master?" I sexily asked as I placed my hand on my belly, gyrating my hips. He caught my meaning.

"Yes," he said lustily. "Let me taste more of your sweets."

I winked at him. I'd practiced earlier that day, wearing my extra long and thick false eyelashes, until I'd been able to wink without my eye getting stuck. Those false eyelashes really made the wink look extra sexy. I then started slowly removing my costume, doing a belly dance that would have made Wendi blush. She would have been proud to see me using some of her moves; I was definitely working it! By the time I'd finished, wearing only my leather thong, heels, and pasties, Dennis was so turned on I thought he would self-combust. I straddled him and started unbuttoning his shirt while we passionately kissed. His hands felt so good as they caressed my body. I felt I could have stayed like that for the rest of the night, but I was no fool. I was going for the gold that night.

"Damn, you feel good," he said, cupping my breasts and flicking his tongue over my nipples. "Now can I have the rest of my dessert?" he said while sliding his hands beneath my butt and lifting my crotch up to his face. As soon as he had me right where he wanted me, he started slowly and teasingly licking and sucking while I laid there with my head rested on his lap and my legs in the air, moaning.

"Oh, baby, I like that. Ohhh, that feels so good," I moaned as I wrapped my legs around his head, enjoying the pleasure he was giving me. My body tensed up and I started shaking from the force of my orgasm. I unlocked my legs from around his head. He grabbed my arms and gently lifted me up, cradling and caressing me while I sat on his lap panting, trying to catch my breath. "Yeah baby," he said, stroking my back, "I like your desserts. Hot. Sweet. Sticky." His words were so intoxicating and the bulge in his pants was throbbing, begging to be set free. As I started kissing him, the smell and taste of myself on his lips took me to another level. I had to have him right then and there. I dropped to my knees, unzipping and removing his pants and briefs so quickly you would have thought I was a magician. I stood back up, straddling him, as he grabbed my butt and licked my navel. I placed my hands on his shoulders and lowered myself onto his rock-hard penis, gasping as he entered me. I continued lowering myself until he was completely inside me. "Ride me, baby," he said, burying his face in my chest and squeezing my butt. And that's exactly what I did. I rode him like he was a horse and I was his jockey. (Hey, maybe that would be the next costume I wore for him.) I don't know what had me more excited, feeling his throbbing dick sliding in and out of me, or the downright nasty things he was saying to me. That just made the sex ten times mo' better.

"Look at ya', girl! You know how to work this pussy don't ya?" he said as he wrapped his arms around me and stood up just as I was cumming. "Ohh Dennis baby," I moaned as my pussy took on a mind of its own; clenching and releasing his dick, drenching it in my cum. "Ohhh yeah baby, this pussy is so hot and tight," he said. I wrapped my legs tightly around his waist while he pounded me fast and furious. I felt him tense up and I knew it was only a matter of minutes before he joined me. "Oh Tara, baby, you feel so good! Oh shit! Umm." We both were talking and moaning so that I couldn't tell which one of us was saying what. All I knew was that I was in heaven and this man had some good sex. "Yes, yes, yes," he moaned as I felt him release.

"I need a cigarette," I said when I'd unwrapped my legs from around his waist and stood there hugging and leaning against him.

"You don't smoke."

"Oh yeah, that's right. Well, I need to lay down. I can't feel my legs." He laughed, picking me up and carrying me into the bedroom.

"I'll be right back," he said. He came back a few moments later carrying two glasses of juice and a wet bath towel. "You just lay there and relax, catch your breath, drink your juice," he said while wiping me down. "I'm not through with you yet."

Boy! He didn't lie about that one. We made wild, kinky passionate love into the wee hours of the morning. That man definitely had staying power. And so did I. We couldn't seem to get enough of each other as we licked, kissed and explored every inch of each other's bodies. Finally, we collapsed into each other's arms, exhausted and spent. We both fell into a deep, sound sleep.

We awoke later that morning around 10:00 a.m. "Good morning," we said in unison, laying there looking into each other's eyes, smiling. We stayed like that for about ten minutes, silently communicating with each other until I rolled him over on his back and mounted him. I knew we didn't have much time and he had to leave, so I didn't mind having a quickie. As I pinned his arms above his head, looking quietly and lovingly into his eyes with my breasts gently brushing against his face, I slowly slid up and down on his throbbing penis until we both simultaneously climaxed.

"Thank you," I whispered while kissing him. "You're welcome," he breathlessly whispered back.

This time he'd brought a change of clothes with him, saving him a trip back to his hotel. As we showered together, I stood behind him, soaping his body with my hands. "You have such a beautiful body," I said, rubbing my hands over him. "But I'm sure you must hear that all the time."

"Yeah, women are blowing up my pager 24/7. Phoning my house, even taking ads out in the paper telling me that."

"Oh, is that right?" I said, smacking him on the ass.

"Hey!" he said turning around and grabbing me. "Watch the rough stuff. I'm only teasing with you, that's all."

"You'd better be," I said as we stood there with the warm water running over our bodies. "Whatever women were doing in the past, I'm not concerned with. I just know that from here on out they better back off."

"Ohhh, it sounds like I've been chosen," he said, picking me up and entering me.

"Yes you have been," I said as we had our second quickie that morning.

* * *

"Dennis," I said, sitting on the bed drying my hair while he got dressed, "Why don't you check out of your hotel and stay here with me? I'll take you to the airport tomorrow."

"Thank you," he said, pulling me to my feet. "Your wish is my command, Jeannie."

"Stop it!" I laughed, blushing.

"Oh, so you're blushing now. Last night you had me blushing. And I wanna thank you for it. Everything about last night was beautiful," he said, cupping my face in his hands. "Thank you, baby. I don't know how I'm gonna get on the plane tomorrow."

"Yeah, I know," I said, hugging him tightly, "but we'll have to be strong for each other. And besides, we still have tonight."

"And I can't wait to get back here. What are your plans for tonight? A cute little nurse's outfit?"

"Yeah," I said, rubbing my hands over his penis. "I'm gonna be the head nurse."

"Oh Lord, give me strength," he said, placing his hand over his heart.

"But first we're gonna let the kid in us come out. We're going to DisneyQuest."

"I've heard about that place. It's supposed to be lots of fun."

"It is. You'll see. You just hurry back," I said, walking him to the door.

"I'll see you later, baby."

I spent the day running errands, thinking about Dennis, reading and answering e-mails, thinking about Dennis, working on the outline for my next book, thinking about Dennis, and thinking about Dennis some more. "Damn! I must be sprung!" I said aloud. I decided to give Connie a call to thank her for intro- ducing me to Dennis and to assure her that I would be placing her in my will.

* * *

"Well, here I am," Dennis said when he returned that after- noon around 4:00.

"Wow! I hadn't expected you back so soon. But I'm glad you're here."

"I want to spend as much time with you as I can. Plus, I think I'm sprung," he laughed, heading for the bedroom with his bags.

"Are you sure it's me you couldn't wait to see, or are you just anxious to get to DisneyQuest?"

"Okay, okay. You got me, it's both. But mainly," he said, taking me in his arms, "it's you. I can't seem to get enough of you. I've spent the entire day walking around with my dick harder than Chinese algebra."

"Well we can't have that, now can we?" I said, unbuckling his pants. "Let me give you a little appetizer of what's in store for you tonight, and show you why I'm the head nurse."

"Ohhh yeah," he moaned as I took him in my mouth. "Ohhh yeah girl, you do that just the way I like it. Now I see why you're the head nurse." I continued licking and sucking until I felt him tense up. (Now I know you're wondering: did she or didn't she swallow. Ha, ha. I'll never tell. Draw your own conclusions.)

"Thank you, baby. Now let me take a quick shower, throw on some jeans, and we can go play," he said, removing his suit.

* * *

We spent five hours at DisneyQuest. I couldn't believe we'd been there so long, but we were busy acting like overgrown kids and having loads of fun, and since they would soon be closing down for good, I wanted to enjoy myself as much as possible. Dennis couldn't get enough of the virtual rafting, and I was in love with the virtual rollercoaster. We had a great time together and I tried hard not to think about him leaving the next day. *Oh well, Tara, be strong. You can do it!* I thought as we shared a kiss.

"I had a ball! That place was more fun than I even expected," Dennis said on the ride back to my place. "I had no idea you were such an overgrown kid."

Me? Kyle and Kianna don't carry on the way you did. Running from room to room, pouting when the ride was over, spilling ice cream all over your shirt."

"Yeah, I guess you're right," he laughed. "But now I'm beat. I can't wait to get back to your place and get some sleep."

"Yeah, me too," I yawned, "straight to bed and to sleep." We cut our eyes over at each other and started cracking up.

"Sleep, my foot. Woman, you about to get a serious workout."

"I hope that's a promise."

"Hey, I can show you better than I can tell you."

And boy did he show me! The sex that night was so, so, so, damn good. I was screaming out his name, he was screaming out my name, and there were times when I think we were screaming out our own names. Ohh wee! That man had every nerve in my body tingling. *Yes, this man is definitely a keeper,* I thought, as we collapsed on the bed panting and out of breath.

"I love you, Tara," was the last thing I heard as we both drifted off into a blissful sleep.

When we awoke the next morning around 11:30, we lay there holding one another, not saying anything. Neither of us was looking forward to his leaving. "Damn you, woman," he said as he ran his hands down my backside. "Why'd you have to go and get all up under my skin?"

"Are you trying to say you're sprung?"

"Like an over-wound clock."

"Ha, ha. Well, you're not alone. You got me sprung, whipped and feeling like a dope-fiend. I'm addicted to you and I just can't get enough of you."

"So what are we going to do about it?" he said, sitting up.

"Dennis," I said, sitting up to face him. "I've fallen in love with you and I'm so glad you came into my life. I'm no more looking forward to you leaving than you are. I wish I could chain you to this bed and never let you leave."

"You wouldn't get any resistance from me on that one."

"Yeah, I know," I laughed. "But we knew what we were getting into before we started this. Now we're just gonna have to be strong and realistic and do whatever it takes to make this work, because I have no intentions of letting you out of my life. I think we'll be spending a lot of time on the phone and running up those frequent flyer miles. I know maintaining a long distance relationship is hard and damn near impossible to do, but if this is what we want, then we'll work it out."

"Woman, where were you five or ten years ago?"

"You weren't ready for all of this back then," I said, running my hands over my body.

"Well I'm ready for it now," he said, pushing me back down and laying on top of me.

"Yes, you are," I said, reaching down and guiding him inside me. I lay there gazing into his eyes as he pinned my hands above my head, slowly stroking me just the way I liked it. Neither of us said a word, just looked into each other's eyes. "Oh, oh, oh," I moaned as he pulled back, hesitated, then plunged inside of me, shuddering.

* * *

An hour later we were in the kitchen preparing lunch. Dennis in his briefs, and me in nothing but heels, at his request. We were sharing jokes with each other; some funny, some down- right corny. By the time we were ready to eat, we were laughing so hard we could barely manage to eat our food without cracking up. But everything was so delicious that we were finally able to get our outbursts under control. While we were clearing the table, the phone rang. "Excuse me," I said, reaching over to grab the phone. "Hello. Detective Barnes, how are you? Uh-huh, yes. That doesn't surprise me," I said as Dennis sat there watching me, patiently waiting for me to hang up. "Thank you for calling. Yes, I won't hesitate to call you."

"That didn't sound too good," Dennis said when I hung up.

"No, it wasn't. Detective Barnes said Aunt June's car was definitely tampered with. He also said he checked with Stan's family in Louisiana. They say he was there, but that was almost three weeks ago."

"So he's back here in Chicago?"

"Detective Barnes thinks so, but he's not sure. He's been by Stan's a couple of times, but he's never there and the young man who's house sitting swears he hasn't seen him in over two weeks. He says Stan called to say he would be home Monday."

"Personally, I think he's here staying in a hotel or some-where he can't be found, and he's using Louisiana as an alibi so he can't be tied to what's going on here," Dennis said, looking concerned.

"Well can't the police check the airport to find out when he left for and returned from Louisiana? Or find out if he's used his credit card to check into any hotels?"

"Yeah, they could if they felt it was necessary, but technically, he hasn't committed any crimes. His fingerprints haven't been found anywhere, yet. He hasn't been seen doing anything. Everything is circumstantial."

"Well I know he's behind this bullshit!"

"Baby, I know he is, too," Dennis said, taking me in his arms. "But I don't want you to worry. I want you to be careful, though, and keep your guard up at all times. I promise you, nothing's going to happen to you."

"How can you be so certain? And besides, I'm not worried about me. It's my family and friends I'm concerned for."

"Tara, I love you and if anybody fucks with you, then they're fucking with me. I don't take too kindly to being fucked with. You do remember that I am a detective, too? I haven't been here in Chicago just working on my case. I've been doing a little detecting of my own and I've pretty much found out the same things as Detective Barnes. But since this is personal for me, I don't plan on resting until you are satisfied that he won't be harassing or threatening you or yours ever again. So even though I'm going back home today, I want you to rest assured that I will make this alright."

"So what do you plan on doing?"

"Shh," he said, placing a finger over my lips. "You let me do what I do best, and you do what you do best."

"And just what is that?"

"Being your sweet, sexy, fine, smart, and funny self. Now put a smile on this lovely face and let me spend the rest of the day showing you how much I love you."

"Your wish is my command, Big Daddy."

* * *

"Well baby, this is it. The moment we've both dreaded," I said when we arrived at the airport later that day, both of us wearing smiles big and bright enough to light up the entire airport.

"Yeah," he said, taking me in his arms, "here we are."

"Is that a tear I see in your eye?" I said, smiling up at him.

"Don't be silly. Of course not. I just have something in my eye."

"I love you, Dennis," I said, clinging to him. "I'm gonna miss you so much. And I'm gonna have such a huge phone bill!"

"Me too baby, me too. But look, I want you to remember what I told you this morning. Keep your guard up and be careful. I'll let you know what I find out about that piece of shit."

"Okay baby, I will," I said as his flight was called. We embraced one another, kissing passionately and hungrily, ignoring the stares of people around us, until we could no longer postpone the inevitable and he headed for his flight. I stood in the terminal and watched until his plane was off the ground, then headed for my car and what would surely be a lonely home. "I guess I'm about to find out what it's like when a hype goes through detox, because I'm about to go through Dennis with- drawal," I said aloud, getting in my car.

TWENTY NINE

"Miss St. Pierre, it's Ralph."

"Yes, Ralph," I said, wondering why he was buzzing me at 10:00 in the morning.

"I have a package here for you. It looks like a gift. Could you come down and get it? I'm here by myself, otherwise I'd bring it up to you."

"Okay, Ralph, I'll be right down." *Dag, my baby sent me a gift already,* I thought as I grabbed my keys and headed down- stairs. "Ralph, I thought today was your day off," I said, going over to the desk.

"It was, but Manny just upped and quit; no notice or nothing. Said something about coming into some money and going back to Mexico."

"Now that was rude and inconsiderate."

"Tell me 'bout it. But at least it gives me a chance to see your pretty face," he said, winking at me.

"Uh-huh. So is this my package?" I asked, eyeing the beautifully wrapped box on the desk.

"Yep, that's it. Looks like somebody's thinkin' of you," he said, waiting for me to open it.

"Yes, well thank you, Ralph. I hope they're able to find a replacement for Manny soon," I said, heading for the elevator. I couldn't wait to see what was inside the box, so I ripped it open while on the elevator. Inside was a videocassette tape. There was no note or return address. I started feeling a little uncomfortable, doubting whether the box was from Dennis. As soon as I was inside, I immediately popped the tape in the VCR and sat down. I watched in stunned silence and disbelief at a tape showing clips of me at various times in my home. I watched as I walked naked through the house; I watched myself using the toilet and bathing; but mostly I watched me and Dennis making love during the days he was here. All of our intimate moments on tape, courtesy of Stan Bishop! Once the tape ended, I sat there paralyzed, unable to move. That motherfucker had again been in my home even after I'd had the locks changed. I started slowly looking around, wondering when and where he'd planted cameras. I thought back to the day I'd come home and was certain I'd smelled his cologne. I calmly picked up the phone and called Detective Barnes.

"Miss St. Pierre, I was just about to call you. There's some- thing I think you need to see. May I come to your home?"

"Yes, please do. There's something I think you need to see, also."

"Alright, then. I'll be there within the hour."

* * *

"Thanks for coming right over, detective."

"You sounded shaken up on the phone. Has something happened?"

"Yes. This has happened," I said picking up the tape. "It came today, very nicely gift wrapped. It's a tape of me here in my home, in my bathroom, even intimate moments in my bedroom."

"I see. So I assume you'd rather I not watch it."

"Exactly. There are some very personal and intimate things on it."

"Well it's obvious Mr. Bishop or someone has had the opportunity to get in here and plant cameras. I'll take a look around and see if I can find any, and I'll also have a specialist come out. But with today's technology and the size of cameras, he could have planted them anywhere and we might never find every one."

"Now that's a comforting thought," I said, rolling my eyes. "I just have no idea how he could have gotten in here. After the rats incident, I had my locks changed. Besides myself, the only ones with keys are my friend Sherita and building management."

"Miss St. Pierre, I think I can solve that mystery for you. I have a tape here you should see. It's from the building security camera." I popped the tape in and watched what appeared to be a pretty normal day of people coming and going. "You can fast forward it," Detective Barnes said.

"Okay," I said, hitting the button on the remote control.

"Okay, stop right there."

I watched as someone stood at the desk talking to Manny. I couldn't tell who it was at first because he managed to stay out of view of the camera, only exposing his arm. I could see the man handing Manny a stack of money and Manny giving the man a set of keys. The man got on the elevator, exiting at my floor, still managing to stay out of view of the camera.

"I tried to talk with Mr. Hermosa about the nature of his business transaction, but it seems he's quit his job and returned to Mexico."

"Yeah, so I hear. That dirty little bastard!"

"But as you can see from the tape, we still have no proof that it's Mr. Bishop because he manages to keep himself from being captured by the camera."

"Oh it's him alright," I said, pressing the rewind button. "Okay," I said, pausing it at the part where Mr. Mystery Man handed Manny the money. "You see that ring?"

"Yes."

"I gave Stan that ring."

"You're sure that's the ring?"

"I'm 110% positive."

"Alright, then that's good enough for me. Mr. Bishop's house guest says he's due home on Monday, so

I'll be there waiting to talk to him. Now I'll take a look around and see if I can't find those cameras."

By the time Detective Barnes was done, he'd found five cameras. He left me with the comforting words of his certainty that there would probably be more. "I'll give you a call and let you know when someone can come out to sweep the place and find the rest of them."

"Thank you, Detective Barnes."

After seeing him out, I sat on the sofa looking around, no longer feeling comfortable in my own home. In a short period of time, Stan had managed to take a place which I'd loved and turned it into a place where I no longer felt relaxed and at peace. My home was no longer home, and no matter what anyone said or did, it would never again feel right to me. As much as I hated to, I knew the only thing left for me to do would be to move. "Out of all the thousands of people who die each day, why couldn't today be Stan's day?" I yelled out, reaching for the phone.

"Hello."

"Hey Dennis, what's up?"

"Nothing much, babe. I was just about to leave for work. Are you okay? You don't sound right."

"No, I'm not okay," I said, fighting back tears. I told Dennis about the cameras and the tape Stan had sent, and the tape Detective Barnes had shown me. I also told him of my feelings about my home and my plans to move.

"Tara, I've got some vacation time coming up. I just need about two days to clear up some things here and then I'm coming to Chicago. In the meantime, why don't you go stay with your family or with Sherita?"

"Okay, baby, I think that's what I'll do," I said as the tears began to fall. "I though that box was from you," I choked.

"I'm sorry, baby," Dennis said as I heard his voice catch. "You just hold it together, okay? Don't let that motherfucker get the best of you."

"Alright, I'll try. You just hurry up and get here. I need you.

* * *

As soon as he'd hung up, Dennis immediately placed a quick call to request some vacation time. After that, he made another call, one, which lasted much longer, and which he hoped would not come back to haunt him. But he would cover his ass as best he could. All he knew was that he would do whatever it took to keep his baby safe and happy.

* * *

After talking with Dennis I felt a little better; glad he would be coming back. I started calling around, setting up appointments to look at some other places. The sooner I was able to move from here, the happier I would be. I knew I wouldn't have any problems breaking my contract since it was partly management's fault that I was moving in the first place. I called Sherita to let her know of Stan's latest piece of work and to inform her that she would be having a houseguest for an indefinite period of time. "Ohhh, that's good girl! Well, you coming to stay with me is good, not that shit Stan did. Now I'll have someone to keep the place clean for me."

"Sherita! Don't tell me you've managed to turn your place into a pigsty again."

"Naw girl, I'm just messing with you. You will be pleased to know that I've turned over a new leaf and I manage to keep the place clean and tidy. But look, Ta, you know you're always welcome at my place, so whenever you're ready, come on over. I won't be in until late tonight, so use your key. And one more thing," she said, stifling a laugh.

"What's that?"

"Bring that tape with you. I wanna see ol' boy in action."

"I will not! You are one twisted sister, you pervert." I laughed, glad for Sherita's ability to always be able to make me laugh, regardless of the circumstances.

I decided to make the most of the day before I left, so after fixing myself a nice meal, I did some cleaning, then packed the things I would be taking with me to Sherita's. Periodically, I would throw up my middle finger, just in case there were cameras Detective Barnes had missed. It was around 4:00 when I was finally ready to leave. As I was heading through the house with my bags, the phone rang. "Hello."

"Tara, I'd almost forgotten how acrobatic you are in the bedroom," Stan said. "If it weren't for the fact that you're a cheating little bitch, I would have gotten turned on watching you in action. I wonder if your fans would like to see you sucking a cock?"

"Motherfuck you, Stan! You are one sick ass piece of shit!" I said, hanging up the phone. I stood there trembling, furious at that crazy asshole, at myself for ever getting involved with him, at his parents for conceiving him, at God for creating him! I looked at my caller ID, surprised to see that he was calling from a 312 area code, which meant he was here in Chicago. His arrogant ass wasn't even trying to hide where he was calling from. I dialed the number and after about ten rings, someone answered. "Hello?"

"Yes, someone just called me from this number and I'm wondering whose number this is."

"Ma'am, this is a pay phone at the Hilton Towers."

"Tha, thank you," I said, totally shaken and surprised to find out that he was only blocks away from my place. I immediately phoned Detective Barnes.

"How long ago did he phone you?"

"Just moments ago."

"Did he threaten you?"

"He implied that he would make sure others saw copies of that tape."

"And you say he was calling from the Hilton Towers?"

"Yes."

"Okay, I'll check into that and see if he's registered there or at any hotels in the area. Are you going to be okay?"

"You know what, detective? I'm sick and tired of this shit! Of being harassed, followed, stalked, taped. Of having my family and friends attacked and being afraid. Now I'm sure you're gonna do your job, but I'm gonna do mine also, and I hope to God that you find him before I do. I can guarantee you if I find him first, I'm gonna put more lead in him than a number 2 pencil."

"Now Ms. St. Pierre, I understand how you must feel, but please let me do my job. Don't go taking the law into your own hands."

"Yeah, whatever," I said, hanging up the phone. I sat there a few moments, giving myself time to calm down before leaving. "Yeah, two can play this game," I said, fishing through my purse. "Now I know I put those keys in this purse," I said, dumping the contents of the purse on the floor. I had no idea what my plan was, but I knew I needed to get back into Stan's house. The only problem was, the keys I was certain were in my purse, were now gone.

THIRTY

As Jeremy and I sat on the sofa facing one another in the early morning hours, with the first signs of daylight beginning to peek through, he looked intently at me.

"Wow. You certainly lead an interesting life," he said as he stood up and stretched. "And it's been, what, four weeks since Stan called taunting you about the tape?."

"Five, actually. Hell, I don't even know why the police are assuming he's missing or why they might think he's dead. Which would be a good thing."

"I did some checking before I came to pick you up, and it seems Stan phoned the young man who was house sitting for him and told him that he would be coming home not on Monday like he had stated, but on the following Wednesday. He was told he could leave on Tuesday, and to stop by that Friday to pick up his pay. Well, it seems he goes by there on Friday as scheduled, finds the front door closed but not locked and when he goes inside there's overturned furniture and blood in the hallway and living room, but no sign of Stan. The police were called and it seems that you stated to Detective Barnes that if you caught Stan before they did, that you planned on doing some harm to him. And since it's now been over four weeks and Stan hasn't been seen or heard from...... Well, I'm sure you see how that looks. His appointment book was found and it seems he had some important business meetings scheduled that his family insists he wouldn't have missed. And based on that, it's being assumed that you might have carried out your promise."

"That's bullshit! Look, I stayed at Sherita's for a couple of days until Dennis got here and then we stayed at a hotel for the two weeks he was here. We spent that time looking for a place for me to move to. As you can see, I still haven't finished unpacking. We had two of the most wonderfully happy, erotic weeks of my life. I would tell you about them but I don't want you trying to steal my man when you two get a chance to meet."

"Oh, now that's cold. You know I would never try to steal your man. Besides, it sounds like you've got the man eating out of your hand and loving your funky drawers."

"Ha, ha. Yeah anyway, I managed to put Stan out of my mind and I didn't think anything about him until Detective Ziegler showed up asking me to come to the station to answer some questions regarding a missing person. He wouldn't tell me who it was until I got there. When he did, I got pissed off and told him if Stan was missing, then that was a good thing. That's when he said I was being uncooperative and placed me in a cell, and I phoned you."

"Ziegler's an asshole. He was just trying to scare you."

"Well he did. With that ugly ass mug of his!"

"Well I've spoken to Detective Barnes and he's agreed to come here and take your statement later today, if that's good for you."

"Yeah, today is cool. I'm leaving for New York tomorrow and I want to get this shit over with. I'll take a polygraph test if necessary. I have nothing to hide because I don't know where Stan is."

"Okay, Tara. I'll call Barnes and set it up for 5:00. Why don't you get some rest and I'll see you then?"

"Alright, Jeremy," I said, getting up to give him a hug and kiss. "Thanks for looking out for me."

"That's what friends are for," he smiled as he headed out the door. As soon as he'd left, I immediately peeled off my clothes, flopped down on the sofa and fell into a deep sleep. When I awoke, it was 3:45. I got up to take a hot bath and eat something before Jeremy and Detective Barnes arrived. I tried to keep myself occupied and not focus on my meeting with Barnes, but I couldn't help feeling nervous and jittery. Finally, Jeremy arrived and Detective Barnes showed up ten minutes later. We sat around making small talk for a few minutes. Detective Barnes apologized because I'd been placed in a cell. "But a man is missing, blood was found in his home, and you did threaten to harm him," he said, looking intently at me. And so began his interview. I managed to stay calm, answering his questions truthfully and convincingly with Jeremy advising me on which questions I didn't have to answer. All in all, it went pretty well and after forty minutes of questions, Barnes said goodnight.

"If I have any more questions, I'll give you a call."

"Alright, but I'm flying out to New York tomorrow for a week," I said, walking him to the door. "You can leave me a voicemail and I'll call you back."

"That will be fine," he said, heading for the elevator.

"Well sweetheart, are you feeling better now?" Jeremy asked, massaging my shoulders.

"Much better. Thank you for everything, Jeremy. I love you."

"I love you back," he said, hugging me. "I'll get on outta here now so you can get ready for your trip. Going to see your sweetie, huh?"

"Yeah, I miss him."

"Well, you enjoy yourself and try to put this business with Stan behind you. But I want you to remember, not only are you one of my dearest friends, but we do have attorney/client privilege. So if there's anything you want to share with me, you know you can."

"Jeremy, I swear I have no idea what's happened to Stan," I said, walking him to the door. *At least not yet,* I thought as I kissed him on the cheek. I knew in my heart that Dennis knew something about Stan's disappearance, and now that I'd spoken with the police and told them the truth—that I didn't know where Stan was or what, if anything, had happened to him—now I could know the truth with a good, clear conscience.

After I'd finished packing, I called Denise to find out how everyone was doing. "Oh girl, we're all fine. The kids were asking about you today."

"Give them a big hug and kiss for me. I'll bring them something back from New York."

"Okay, I will. Aunt June is at the boat cleaning out the slots."

"Man, that woman has great luck with those machines," I exclaimed.

"Girl, don't she? And she says to hell with anyone who has something to say about her going to the boat to gamble," Denise laughed.

"Hey, I ain't mad at her. So how's Houston doing?"

"He's fine. Right now he's in the garage working on my car."

"Did he ever tell you how he got that gash on his head?"

"He says he slipped and hit his head on a locker one night when he and Dennis was out playing basketball with his friends Dennis, when Dennis was here in town a couple of weeks ago. But it's healed up pretty good. You can hardly see it, considering it happened about three weeks ago."

"I think it was more like four weeks ago," I said slowly. "Well Denise, I just wanted to talk to you guys before I left. I'll call you when I get back. Love ya."

"We love you too, Tara. Give Dennis a hug for us."

"Will do," I said, hanging up. I sat on the couch with my mind racing, trying to remember every second and everything that happened when Dennis was here. How many times was he away from me? Was he gone for long periods of time by himself? How many times did he and Houston get together to go hang out? Yeah, I couldn't wait to get to New York.

THIRTY ONE

"Hey pretty lady," Dennis said, walking up to me in the terminal. "How was your flight?"

"Oh, it was a typical flight, very boring. But I'm here now and damn, you look good!" I said, looking him up and down. He was wearing a white mesh tank top and white shorts which made his glistening chocolate skin look even more beautiful. I caught women and a few men giving him appreciative glances. One woman even had the nerve to come over fronting like she wanted to meet me! "Hey, you're Tara St. Pierre! I love your books. You're one of my favorite authors," she said, never once looking at me, but keeping her eyes glued on Dennis. "Is this your husband?" she asked.

"No," Dennis replied. "This is her very much in love and committed man."

"Oh, I see," she said, somewhat embarrassed. "Well, it was a pleasure meeting you," she said walking off.

"The vultures are out today," I laughed. "But I ain't mad at miss thang 'cause you are the finest thing in this airport. You got me getting moist just looking at you."

"Then come on over here and show me how glad you are to see me," he said, pulling me close as we shared a deep, intimate kiss, drawing even more attention.

"We'd better get out of here before someone calls security," I said, reluctantly stepping back.

"Hey, I'm the law and if I wanna play tongue hockey with my woman…"

"Tongue hockey! That is so ghetto," I said, laughing and punching him on the arm.

"Well if you think that's ghetto, I hope you're not offended by the Nova I drove here to pick you up in."

"A Nova! Yeah right. I'd like to see you fit into a Nova," I said as we walked outside and I scanned the area looking for his car. As we approached the curb, a limo pulled up.

"Nothing but the best for the best," he said, opening the door.

"Wow, I'm impressed," I said, getting in while he put my bags in the trunk.

"Are you comfortable back there, little lady?" the driver said, turning around.

"Jerome! Man, how you doing? I can't believe you guys. What'd you do, beat up some drug lord and confiscate his limo?" I laughed.

"Tara, I'm offended. You know we would never break the law," Jerome responded. "Just enjoy the ride, woman, and let me do my job," he said, closing the partition.

"You know, gorgeous," Dennis said, scooting closer to me, "I've missed you. A lot."

"Uh-huh," I pouted. "Then why weren't you there for me when I was chilling in a jail cell waiting for my attorney to come get me?"

"I know, baby, and I'm sorry you had to go through that, but it's over now," he said, running his fingers over my neck and chest. "But you were treated alright while you were there, weren't you?"

"Yeah, I guess so. At least they didn't have me handcuffed like some common criminal," I said, closing my eyes as he began kissing my neck.

"Being handcuffed is not always an unpleasant experience, you know," he whispered in my ear.

"Says who?" I started to say. "Hey! What tha…" I exclaimed, opening my eyes as I felt metal on my wrists. "Dennis! Take these cuffs off me."

"I will, baby. I just want you to see that being cuffed can sometimes be a good thang," he said, pushing me back on the seat as he began unbuttoning my blouse and letting his tongue work its magic on my breasts. After a few moments of pleasure, he stopped and cupped my face in his hands. "So, has your opinion changed now?"

"No!" I said stubbornly. "There is no pleasure in cuffs."

"Okay then," he said, shrugging his shoulders and sliding down on the floor. He ran his hands up my legs and started kissing my inner thighs while raising up my skirt.

"Have you lost your mind, man? Stop that!" I said as he pulled my panties to the side and started sucking and letting his fingers do the walking. In no time at all, he had me singing a different tune. "Ohhh baby, that feels good," I moaned.

"Um, hum," he mumbled as he continued pleasuring me until I came. "So, whadda you have to say now about being cuffed?" he asked while straightening out my skirt and removing the handcuffs.

"Do those come in 24kt gold?" I asked breathlessly.

"Well lady and gent," Jerome said, lowering the partition as he pulled in front of Dennis' apartment complex, "we've reached your destination. Kindly exit the vehicle and leave your tips on the seat."

"You got it, bro'," Dennis said, getting out and coming around to open my door.

"Tara, it's good to see you again. I'll catch you later," Jerome said, winking at me. "Dennis, I'll give you a call later. Now I'd better get this limo back before it's missed." I shook my head, not even wanting to know how and where they'd managed to get the car from.

"Well, here we are. Home sweet home," Dennis said as we entered his apartment. "Yeah, yeah, I know," he said as he caught me looking around. "I should get a decorator in here."

"Baby, this is such a beautiful place. You really should fix it up. And a couple of plants would be nice."

"Hey, I'm a bachelor. We're supposed to have sparsely furnished apartments."

"Says who?"

"Uh, I think I heard it on Oprah. Besides, I'm rarely at home anyway. But if it'll make you happy, I'll get a decorator in here—one day. Now get over here and show me how much you've missed me," he said, dropping my bags.

"Well, I've missed you a lot," I said, wrapping my arms around him. "So I hope you're ready for what I'm about to do to you."

"Ohhh weee! Hurt me girl!" he said as we began removing each other's clothes. After about an hour of showing each other how much we'd been missed—and boy had we missed one another—Dennis wanted to go by his mom's house. She'd been pretty sick lately and he wanted to check on her. So after we'd finished our afternoon tryst, we showered, unpacked my bags, and left for his mother's.

Sick or not, Dennis' mother was a non-stop talker, and her favorite subject was Dennis. She shared with me numerous stories about the trouble he would get into as a little boy and how athletic and smart he was. But the stories that interested me most were the ones about his previous girlfriends. "Chile, I don't know what you done to this boy, but all them women that used to call and come by here looking for him have disappeared. I don't know why he ever had 'em calling my home in the first place. He shoulda gave 'em his own number!"

"Aw Momma, that was just a playa's move. And besides, I'm here more than I'm at my place, anyway. Now would you stop telling Tara all these stories before you have her thinking she got me whipped and wrapped around her little finger?"

"Hmph. She do. I heard you talking to your Uncle Lonnie about her."

"Is that right?" I said. "And just what did he say about me?"

"Momma!" Dennis said, grabbing his mother in a bear hug and lifting her off the floor.

"Boy, put me down!"

"Only if you promise to knock it off."

"Oh alright. I promise I won't tell Tara you said you love her and no other woman has ever made you as happy as she makes you."

"Thank you, Momma, for not telling her that," Dennis said, putting her down and giving her a kiss on her forehead.

"You're welcome," she said, smiling at me.

"Is there anything you need done, Momma?"

"No, baby. I'm okay."

"You sure? You don't need anything from the store or me to cook you dinner?"

"Dennis! Boy, stop perpetrating. You know you can't cook worth a damn," she laughed. "Your sister should be here in a little bit. She's gonna fix dinner. Her cooking is edible."

"Momma, that's cold," Dennis said, pretending to be hurt.

"Don't cry, big baby," I said, patting him on the back. "You can cook for me anytime."

"Girl, you must really be in love or else you like living life on the edge."

"Miss Sadie, you are so crazy," I laughed. "Now I know where Dennis gets it from."

"Well Momma, we're gonna cut out now. I'll call you tomorrow," Dennis said, giving his mother a kiss.

"Bye, Miss Sadie. It was such a pleasure talking with you, I'm sure I'll get a chance to see you again before I go back to Chicago."

"Tara, I'm glad you came by and you're always welcome here," she said as I gave her a hug. As Dennis and I were getting in the car, I started laughing.

"What's so funny?" he asked.

"Oh I was just imagining your mother and my Uncle Sammy in a room together. Now that would be too wild."

"Yeah, judging from what you've told me about your Uncle, I agree. That would be a hell of a combination."

"So what are we gonna do now?"

"Well first we're gonna stop by this little boutique not far from here, then we're going home and I'm gonna fix us a nice meal."

"Are you sure you want to do that?" I asked, looking at him skeptically.

"Yes, I really want to stop by the boutique."

"You know that's not what I'm talking about," I said, slapping his leg.

"Look woman, I might not be much with a stove, but I'm hell with a grill."

"Sorry," I said.

"After our four star meal, we'll go by the club for a while, then come back home and I'll tattoo your forehead with the imprint from my headboard."

"Ahhh," I burst out laughing, "ha, ha, ha. That's a good one, Dennis," I said, wiping my eyes, laughing uncontrollably.

"So, what's up with the boutique?" I asked as we parked the car and headed inside.

"I saw this cold dress that has your name all over it."

"Oh, really? So tell me, do you shop here often? And if so, then for whom, 'cause I can only think of two scenarios for you coming here. Either you're here shopping with some other woman, or you're a cross-dresser. Please say it ain't so!"

"Tara, now you know I wouldn't cheat on you."

"Oh God, no! You're a cross-dresser! God, please don't let him look better in a dress than I do," I said, looking up to the heavens.

"Come here, miss funny lady," he said, grabbing me around the waist. "You'll be happy to know that neither of your scenarios are right. My cousin Yasmine owns this boutique. Now let me show you the dress I'm talking about," he said, picking out a long, powder blue dress with a slit up the front, plunging neckline and the back out. Dennis' cousin came over to greet us. "Dennis, sweetie," she said, giving him a big hug. "And this lady needs no introduction," she said turning to me and holding out her hand. "Tara, it's a pleasure to finally meet you. If I hadn't recognized you from your books—which I loved—then it would certainly have been from Dennis describing you. He talks about you all the time."

"Thanks, Yasmine. It's good to meet you, too. I'm gonna slip in the fitting room to try this gorgeous dress on. I'll be right back, baby." As I came out of the fitting room, Dennis and Yasmine stopped their conversation mid-sentence. "Damn, baby! You look so good in that dress," Dennis said as his eyes lit up.

"Yep, you were right, Dennis. That dress was certainly meant for her," Yasmine said admiringly.

"Yeah, my baby rockin' that dress!"

"Thank you," I said, giving him a peck on the lips. "You do have good taste."

"I chose you, didn't I? Yasmine, ring it up and throw in a pair of matching earrings and necklace," Dennis instructed Yasmine while I went back into the fitting room.

On the ride home, I reached over, gave Dennis another kiss and thanked him again for the gifts. "You're welcome, baby. You know there's nothing I wouldn't do for you." Hearing him say that, I decided it was a perfect cue.

"There is one thing I would really like for you to give me."

"Yeah, what's that?"

"Information. Dennis, I really need to know what happened to Stan. And I know you know."

"No," he said, looking straight ahead.

"No, what?"

"Let it go Tara, okay? Some things are best left alone."

"Dennis, I...."

"No, Tara," he adamantly said. "Now I hope that wasn't your reason for coming out here. I'd like to think you missed me and wanted to be with me."

"Dennis baby, I love you. I came here because I do miss you and if you don't want to tell me what happened, then I'll leave it alone," I said, rubbing his arm.

"Yeah, like hell you will," Dennis said, shaking his head.

Yeah, like hell I will, I thought to myself, smiling at him. *I'm not dropping shit! He's gonna tell me what happened if I have to choke it out of him.*

THIRTY TWO

"Ohhh baby, that feels so good," Dennis whispered as he lay face down, spread eagle on his bed that night while I slowly ran my tongue and a feather over his body.

"You have such a beautiful body," I whispered back, running my tongue lightly down his tight, firm ass and continuing to make my way down the entire length of his body. "Get on your knees," I commanded. He eagerly obeyed. I reached around from behind him with one hand, grabbing his rock hard, throb-bing dick while with the other hand I gently massaged his balls.

"Damn girl, you go' make me lose control in here," he gasped.

"You like that, baby?" I asked as I rubbed my breasts over his back while continuing to stroke him. "You like the way I stroke this dick? Is this my dick, baby?"

"Ohh, yes! Yes. Yes," he moaned, tensing up. "This dick is all yours."

"I love the way your dick feels in my hand," I breathed lustily in his ear. "Hard, hot, throbbing."

"Where else do you like to feel it?" he asked, wrapping his hand around mine, both of us masturbating him as he began to reach his climax. "Aw baby, I like it everywhere; my hand," I said, running my tongue down the side of his neck, "my hot, wet pussy…"

"Oh yeah, baby. That's it, that's it."

"And you know where I really like to feel this dick?" I asked, rubbing my hot, wet pussy up and down his leg.

"Where baby, where?"

"I love feeling this dick in my mouth. Oh yeah, I like that."

"Ohhh shit, Tara!" he screamed out as he came, hot juices flowing down our hands as we collapsed onto the bed.

"Damn, girl," Dennis laughed as he grabbed me, squeezing me tight. "You need to get a job working for the sperm bank. You sho' know how to get it out of there!"

"Oh, so you won't mind me handling some other man's johnson?"

"Woman, if I even thought you were entertaining the idea of doing to another man what you just done to me, I'd rip both your hands off."

"Well, sweetie," I said, kissing his chest and placing his hand between my moist thighs, "I guess my hands are safe because I belong to you. Now you catch your breath suga'. I'm not done with you."

"Is that right?" he said with excitement in his voice.

"Uh-uh. I'm gonna work you like a part-time job." And that night, that's exactly what I did; and he worked me right back. Hey, why waste time trying to choke information out of him? This way was much more pleasurable.

* * *

"Good morning, sunshine."

"Good morning, baby," I said, snuggling up next to him. "Thank you for last night. Is it my imagination or does sex with you continue to get mo' better?"

"Yeah, we do seem to compliment one another perfectly. Your little hot ass brings out the beast in me, you freak," he said, pulling me on top of him. And just like that, we were at it again.

"Tara, I love you. You're the best thing to happen to me," Dennis said to me later that day as we relaxed on the patio enjoying the day and each other. "I have something for you."

"Really," I said curiously as he moved closer to me. He took my hand in his and placed a gorgeous platinum and gold ring with a heart-shaped diamond in the center, on my finger. "Dennis! This is so beautiful!" I exclaimed.

"It's a promise ring," he said, looking deeply into my eyes. "Tara, I promise to always love you, to protect you, and to always make your happiness my number one priority. I realize having a long distance relationship is gonna be a challenge. Damn, is it a challenge! Knowing that you'll be leaving in a couple of days is killing me, but I'm willing to take this as slow or as fast as you want to take it, because I'm all yours."

"Thank you, baby," I said, fighting back the tears. "I love you, Dennis. I love you so much. You mean everything to me and I promise we will always be a part of each other's lives. I would never do anything to hurt you."

"I know, baby. I know," he said, gently kissing me.

"Dennis," I said, gazing into his eyes.

"Yeah, baby?"

"Please tell me what happened. I need to know."

"Tara," he sighed, "you're right. You have a right to know. Just promise me you'll never make me regret having told you."

"I promise."

As he got up to fix us a couple of drinks, I sat there with a mixture of anticipation, excitement, dread and fear coursing through my body, eager to finally find out exactly what had become of Stan.

THIRTY THREE

SECRETS REVEALED

"Hey Houston man, it's Dennis," Dennis said when Houston answered his cell phone.

"What's up, D? Is tonight the night?"

"Yeah, man. I'll only be in Chicago for two more days, so it's on. You sure you still wanna do this? Me and Earl can handle it."

"Come on, man, don't play me like that. I'm in. I've already told Denise we were thinking about meeting up at the gym tonight for some hoops, so just tell me when and where and I'm there."

"Well, I don't want to make you out to be a liar, so I'll meet you at the gym at 7:30."

"Cool, I'll see you there."

*   *   *

When Houston pulled up in front of the gym at precisely 7:30, Dennis and Earl were already there waiting for him. He parked his car and got in the car with them.

"Houston, this is my man Earl. He's been keeping an eye on our elusive friend for the past three days, checking out his routine."

"Hey, what's up Earl?" Houston said, giving him some dap. "Now how is it the cops can't seem to find him, but you're able to find him and keep him under surveillance for three days?"

"Well, not to take anything away from the boys in blue, but let's just say I have much better contacts and resources than they do."

"Not only that," Dennis said, "but there's not a lock he can't pick or any place he can't get in to."

"I'm impressed," Houston remarked. "I'll keep that in mind should I ever decide I want to take a tour of Fort Knox after hours."

"Ha, ha," Dennis laughed as they headed for Oak Park.

"Yeah, your boy is pretty slick," Earl said as they circled Stan's block then headed two blocks over to park the car. "He's registered in a hotel down the street from Tara's condo under one name, and registered in another hotel on the Westside, not far from where he grew up at, under another name. Every night around 10:30 he takes a cab and gets out about a block away from his home, then he jogs home. And get this, in back of his house are a lot of shrubs, so he jogs around back and ducks into the shrubs. And the boy is quick! I mean he disappears so fast it's as if he was never there."

"So what then?" Houston asked. "He hides in the bushes until he's sure no one's watching, then sneaks his punk ass in the house?"

"Man, it took me awhile to figure out where the hell he'd disappeared to, but finally I found it."

"Let me guess," Dennis interjected. "There's a hidden door somewhere."

"Bingo!" Earl said as they headed down the street to Stan's house. "Right behind the shrub is a door that's so obscure you'd have to be a genius to find it. Damn, I'm good, 'cause I found that bad boy."

"So I guess this is where your lock picking skills comes in," Houston said nodding to the bag Earl carried, as they made their way up the front steps.

"Naw man, we're gonna save those skills for later. For now we're gonna get in the old fashioned way," Dennis said, holding up the keys to Stan's house. Upon entering, they turned on their flashlights and started looking around.

"Whew! This is some kinda layout," Earl exclaimed.

"Yeah, it is," Dennis said, shining his light around. "Let's get to the garage and find the control box for these hidden rooms so we can really see what's going on here."

After about five minutes of working with his equipment on the control box, Earl was able to get the codes and all lights were green, including the one Tara was unable to figure out.

"Damn, you are good," Houston marveled.

"The best in the west," Earl said, matter-of-factly. "But now that we bust this cherry open, let's get down to business."

"Let's go upstairs first. I doubt if we'll find anything down here," Dennis said as they headed for the staircase.

"Would you look at this shit!" Houston whispered as they entered the guest bedroom, the one which was painted all black. The room was completely empty except for a life-sized photo on one wall of Tara, nude. It had been altered to show a grotesquely large rat seemingly copulating with her.

"You sick motherfucker!" Dennis shouted as he started ripping it to shreds. "As soon as he shows up, I'm'a kill him!"

"No, *we're* gonna kill him," Houston said, shaking with rage.

"I feel you," Earl said, shaking his head. "But we still got a while before he should be showing up, so why don't we finish up our tour."

They went into Stan's bedroom, carefully searching through the dresser drawers and the closet, but they could find nothing out of the ordinary. "Come on, let's go up to the attic," Dennis said, heading out the room. Once in the hallway, he made his way to the mirror and felt along the top for the latch Tara had told him about. "Bingo!" he said as the wall slid back, revealing a staircase. Earl propped a screwdriver at the top of the door to prevent it from closing. Once they'd made their way up the stairs, they found the door which concealed the attic open, and they eagerly stepped inside. As they stood in the attic, they were all momentarily speechless as they looked around at the hundreds of pictures of Tara. The walls were covered with them, ranging from wallet size to life size. There were various articles and press clippings about her. There was even some of her under-wear hanging from the walls. In one corner of the room was a mannequin wearing some of her clothing and jewelry. The room reeked of her favorite perfume.

"This has got to be the most bizarre shit I've ever seen," Houston remarked.

"Yeah man, this motherfucker is seriously twisted," Dennis replied.

"What 'cha think he's planning on doing with this?" Earl asked as they walked to the center of the room where there was a large cage bolted to the floor. In the corner of the cage was a large bucket. As they got closer, they were able to get a good look at the floor of the cage.

"Well, I guess we know what he intended to use this cage for," Houston said, astonished.

"Yeah, man," Earl joined in. "Dennis, I think this is supposed to be your new home." They stood there looking at the floor of the cage which contained a large photo of a bloated corpse on which a picture of Dennis' face had been attached. At the bottom was a banner which read: "My Home Sweet Home."

"Man, what time is it?" Dennis calmly asked.

"It's 9:50. We've still got a little time before this fucker gets home, so what'll we do now?" Earl asked.

"We rip down all of his little mementos and trash 'em."

"I'm with you, D. Maybe we should..." Earl started to say. "What the fuck was that?" They were startled by a noise coming from behind the desk. Dennis pulled out his gun, slowly going over to the desk and peering behind it.

"What is it, D?"

"Come look at this shit," Dennis said as Earl and Houston cautiously walked over, looking behind the desk.

"Goddamn! D, shoot that motherfucker!" Earl shouted, with a hint of fear in his voice.

"What the hell is this dude's fascination with rats?" Houston said angrily as they stood looking down at a cage containing a very large rat.

"Familial ties," Dennis said, walking away.

"Look man, I'm going downstairs to get a couple of garbage bags so we can take care of this shit up here and wait for this asshole to come home," Houston said, heading for the door. He made his way quickly down the stairs, heading for the kitchen where he proceeded to look for garbage bags. Finding a box of them in the pantry, he was heading through the living room when he got a very uneasy feeling. He stopped, tensing up his body as he realized he was not alone. Instinct made him crouch down and swing abruptly around, but he wasn't quick enough to avoid the blow which caught him on the temple. Ignoring the pain and the blood running down his face, he lunged forward, grabbing Stan in a bear hug as they crashed into the cocktail table. Anger and hatred took over as Houston started punching with every ounce of strength he could muster. They fought from the living room to the foyer where Stan viciously kneed Houston in the groin. As Houston went down gasping, Stan reached for the front door, struggling to open it as blood poured down his face.

"Open it, motherfucker, and the only thing that'll be on the other side are your fucking brains!" Dennis said, holding his gun to the back of Stan's head. Stan took his hands off the doorknob and Dennis savagely punched him in the kidneys then stood back as Stan slumped to the floor. "Are you alright, man?" he asked, turning to Houston.

"Yeah man, I'm okay, but my 'boys' are gonna need a couple days bed rest," he said, gingerly massaging his groin.

"Earl, look in the bathroom for some bandages so we can take care of Houston's cut before we drag this sack of shit upstairs."

"I'm on it, D."

After dragging Stan's limp body up to the attic, they dumped him in the cage, closed the door and waited for him to regain consciousness.

* * *

"Well, well, well, the master rat has awakened," Earl said when after ten minutes of waiting, Stan started to come around.

"You motherfuckers better open this goddamn door and let me the fuck outta here!" he furiously shouted.

"You best be careful what you ask for, man," Dennis said, walking closer to the cage. "I guarantee you if we open this door the only thing that'll be left of your ass will be a brown puddle in the middle of the floor, 'cause we'll happily stomp the shit outta you."

"Yeah, right," Stan remarked, yawning and looking at his watch. "Look Mr. Big Shot De-tec-tive, fuck you and your boys. And I guarantee *you*, when I get outta here all you motherfuckers are dead."

"Naw pal, I think you got it twisted. You're the dead motherfucker. What, you think we just go' let your ass go after all the bullshit you've done to my woman?" Dennis said, opening the cage and stepping inside.

"Your woman? Man, the first one of you motherfuckers I'm comin' after is that bit...." He never got a chance to finish the sentence. Dennis viciously punched him in the face, crushing his nose. Stan grabbed onto the bars to steady himself as he tried to breathe through his broken nose. Dennis grabbed him by the throat, squeezing. "I should kill your sick ass right here and now," he said, applying more pressure. "But naw, a quick death would be too good for you," he said, letting go and casually walking out of the cage, slamming the door.

"Yeah man," Earl said, stepping up to the bars. "But I got something here for you," he said, reaching inside his jacket pocket and pulling out a Snickers candy bar. "You won't be going anywhere for a while. Actually, never."

"Good one Earl," Dennis chuckled.

"So Dennis, what're we gonna do about these pictures?" Houston asked.

"Leave 'em. He can have his shrine. Earl, make sure that clown'll never be able to get out."

"That won't take but a minute," he said, removing a miniature soldering iron from his bag.

"Whooaa," Houston said, stopping Earl. He made his way to the desk, pushing it aside and cautiously lifting up the cage containing one huge, mean and ugly looking rat. Earl and Dennis looked at one another, giving a nod of approval. "Nice touch," Dennis said, giving him the thumbs up.

"Now it'll definitely be 'home sweet home'," Earl laughed as he opened the cage door for Houston who set the smaller cage inside, opening the door.

* * *

"You think that rat'll be okay in there with him?" Earl asked as they headed down the stairs, jamming the mechanism on the doors, making them literally impossible to open.

"Naw, I doubt it," Dennis remarked. "He'll probably make the rat wanna leave his ass alone, too." As they entered the garage, Earl removed the control box from the wall, sliding a cabinet over to cover the bare spot on the wall.

"Well, gentlemen, it looks like our work here is done."

* * *

"Damn!" was all I could say when Dennis finished recoun- ting the events of that night. I was left totally speechless as I tried to process what I'd just heard. Dennis reached over, removing from my hand the glass I was holding in midair. He went inside and came back with a glass of ice water and a cold towel. "Tara, breathe," he said, placing the glass in my hand and the towel on my forehead. "Are you gonna be alright?"

"Damn!" I said again, beginning to gulp the water down as I regained my composure. "You did that for me?" I asked, pulling him closer. "You really do love me," I laughed, giving him a big hug. "This is some really wild shit! And I assure you, this goes no further than here. Although I must admit, I would love to share this with Sherita. But I realize the seriousness of it, so my lips are sealed." *One day I'm gonna have to write a book about this,* I thought to myself.

I stayed in New York four more days, four glorious days with Dennis. We spent a lot of time talking. Talking about us, our future, our secret. We both needed to know if we were still okay. We were. We needed to know if this deed had shattered the foundation of our relationship. It hadn't. We were still on the same page and our feelings for one another had not been changed or stilled. I felt calm in that knowledge as I flew home on the fifth day. I was pretty solid about my feelings for Dennis, but as I sat there alone with no distractions, just the beautifully clear, blue sky before me, I had to truly examine my feelings for Stan. He was someone I'd known since childhood. Known and loved. Could I really live with myself knowing and never revealing what had become of him? And then I thought about the hundreds and thousands of women you either hear about or know, who have the misfortune of finding themselves in a similar circumstance. Being intimidated, harassed, stalked, and even killed. How many of them tried to do the right thing by letting justice prevail? Sometimes it even works. But then sometimes you gotta let the ghetto laws prevail. Maybe not to the extreme as was the case with Stan. Sometimes a good talking to will do the trick. Sometimes it might take a solid ass kicking. But then sometimes it's necessary to take it to another level. Stan picked the wrong person to try to victimize. So yes, I smiled as I looked out at the picturesque view, I could live with myself knowing what I knew. I just wished more women had men in their lives like Earl, Houston, and my baby, Dennis.